Also by Alan Thompson

The Peninsula

Wolf Isle

The Order

The Onyx Unicorn

Juvenal's Lament: A Political Fable

The Nun's Dowry

Lucifer's Promise

Gods and Lesser Men

The Kingfishers

The Black Owls: An Oxford Nightmare

A Hollow Cup

NIMROD'S TOWER

ALAN THOMPSON

W & B Publishers

For information:
W & B Publishers
9001 Ridge Hill Street
Kernersville, NC 27284

www.a-argusbooks.com

ISBN: 9781635543049

This is a work of *fiction*. All of the characters, organizations and events portrayed in this novel are either products of the author's imagination or used fictitiously.

Book Cover designed by Alan Thompson

Printed in the United States of America

For my friend, Bob Rasmussen: *Requiescat In Pace*

NIMROD'S TOWER

PROLOGUE

> *And they said, Go to, let us build us a city and a tower, whose top may reach unto heaven; and let us make a name, lest we be scattered abroad upon the face of the whole earth* – Genesis 11:4

THE GUNFIRE began at an army garrison near Seoul, South Korea, and ended at a naval air station on the coast of Iceland. In the seventeen hours between first and last, gunshots rang out on hundreds of military installations and naval vessels around the world. In every place, the ritual was the same – a single gun fired a single shot as the sun appeared over the horizon, fired again every half-hour, and loosed its last shot as darkness fell. Flags were lowered to half-staff. The formal mourning for the President of the United States of America had begun.

The president's casket lay on a high black catafalque in the center of the East Room. For twelve hours official Washington came to the White House, some to pay their respects, others to make sure he was dead. The first to arrive were Executive Branch officials, presidential appointees and White House staff. The Justices of the Supreme Court, all of whom he had elevated to the Court, came next, followed by Members of the Senate and House of Representatives, then State and Territorial Governors. The Chiefs of Washington's 177 diplomatic missions were the last to view the body, following which the president was left with an honor guard – enlisted men and women in full dress uniforms from each branch of the Armed Services – whose members were changed out every hour in precise, choreographed symmetry.

Except for the president and his guardians, the room was empty, but they weren't alone. Three television cameras aimed at the catafalque, one from above and the others on either side, broadcast his repose unblinkingly to the nation and the world. It was one of the suggestions he'd made when queried after his election about a potential funeral. "The ratings will be huge," he said, perhaps jokingly. An impresario even in death, other changes to past practice included more television at the Capitol and Arlington, a greater than usual show of military might, and fireworks after the burial.

Early the next morning the queue for the procession to Capitol Hill began to form just outside the East Room. Thousands of troops lined both sides of the route the cortège would follow – North Portico Drive onto a remnant of Pennsylvania Avenue, down 15th Street to Pennsylvania again, then on to Constitution Avenue and the East Plaza of the Capitol. Television cameras were positioned along every block. The Goodyear blimp provided aerial coverage.

The procession began promptly at noon under leaden skies. In the lead was a squadron of mounted patrolmen from the District of Columbia Metropolitan Police followed by dignitaries in limousines. Next, where a military band might ordinarily be placed, there was only a corps of drummers with muffled instruments. Behind them were two more limousines carrying the president's honorary pallbearers, the nine Justices of the Supreme Court. Then came a special honor guard comprised of the Joint Chiefs of Staff and White House military aides, followed by a sailor carrying the flag of the United States, all on foot.

A caisson bearing the president's coffin – surrounded by eight military body bearers – came next, then a caparisoned horse and the president's flag. After that, in order, were immediate family and the new President of the United States in automobiles, and more policemen. Bringing up the rear were six march units representing each branch of the Armed Services.

The four-wheeled caisson was a wooden wagon originally used to transport cannon during World War I. It was drawn by three pairs of gray horses, all saddled though only those on the left bore riders, and the casket it carried was draped with an American flag. The caparisoned horse, riderless, was jet black. Led by a marine in full dress blues, the stallion wore a saddle blanket, saddle and bridle, all black, and carried a pair of boots turned backwards in the stirrups.

The pace was slow and measured, the only sound the muffled drums and the occasional word to the horses. As the skies opened, hundreds of thousands of citizens stood behind the military cordons along the route, silent. Tens of millions of others, too far away to come to Washington on such short notice, watched on television. When the procession reached the intersection of Constitution Avenue and 4th Street, twenty-one fighter jets – one in the lead followed by five flights of four planes each – flew low over the crowds. As the last flight approached, its number three aircraft peeled away from the others and disappeared over the horizon.

At the Capitol, another military cordon lined the center steps at the east front. A joint band from the Army, Navy, Air Force and Coast Guard sounded four ruffles and flourishes and played "Hail to the Chief" at dirge adagio – eighty-six beats to the minute – followed by the Navy hymn, "Eternal Father, Strong to Save." At the first note of the hymn, a battery from the Army's 3rd Infantry, the "Old Guard," fired a twenty-one gun salute with five-second intervals between rounds.

A perfect silence greeted the final volley, broken by gruff commands from the chief of the body bearers. They lifted the coffin from the caisson and carried it up the steps, pausing as each foot gained the next tread. The former First Lady and the president's children, joined by the honor guard, honorary pall bearers and the new president, followed the casket into the Capitol Rotunda. Rumors that the rotunda, under the joint control of the Senate and House of Representatives, might not be made available for the ceremony proved groundless.

The body bearers raised the coffin to the Lincoln catafalque and opened the head panel, another request from the dead president. The catafalque, a wooden trapezoid draped in black fabric, was situated in the center of the room. Members of Congress entered the rotunda from their respective sides of the Capitol and listened to a brief eulogy delivered by the Chief Justice. Thereafter, heads of foreign states, former presidents, the Cabinet, the Dean of the diplomatic corps and the president's personal staff shuffled past the catafalque. Thirty minutes later, everyone was gone, leaving him again with his honor guard and three television cameras.

And then the doors were opened to the people. As they entered the rotunda, wet and still silent, they were divided into two lines that passed on either side of the catafalque. Thirty-five hundred mourners an hour, twenty-four hours a day, said goodbye. Though the president had directed that his body lie in state as long as anyone wished to see him, the powers-that-be deemed that "impossible" and "unprecedented" and, with no end in sight, closed the rotunda after five days and banished him to his grave at Arlington National Cemetery. After a tense confrontation with Capitol Police the people, sullen, melted away.

A cortège similar to the one that took him to the Capitol carried him down the National Mall, past the charred stump of the Washington Monument, around the Lincoln Memorial and across the Potomac to Arlington. It was an Indian summer afternoon, blue skies and bright sunshine, and the people again lined the route beneath elm trees just beginning to turn yellow. Instead of the muffled drums, a fife and drum corps marked the cadence.

As the mourners gathered in ranks around the grave, a roar began to build in the west. Military airplanes in vee formations – thousands, of every description – approached. Each wave flew straight and true, directly over the cemetery. After the last one had faded into the distance, it was quiet for a moment, and then a single aircraft, a blue and white Boeing 747 with an American flag on its tail, flew close to the ground and dipped its wings.

The reluctant tribute below continued. As the caisson approached, the Marine Band played ruffles and flourishes and "Hail to the Chief." A wizened old man in a black robe, the pastor from the president's sometime church at the winter White House, waited by the gravesite. The body bearers raised the casket from the caisson for the final time and set it beneath a black canopy emblazoned with the presidential seal. A great horned owl, perched in a nearby oak tree, looked on solemnly.

He'd never served a day in the military, and his detractors, who had likewise refused military service, sniffed at all the spit and polish. They deemed burial at Arlington a bridge too far, but no one said so publicly. Some of his more perceptive enemies suspected that he was mocking them one last time.

The preacher spoke a few words. Because he did not wear a microphone or because it didn't work, they were mostly lost to the world's television audience. The combined Glee Clubs from the United States Naval Academy rendered the first and last verses of "The Battle Hymn of the Republic" a cappella, the benediction was given, and a three-volley salute from seven rifles – once invoked to clear battlefield casualties and re-start the hostilities – was executed.

The pace of the ceremony picked up as if the participants were impatient to have it over. The flag that draped the coffin was folded twelve times by the body bearers and presented to the widow. A lone bugler played *Taps,* and the twenty-one gun salute was rendered again by the Old Guard. As the people turned away, four Special Forces troops, unbidden, stationed themselves at the corners of the president's grave. His fireworks could be seen and heard over the Mall.

The gunshots that began the world-wide mourning six days earlier sounded again, this time simultaneously. As flags were lowered at military bases and aboard Navy ships, fifty more shots were fired, one for each State in the Union. The forty-fifth President of the United States of America went out as he came in, not with a whimper but a bang, and the cadre he derided as "the Swamp," having afforded him these laurels through gritted teeth, prepared for a return to business as usual.

The citizens, more rooted in the reality of the nation, braced for something more.

ONE

We find ourselves in the peaceful possession, of the fairest portion of the earth, as regards extent of territory, fertility of soil, and salubrity of climate – Abraham Lincoln, 1838

THE PRESIDENT of the United States looked over her morning cup of coffee. "The Secret Service is having a fit," she said. "They want me to move into the White House *now.*"

"Why?" I said.

"My place isn't secure enough to suit them. No fences, too many neighbors. You know."

"So why not move?"

"It's still just too – raw. I don't want to provoke half the country." She paused. "I'd like to wait until after the election."

I nodded. A series of unlikely events had culminated in the most extraordinary political circumstances in the country's history. Two years earlier, the sitting vice-president had been killed when the National Cathedral was destroyed by domestic terrorists calling themselves the Sons of Liberty. In what he described as an effort to heal an increasingly bitter divide, the president–a man with no ideology to speak of–reached across party lines and chose the woman sitting across from me, Lucinda Trent Vere, to be the new vice-president. Her supporters gaped, then applauded, while his party leaders were speechless with fury.

She stood for everything the president did not. During an earlier stint as Chief Justice of the United States, she had deemed his signature legislation unconstitutional. She was her party's favorite to run *against* him in the next election and, after a few months of polite posturing, she announced her intention to succeed him. Thereafter, Washington returned to its new normal – a spiteful, factional gridlock – while the country continued its downward spiral into bedlam.

Six weeks before the election, the president died of a liver disease never disclosed to the public. Politicians and experts of every stripe mounted a furious campaign to explain the unremarkable circumstances of his death, but citizens outside the beltway – those who loved him and those who hated him – refused to believe them. Assassination, whether perceived as a virtue or a sin, was on everyone's lips, and the antipathy among them was palpable.

The election, now five weeks away, was a foregone conclusion. The conventional wisdom was that half the country would vote for Lucinda Vere, the other half would stay home. Down-ballot races would mimic the presidential vote. She and her partisans, though giddy with the prospect of undiluted power, tried to project concern for the perilous state of the nation.

"Half the country's already provoked," I said. "And that's putting it mildly." She was now the sitting president and fully entitled, obligated even, to live in the White House. "The election won't change that. It'll make it worse."

Our first meeting, two years before, had been an early sign of the approaching turmoil. She was Chief Justice of the United States, I was a very junior congressman charged by my colleagues with removing her from office. My inability to do so – despite her acknowledged corruption – was another indication that the country, as reflected by its representatives in Washington, D.C., was in dire straits. After she was acquitted by the Senate other, even more malignant circumstances had thrown us together again.

After my wife died, I went home to New Hope and moved into my mother's old white colonial on Battle Lane. A few months later, I returned to Washington for my third tour – fourth, counting college in the 90s – ostensibly to help Azure County's new congresswoman maneuver the corridors of power, but the real reason was Lucinda Trent Vere. Ours was a complicated relationship – her politics and mine were polar opposites, she was unavoidably in the public eye while I evaded it at all costs – but we had learned to tolerate our differences and embrace the things that mattered. Chief among the latter was a shared sexuality that was as intense as it was surprising.

A Brahmin from Boston, her pale skin, aqua eyes and fair shock of hair, combined with a reserve passed down for generations, had earned her a sobriquet, "the ice maiden." When she was appointed to the Supreme Court, speculation among the less refined in Washington was that she, at age thirty-five, was still a virgin. Facts turned up during her impeachment not only belied that notion, they revealed a woman whose capacity for sex, and the emotions that went with it, was almost limitless.

Since my return to the Federal City, we had sparred over the terms of our intimacy. A twenty-four hour news cycle and the peeping toms who perpetuated it made a normal relationship impossible. She was far more prominent than past vice-presidents, and appearances in public with me in tow would be problematic at best. She had remained in her townhouse on Dupont Circle rather than move into the vice-president's official residence at the Naval Observatory, which rendered any sort of privacy on her end illusory.

As a consequence, we usually met at my home, an 18th century mansion in Georgetown Heights. We weren't a secret, but we weren't obvious, either. The great house on 28th Street was mine because my wife, whose family had built it before there *was* a United States, was killed in the attack on the National Cathedral, and our daughter had died in a blaze on Mason's Island a few years before. It had extensive grounds and walls and gates, and the monuments remaining on the Mall were visible from the back steps.

It also backed up to Oak Hill Cemetery, whose relative isolation allowed Lucinda to come and go unmolested. That arrangement, however, could not survive her promotion – we would have to be more creative about our trysts for the foreseeable future. Neither of us wanted to become fodder for the tabloids, paper or electronic, though it was probably inevitable.

She looked at her watch and rose. "I'll see you at your next gaggle," I said.

She smiled and kissed me on the cheek. "Toss me a softball, Tommy. I'll probably need it."

How long could we last? Our differences – my laissez faire attitude versus her absolutist view of life – were fundamental, and her new job gave her the opportunity to impose her beliefs on others. It seemed only a matter of time before I would have to choose between her and the lot I had cast for myself.

The sun and the trees created light and shadow for her to pass through. I watched her walk down the white gravel path, past the temple and the statuary and the fountains, and disappear through the back gate into the cemetery. She didn't look back. An ideologue completely immersed in her creed, she was in charge now, and the pieties of her secular faith – gradually ascendant for almost a century – would be granted a new urgency. Lucinda Trent Vere was a true believer, and she wouldn't allow the current crisis to go to waste.

THE NEWSROOM at the *Georgetown Star* was an anachronism, a throwback to a time when newspapers were many, prosperous and respected. The scene recalled *All the President's Men* though the tools in use had been updated. Carrels around the perimeter and desks in the middle of the room were crowded with reporters and columnists and editors speaking into cellphones and tapping on keyboards. Screens flickered and glowed. The noise was different, too – the rise and fall of human voices was no longer interrupted by the clack of teletype and typewriters or the jingle of phones with cords and cradles.

A few years earlier, the *Star* had been struggling to survive. The last of the country's great afternoon broadsheets, its revenue and circulation were plummeting, its staff depleted, its influence – once equal to that of the city's morning behemoth, the *Post* – nil. It was shopped around at a bargain-basement price for months, but there were no takers until Martin Luther Jones stepped into the breach. Jones, a wealthy eccentric from Atlanta, was looking to fill a prominent void in the nation's capital.

He explained it over lunch at The Palm. "This town – this country – needs another point-of-view," he said. "I'm going to provide it."

I'd known him in an earlier incarnation, when I was practicing law in Atlanta and he was developing the unique real estate market that made him a billionaire. "That's a tall order," I said. "Others have tried."

He nodded. "They weren't all in. There was always something else. Politics. Crusades. Dinner invitations." He paused. "There'll be no such distractions with the *Star.*"

"Meaning?"

"Whatever I have –" he smiled "– and it's considerable, will go into the newspaper. No economizing, no corner-cutting. It'll be the finest, most widely-read paper in the world."

"Just to provide another point-of-view?"

He shook his head. "In five years, the *Star* will be the *only* point-of-view."

In short order, Jones – Marty to his friends – had moved to back up his boast. He doubled, then re-doubled the staff at the *Star*, and opened news bureaus all over the world. He financed and promoted bloggers and podcasters affiliated with the paper. He supported social media "influencers" who shared his "point-of-view," and purchased radio and television stations in every region of the country. His most recent venture, still in the start-up stage, was an ad-free alternative to the Internet called the "Grapevine."

But the *Georgetown Star* was the jewel in his crown. Newspapers had been in decline for years, gutted by internet publishers and social media where the news was "free." Traditional sources of revenue like classified advertising had dried up. Bankruptcies of old-line papers were announced every day. Increasingly, the news was produced in just a few places – the Boston/New York/Washington corridor and the crescent bounded by Seattle, San Diego and Phoenix. Jones added a slogan to his masthead – "And the truth shall make you free" – and set out to challenge all that.

Money was no object. For the flagship paper, intended for Washington and environs, he restored all the features abandoned over the years and added new ones. The news itself emanated from the newsroom of the *Georgetown Star* – wire service content was *verboten*. Every edition of the paper came with a four-color section of most of the country's syndicated comic strips – only those with a political bent were excluded.

He paid particular attention to younger readers. Readership among those under fifty had been dropping for years, accelerating with the growth of the Internet. Exploiting the growing disgust with the excesses of the new media, he highlighted the lies and half-truths as news, and sued to challenge the theft of the *Star's* content. His pockets were deeper than those of the plagiarists, and they often stopped stealing his product rather than fight him in court.

He bought or established local papers in all fifty states. Their content varied, but always contained the national and international news reported from the *Star's* newsroom, the editorial page and the comics. Jones wrote the editorials himself.

All that was in the future the day we met for lunch at The Palm. The usual uproar among the patrons, all speaking at the same time, made it hard to hear. "I want you to come work for me," he said, leaning closer.

"Doing what?"

"Reporter. Columnist." He paused. "News seems to find you. I want you to write about it for the *Star.*"

"I'm no journalist."

He laughed. "Have you ever looked up the definition of –" he made air quotes with his fingers "– journalist? It's somebody who writes for newspapers or reports the news on television. Nothing special's required."

"Journalism school?"

He shook his head. "Most of them are sociology majors. Journalism's not a profession, it's a construct. The First Amendment's a license to pros-elytize for fun and profit."

Three months later I resigned as chief of staff for the Azure County congressional delegation and assumed a perch at the *Georgetown Star.* My column appeared in the paper whenever I had something to say, usually in the opinion pages. My colleagues were mostly younger, recruited from schools and newspapers in the South and Midwest because, as Marty Jones put it, he didn't want his newsroom "infected with the groupthink" so wide-spread on both coasts.

"There's no self-awareness," he said, refer-ring to the reporters and editors responsible for the bias. "They actually raised a shrine to themselves, and it closed for lack of interest."

"It's not intentional?"

"At the upper levels, maybe, but most of them probably can't help it. They are a product of the places where they live and work, and their re-porting reflects that environment. They would have to *actively* reject what they think and feel about a particular story. That's hard, and most of them aren't up to it." He paused. "Plus, they aren't paid worth a damn. I'd be pissed off all the time, too."

I leaned into the only door that opened off the newsroom, that of the owner and publisher. "You wanted to see me?" I said.

"Yes, Tommy," said Marty. "Come in." Small, very dark and completely bald, he seemed lost be-hind the enormous desk. His three-piece suit, one of many imported from Savile Row, was disarranged – the coat on a rack in the corner, the vest unbut-toned, the trousers secured by loose silk braces over a pin-striped shirt. His yellow club tie was knotted to the throat. The glare from a lamp on the desk, reflected in his horned-rimmed glasses, concealed large green eyes.

The room was wired for sound. A few months earlier, he'd been accused of sexual harassment by a disgruntled former employee, and seethed over the media's gleeful acceptance of her word over his. To all outward appearances, his office was that of a prosperous newspaper publisher, but it was also a virtual recording studio, a fact known only to his closest associates.

He pushed an envelope across the desk. "That arrived this morning," he said.

Addressed to "The Georgetown Star," it was postmarked "Alexandria, VA." The message, an assembly of headline type cut from the pages of the *Star,* was brief:

I KILLED HIM TO SAVE THE COUNTRY

I looked up. "Every paper in the country probably got one of these," I said. "So what?"

He handed me a smaller envelope. "This came with it."

I thought it was empty at first, but closer examination revealed a clump of reddish hair. "I've had it checked," Marty said. "It's the president's DNA."

"How do you do that?"

"The spooks have been collecting presidential DNA for years. I have my sources."

"What do the cops say?"

"I haven't talked to the cops."

"Why not?"

"You said it yourself. These 'confessions' are a dime a dozen."

"Not with a packet of the president's hair." He didn't respond. "What're you going to do?"

"You mean, what are *we* going to do?" I smiled. "*I'm* going to have the envelopes and paper examined for fingerprints and whatnot. More DNA, maybe." He paused. "*You're* going to look into the President's so-called liver disease. Test the government's story. If there's something to write about, write it. I want the truth." He stopped again. "I'll keep the envelope and hair. You take the note."

I found an empty desk in the newsroom and sat down, pondering his final remark. *Truth* was the "point-of-view" he demanded at the *Georgetown Star.* While others insisted that there was no "truth," or that everyone was entitled to his own version, Marty was old-fashioned. He insisted on the definition in the dictionary — "the real facts about a situation, person or event."

He also refused to tolerate bias in the way those facts were reported. To the extent they had ever operated without prejudice, the national newspapers, and broadcast and cable news, had given up. They now only purported to "manage" the bias of their reporters, to provide their readers and viewers with their best news "judgment." Worse, they catered to the prejudices of their customers, thereby enabling polarized voters and, thus, polarized politicians and a polarized country. Most of the media didn't report the news — it *was* the news.

At any other news outlet, the story about the anonymous confession and the President's hair would already be on the street or part of a "Special Report." It wouldn't appear in the *Star* until Marty Jones was satisfied it was real news and not just some poor soul's effort to make himself important.

Today's front page was spread across the computer screen in front of me. There was other news out there – drought in Kenya and Ethiopia giving rise to predictions of mass starvation, unparalleled winds and rain around the globe, a late-season tropical storm gaining strength off the Cape Verde Islands. The death of a single man seemed small in comparison to the misery being inflicted on the rest of the world.

Nevertheless, I needed to prepare the way now in the event there was something to write about later. I opened a new page, and began to type:

A CONSPIRACY CRISIS?
Tommy Sawyer

For the past four years, it has been a matter of faith among the mandarin class that our deceased president was the wellspring of all the country's ills, a fixation that had assumed Orwellian proportions at the time of his death. But for him, they said, ours would be the land of milk and honey it used to be. Truth, justice and the American way would still be the order of the day, our politics would still be virtuous, and our citizens – whatever their race, color or creed – would still live in harmony. And, not coincidentally, their own status would still be unquestioned.

He's gone now, and those dubious assertions will undoubtedly be exposed for the agitprop they really were. Having ruthlessly exploited, and widened, the country's fault lines, our self-anointed overlords will have to find another excuse for the chaos they've created.

The honest ones, or those who simply want to retain some credibility, will acknowledge that our problems began long before he was elected and won't disappear with his death. Our institutions – schools, civic organizations, government – have been failing for years. We are in thrall to the cult of the individual and the nihilism that accompanies it. Factions, each with its own brand of Caesarism, vie for power, and odious imprecations are hurled from every side. "Race" explains everything. Crime and domestic terrorism are on the rise. The pursuit of happiness has become a slough of despair. In short, the poet's inferno has nothing on the United States of America.

Reactions to the president's death reflect the depths to which we've fallen. Unseemly jubilation and overwrought anguish have been subsumed by the near universal certainty that he was assassinated. This, in spite of assurances from everyone in his administration that he died from liver disease, and not a particle of evidence to the contrary. But the disbelief is complete. No one trusts our elected officials now, or one another, and the consequences for the country could be catastrophic.

The last president to die in office was *assassinated, and conspiracy theories of how it happened are with us six decades later. For now, the current suspicions are "theories" as well. God help us if they prove to be more than that.*

TWO

*We find ourselves under the
government of a system of political institutions, conducing
more essentially to the ends of
civil and religious liberty,
than any of which the history
of former times tells us* –
Abraham Lincoln, 1838

CONGRESSIONAL QUERIES into the president's death began a day after he was buried. A
joint committee of senators and congressmen had
been proposed by the new president and rejected
because neither chamber was willing to be "ob-
structed" by the other. Hence, the House Select
Committee convened in the room usually reserved
for Ways and Means at 10:00 AM, and the Senate
Select Committee met at 2:00 PM in the Judiciary's
hearing room.

The House Caucus Room was typical of
Washington – banal symbolism gone to ruinous ex-
cess. Cost, of course, was no object. Molded swags of
foliage and ribbons, and plaques and classical
masks, adorned the walls. Stars covered with gold
leaf encircled the ceiling, and four monumental ea-
gles – framed by plaster sunbursts and baskets

overflowing with flowers and fruit – surveyed the room from atop a marble platform.

The upper and lower rostrums, where the committee and its helpers would sit, were made of American walnut, barely visible behind more ea-gles, wreaths and stars. Portraits of past worthies looked down from places designed especially for them. Financed with plunder extracted from the citizens at the point of a gun, it was just one exam-ple of the opulence that our "servants" in Washing-ton lavished upon themselves.

Owing to my previous service as a member of the House, I was able to schmooze with the Chair-man of the House committee briefly, and secure a seat in the front row of the gallery. Television cam-eras were positioned around the perimeter, and re-porters with microphones were stationed in the hallway. All the seats were taken. Latecomers stood two-deep along the walls, and still photogra-phers knelt before the rostrum where the members sat.

Five witnesses, four medical professionals and the White House chief of staff, were sworn in and made opening statements. The medical judg-ment was unanimous: The president had died of complications – multiple-organ collapse and brain death – resulting from hyperacute liver failure, a rare condition that afflicted fewer than 2,000 peo-ple in the country every year. The onset of the ill-ness was sudden, its progress rapid. By the time it was diagnosed, it was too late to save him though every medical procedure, including a liver trans-plant, was employed.

The chief of staff testified that the president had complained of fatigue and nausea and a pain on his right side just below the ribs, but waved off a suggestion that the White House doctor be called in. Two days later, he was found asleep at his desk and, when awakened, appeared not to know where he was. Seconds later, he threw up in the waste basket next to the desk. The doctor was summoned over his objections.

The White House doctor, who'd been the president's family physician for decades, stated that he didn't suspect liver failure at first. There was no history of the disease, and there were many potential diagnoses far more common than liver failure. During his examination, the president grew more confused and incoherent, and the decision was made to transport him to Walter Reed via helicopter where he was placed in the intensive care unit.

After considering and discarding various possibilities, the staff at Walter Reed performed a biopsy, whereby a needle was used to remove tissue from the liver. While the tissue was being analyzed, the president's "encephalopathy," the decline in his brain function, reached a critical stage and he fell into a coma. A scan revealed increased swelling in his brain. A liver transplant was ordered.

Because Walter Reed didn't have the facilities or personnel to perform a liver transplant, the president was loaded aboard Marine One again and flown to George Washington University Hospital, four blocks from the White House. After the donor liver was secured, the transplant surgery began but it was too late. He died on the operating table. The hepatologist testified that there was little chance that the transplant would succeed, "given the extent of the encephalopathy and the pressure on the brain."

"Why do it, then?" said one of the junior panel members from California. "Aren't there protocols about who can have a transplant? A waiting list?"

"Well – yes. But patients with acute failure have a special status." She paused. "And he *was* the President of the United States."

"So you just arbitrarily moved him to the head of the line?"

The doctor hesitated. "Yes."

"And wasted a liver that might've saved someone else's life?"

There was no response.

The Medical Examiner for the District of Columbia spoke last – her autopsy confirmed the final diagnosis. "The overall mortality rate for acute liver failure is about forty per cent," she said. "In this country, most of it is the result of drug overdose. A transplant is generally the only means by which such a patient survives."

"Are you suggesting," said the Chairman, a rising star from Oregon, "that the president died of a drug overdose?"

"No, no. Blood tests eliminated that possibility."

"What caused it, then?"

"As I said, over half the cases are drug-related, usually pain pills like Tylenol and Vicodin. Other victims also suffer from some type of hepatitis. Fully twenty per cent are enigmatic."

"Enigmatic?"

"Unknown."

"Was the president suffering from hepatitis?"

"No."

"So the cause of his death was – enigmatic?"

"The cause of the cause of his death. Yes."

I sensed a change in mood. Whereas her colleagues had limited themselves to dry, non-controversial medical observations, the Medical Examiner had cleared the way for the exercise of partisan imagination. The president's blood had been tested for drugs, never mind the result, and "the cause of the cause of his death" was "enigmatic," an especially curious term for a medical condition. Several reporters, cellphones at the ready, left the room to call in the story so far as the committee members continued to question the witnesses.

Addressing the president's chief of staff, the ranking member from Georgia, nearing the end of his eighteenth and final term, said, "Let's see if I've got the timeline straight: The president told you he wasn't feeling well. Nausea and pain on his right side. Right?"

"Yes, sir."

"Had he said anything earlier?"

"Not that I recall."

The congressman blinked for a moment. "You mean he *might* have?"

"I can't be sure."

Another pause. "And two days later, he fell asleep at his desk, appeared confused, and threw up?"

"Yes."

"Are you sure it was two days? Could it have been three? Or four?"

"I – I don't think so. I think it was two."

"And you called his doctor?" The witness nodded. "Did he come immediately?"

"Within a few hours."

"Four? Six?"

"No more than four."

"And you sent the president to Walter Reed?"

"Yes. The next morning."

"The next morning? Why?"

"The president didn't want to go."

"Did you think he was capable of making an informed decision by then?"

The witness shrugged. "I don't know."

"How long was he there?"

"From 7:00 AM until about 5:00 PM."

"Walter Reed's what? Ten miles from the White House?"

"Yes, sir."

"And ten miles back to George Washington Hospital?"

"Yes, sir."

"How long before the surgery started?"

"I'm not sure. There was some trouble finding the donor liver. It was the next day."

"Morning or afternoon?"

"Afternoon. He died around four o'clock."

The congressman looked at the doctor from the University hospital. "Doctor, what's the typical time from infection to death in cases like this?"

"I can't say there's a 'typical' period of time, Congressman. Some people *do* recover from it. Others die within a few days."

"How few?"

"Five or six. It's difficult to measure because the onset is so hard to detect."

"All right. Thank you."

The congresswoman from New York was recognized. She spoke to the president's doctor. "Doctor Cohen, am I correct in understanding that the president rejected the best medical advice during this episode? On at least two occasions?"

"Well, I –"

"I mean, he refused to call you in at the outset?"

"That's my understanding."

"And he delayed the trip to Walter Reed?"

"Yes."

"One of the causes of this illness is drug overdose?"

"Yes, but –"

"That's all I have. Thank you, Doctor."

"You tested his blood, correct?" said the ranking member.

"Yes, sir."

"And found no drugs?"

"That's right."

"But," said the New York congresswoman, "that was several days after he fell ill. Right?"

"Yes."

"So the – evidence of drug use might've disappeared by then?"

"Congresswoman, I can't –"

"Thank you, Doctor. You've been very helpful."

The member from South Carolina spoke up. "Are you telling this committee that you don't know how the president died?"

The Medical Examiner responded: "No, ma'am. The president died of complications resulting from acute liver failure. What we don't know is what caused the liver failure."

"Why not?"

A hint of exasperation passed over the woman's face. "Because we don't know everything. Medical science has determined the cause of eighty per cent of these cases. We're still working on the other twenty per cent."

"And the president's case just happens to fall into that twenty per cent?"

The M.E.'s face darkened, but she made no response.

The hearing continued for another hour but the lines had already been drawn. Instead of considering the situation actually presented to them, the members of the committee preferred to speculate on things that *might* have happened. One faction seized on the sequence of events to suggest that the "delays" leading up to the transplant had doomed the president. Predictably, there were barely concealed hints that they were intentional.

Others implied that he died of a drug overdose, despite the testimony to the contrary, and his refusal to seek help was evidence of a "cover-up." The congresswoman from South Carolina flatly refused to believe that, "in this day and age," the medical community could not pinpoint "the cause of the cause" of death. "Where's all this science when you need it?" she said. "I don't buy it." For one or two, the real news was the "violation" of the transplant protocol and loss of the donor liver.

All this was immediately injected into the country's bloodstream by the social media and, with slightly less speed and conjecture, by the nation's newspapers and networks. By the time the Senate committee convened that afternoon, the story-lines had been set, ready to be embellished, challenged and defended by media and citizens alike.

Moreover, the knowing, sarcastic mockery that was now the hallmark of social media and too many traditional news organizations added to the stew. Remarks like "the president's been brain dead for years," and "he never made an informed decision in his life" were typical. Naming an "old crony" as White House physician, rather than a "well-qualified" government doctor, was ridiculed, "a disaster waiting to happen." The intended audiences, those who reacted with delight and those who exploded with rage, performed as expected.

RATHER THAN temper the familiar surge of suspicion and ill will, the Senate hearing, featuring the same witnesses, made matters worse. The Judiciary's hearing room, only slightly less sumptuous than the Assembly Room, was packed. As soon as the White House doctor finished reading his opening statement, the chairman of the committee, an old bull from Louisiana, said, "When did liver failure first occur to you?"

"At the conclusion of my initial examination. It was one of the options we were considering when we sent him to Walter Reed."

"Did you order a transplant then?"

"No. We were —"

"Walter Reed has no facilities or doctors to perform a liver transplant?"

"That's correct."

"Isn't it true that almost nobody recovers from this disease without a transplant?"

"Yes."

"And yet you made no effort to get the ball rolling after your examination revealed the potential for acute liver failure?"

"There were other —"

"In fact, you sent him to a hospital in Bethesda, Maryland, a hospital without the means to perform a liver transplant, instead of the hospital down the street that *could* perform the operation. Correct?" There was no answer. "Well?"

After a prolonged silence, another senator, a woman from Tennessee, said, "What about mushrooms?"

"Mushrooms?" said the president's doctor.

"Yes. It's my understanding that certain mushrooms can cause liver failure."

The witness, bewildered, looked at his fellows. The Medical Examiner responded: "You're right, Senator. Ingesting the 'death cap' mushroom causes severe liver damage."

"Did he eat one?"

"Not that I know of."

"Did you check?"

She shook her head. "Things were moving too fast. After the biopsy confirmed the diagnosis, all our efforts were directed at the transplant."

"What about at the autopsy?" The M.E. shook her head again. "So it could've been mushrooms?"

"It's possible. But very unlikely."

One final note of uncertainty was sounded a moment later. "Did your autopsy consider poison?" said the senior senator from Texas.

"Only in a cursory way," said the Medical Examiner. "The evidence of liver failure was overwhelming."

"But the actual cause of death was the failure of multiple organs, right?"

"Yes. And brain death."

"The brain's an organ, isn't it?"

"Yes."

"And the liver?"

"Yes."

"And there are poisons that kill by attacking the organs? Botox? Thallium?"

"Yes. But the president died from organ destruction brought on by acute liver failure."

The news from the "responsible" media that evening was that the president had died of acute liver failure after an all-out effort by his staff and doctors to save him. None of them, however, failed to mention the alternatives proffered at the hearings – poison, mushrooms, drug overdose, intentional neglect, the president's own stubbornness – no matter how outrageous. And as day follows night, each one quickly found adherents in the body politic – the potential for botox poisoning was especially appealing. The indignation, real and feigned, continued and, in certain precincts, newspaper circulation rose and more and more screens attracted more and more eyeballs. He was dead, but he was the gift that kept on giving.

My charge was to test the government's story, and write about it if there was something to write about. The hearings were fact and I wrote about them, fully aware that I was adding fuel to the fire, but they were the beginning of the government's story and had to be reported. The liver diagnosis would be tested, and overdoses, poison and mushrooms considered. That the hearings themselves reflected the country's ongoing disintegration went unsaid.

THREE

*We, when mounting the stage
of existence, found ourselves
the legal inheritors of these
fundamental blessings —*
Abraham Lincoln, 1838

AS THE first significant act of her presidency, Lucinda Vere offered blanket amnesty to the Sons of Liberty. The Sons, thousands of young men whose manifesto lamented their failure to find happiness in the United States of America, were responsible for the destruction of the Washington Monument, the National Cathedral and one of the buildings at the Library of Congress. In the process, they had murdered several hundred people, my wife among them.

The media's response was unsurprising. News reports barely mentioned the carnage, concentrating instead on the secret negotiations that had begun even before she became president. Speculation regarding the success of her effort was widespread. A few editorials gave lip service to "law and order," but hastened to point out that the country *was* "deeply flawed," and its moral bankruptcy a true source of resentment. Still others welcomed a fresh approach, "so unlike the previous administration."

President Vere had immediately adopted one of her predecessor's signature innovations. There would be no daily press conferences at the White House, and no White House Press Secretary. Instead, the media would get its presidential news straight from the horse's mouth, most often during her strolls across the South Lawn to and from Marine One. These press gaggles had been bitterly criticized by reporters accustomed to posing gotcha questions and bullying a functionary who knew only what she was told, but the edict from President Vere was met with no more than grumbling resignation.

I had attended her first gaggle a week earlier. Against a backdrop of the helicopter's roaring engines and the thump-thump-thump of its rotors, anonymous reporters shouted questions, some of which she chose to answer, most of which she ignored. Like the man before her, she was in total control – questions from what seemed to be an unruly mob were barely heard while her answers, enhanced by microphones, were whatever she wanted to say. There was no haggling over past discrepancies and no follow-up questions and, when she'd had enough, she waved and climbed aboard the chopper.

Two days after the amnesty announcement, the gaggle began with a brief statement from the president: "I'm pleased to report that the Sons of Liberty have accepted our offer of amnesty. There will be no more attacks. Our children are coming in from the cold." The cacophony of questions, mostly about the details of the amnesty, began. It was "unconditional," she said, and included measures to ensure that the Sons "were re-integrated into society."

She pointed at me, and smiled. "Tommy?"

I decided against the softball question. "How are you going to 're-integrate' all the people they killed?" I said. "Raise them from the dead?"

The gaggle fell silent. She glared and turned away. The shouting began again, but she refused to turn around and, seconds later, disappeared inside Marine One.

"Way to go, Tommy," said the reporter from the *Post*. "Lover's quarrel?"

I ignored her. Our liaison was well-known among the media, but they had declined to reveal it to the public on the assumption it would damage the president politically. They regarded sex in all its iterations as inviolable, though the heterosexual variety was now viewed with some suspicion, but her supporters might question her loyalty, and her judgment, if they knew she was sleeping with a troglodyte like me.

I had mixed feelings about the pardon. I was shocked, but I wasn't surprised. It was the inevitable result of a creed that valued doctrine over life. I wanted Lucinda to succeed, but the Sons of Liberty were pardoned not for humanitarian reasons or to heal a wounded country, but because their politics lined up with hers. It didn't bode well for the rest of her time in office.

While the political and cultural agglomerates on both coasts applauded the amnesty, the reaction in the rest of the country was mixed. In rural areas and small towns it was seen, not as the jaw-dropping abomination it would've been only a few years before, but as the continuing, inevitable decline of the once-hallowed place where they were born and raised. Their slogans – "Our Country, Right or Wrong" and "America – Love It or Leave It" and "Make America Great Again" – had faded, leaving a blank space on the bumpers of their pickup trucks and SUVs. There was nothing left to believe in and, worse, nothing left to die for.

A few redoubts in the hinterlands were fighting a rearguard action without much success. They no longer controlled the message, and the children had been kidnapped while their parents weren't looking. The prevailing dogma became the "truth," not because it convinced others but because those with microphones promoted it relentlessly while denigrating the alternatives. Combined with the indoctrination of their offspring, the propaganda had rendered the people impotent.

A week earlier, the Governor of Idaho had erected barriers across all the roads leading from Oregon and Washington State, preparatory to building a wall along Idaho's entire 479-mile western border. She acknowledged that it was only a gesture – the "wall" was really just a chain-link fence – that would not keep the people from Washington and Oregon, or their ideology, from penetrating her state. "They ruin the places where they live, and move here to escape it," she said. "Then they insist on the things that made them move in the first place. It's crazy."

There were also some radical organizations, mostly in the South, that condemned the administration's "servile complicity in murder and annihilation." Chief among these were the Martyrs for Christ, headquartered in Bessemer City, Alabama. Likening the Vere Administration to Vichy France, its leader, one Earnest Pogue, excoriated the federal government as Nazis and traitors intent on dictatorship. "Lucinda Vere is a fifth columnist," said Pogue, "who intends to take over this country. Her entire career has pointed in that direction. Pardoning traitors and killers and giving them jobs in business and government is just another step along the way."

Pogue had clashed with the government two years earlier. Charged with "aiding and abetting" the Sons of Liberty during their reign of terror, he'd been convicted on questionable evidence and sentenced to ten years in a federal penitentiary. As he passed through the prison gates, surrounded by the media who had plumped so vigorously for his conviction, the presidential helicopter touched down just inside the walls, whereupon the former president emerged and announced that he was granting Pogue a full pardon.

The gnashing of teeth in the nation's newsrooms was audible. Pogue was everything they despised. An unctuous, phony religious fanatic who never missed a chance to condemn the "godless," he was a racist and a redneck who ostentatiously held hands with his second wife – he called her "Mother" – in public. He spoke so slowly that every syllable could be heard, assuming his listeners had the patience to do so. His string ties, seersucker suits and white socks were lampooned mercilessly. The pardon was under attack from dozens seeking to pre-serve "liberty" and "justice."

The Martyrs for Christ, in protest of Muslim services held at the Cathedral, had occupied it a few days before it was destroyed, and staged a rally at the Lincoln Memorial at the same time the Sons blew up the Washington Monument, a serendipity that led to Pogue's arrest. He was widely reported to be a figurehead controlled by "a cabal of white supremacist billionaires."

Once numbering fewer than 100 members, the Martyrs had grown rapidly over the past two years. Dozens of chapters had formed a network promoting resistance to government at all levels. Initially limited to the southern states, they had spread to all regions of the country. A well-funded legal team routinely filed suit to obstruct govern-ment programs deemed "un-American." Sympathet-ic judges, ignoring the law and the Constitution, often saw things their way.

Their membership and their objectives had changed. Religion had been downgraded to politics – the organization now purported to speak for every "blue collar" worker in America, blue collar loosely defined as those without a college degree, about two-thirds of the working population. Labor unions – plumbers, electricians, truck drivers – had be-come affiliated, as did their counterparts – fire-fighters and policemen – in the public sector. The military, whose rank-and-file and non-commis-sioned officers were overwhelmingly blue collar, was a fertile recruiting ground.

The Martyrs had come under intense scruti-ny recently after an F.B.I. agent who had infiltrated the group turned up dead under a pile of gravel near Bessemer City. The cause of death was "asphyxiation." The investigation had so far yielded nothing.

WITH THE elevation of Lucinda Trent Vere to the presidency, the scrum for money and power on Capitol Hill was in full swing. No longer restrained by the fact of a contested election, one wing of the political establishment squabbled openly, while the other prepared for its journey into the wilderness. The nation at large, equally fractious, was more nuanced. Victims and oppressors, mostly unaware of their status despite the best efforts of media and government, carried on in relative harmony, though the pall of assassination hung heavy over the landscape.

Official Washington had already moved on. *He* was forgotten, and his death was only something else to exploit. What mattered was the upcoming changing of the guard, one that might last for generations. Utopia was just around the corner.

Utopia's designated rulers, however, inspired little confidence during the frenzied aftermath of the president's death. The disarray was most evident in the House of Representatives. Caucuses, each vying for territory and influence, sprang up overnight. Because the opposition – dubbed the "Rich White Caucus" by the media – was about to be obliterated by the upcoming election, there was no incentive for the many factions in the other party to cooperate. Every compromise was undermined by new demands, every deal gutted by shifting coalitions.

As a consequence, they became further atom-
ized. The Queer Caucus gave rise to the Lesbian,
Gay, Transgender, Bi-Sexual and None-of-the-
Above Caucuses. The Men's and Women's Working
Groups were split by generation, and became members of the Silent, Boomer, X or Millennial Caucuses. The Poor Caucus divided itself into a hierarchy
based on complex calculations of relative poverty,
while the factions within the Undocumented Caucus were identified by the laws they wanted to re-
peal.

This growing divide led to deadlock. Questions of loyalty and turf were paramount and had
to be resolved before a post office could be built in
Jersey City. Every faction demanded its share of
whatever was doled out and, since every member
belonged to more than one group, the potential for
conflict and confusion was never-ending.

For example, the Chairperson of the Brown
Caucus, a sub-set of the Colored Caucus, had to
contend with her fellow peoples of color – the Black,
Red and Yellow Caucuses – before negotiating with
the Lesbian and Boomer Caucuses, of which she
was also a member. The relative worthiness of each
faction, and thus its authority to dispense government largesse, was usually determined by the media and "cultural" cues – movies, books, television –
that measured their levels of victimhood. The calculus changed constantly, and the struggle to mediate
between her sexual orientation and skin pigment
left her exhausted. The Boomer Caucus, very low
on the victim totem pole, provided a place to relax.

Assured of a massive majority, contentious
policies that even their partisans didn't condone

took center stage. Bills supporting abortion "any-time" and mandatory universal union dues, as well as a crusade against global warming, were readied. Massive tax increases were planned. "From each according to his ability, to each according to his needs," was resurrected. The "fundamental trans-formation" of the country was about to get under-way and, as expected, President Vere did nothing to discourage it.

Because it largely supported these policies, the press treated this political upheaval with faux objectivity. Reporters sought comments only from experts and academics who agreed with them. Polls, studies and surveys were created, not to pro-vide objective information, but to bolster pre-determined certainties. In an earlier time these distortions might have moved public opinion but, having endured similar efforts for years, the people were now too jaded to drink the Kool-Aid. Never-theless, the unrelenting repetition of a single point-of-view added a dystopian cast to the national con-versation.

The un-elected "intelligentsia" cheered the politicians on. From cities on the coasts, where they lived well apart from the objects of their anxiety, they clamored for "social justice." Spurious self-abnegation, combined with a refusal to recognize the perils of *their* future in the brave new world, made them a perfect foil for the true revolutionar-ies.

While all this churning was going on, the country was largely ungoverned. It wasn't a new phenomenon – neither faction had accomplished anything beyond dividing the spoils for years, and the nation's infrastructure was approaching third-world status. Washington was a case in point: On the surface, it maintained its "City Beautiful" façade for tourists and residents alike, but sidewalks, roadways and bridges were allowed to decay.

Of particular note was the deterioration of the city's drainage system. Washington was situated alongside the Potomac River, a powerful stream that dropped 3,000 feet from the West Virginia mountains to the Atlantic Ocean. It flooded often, and sometimes the water reached the Federal Triangle, the parcel next to the river defined by the National Mall, the White House and the Capitol. Plans to repair levees and upgrade flood walls, long on the books, had never been funded by the Congress.

A FEW members of the opposition finally roused themselves. Faced with an existential threat, they held meetings around the country in an effort to mount some kind of defense. The highest priority was finding someone to replace the dead man at the top of their ticket, someone their adherents could vote for and perhaps save some of the candidates further down the ballot.

There had been no competition for the party's leadership for four years, no real campaigning and no attempt to be anything other than one of the president's men. His vice-president, who might have served as his surrogate, was the other party's candidate. Contrary to the ordinary course of events, no one was eager to step into the breach. His new running mate, Jeremiah Jefferson, was a political neophyte.

Jefferson, a Mississippi native, had only recently switched parties and was its first black vice-presidential candidate. He had never run for political office, and had resisted the president's offer of a spot on the ticket but, citing the country's "headlong descent into anarchy," he had ultimately acquiesced. Because he was Chairman of the National Confederation of Black Churches, his selection was portrayed by the media as a cynical effort to court black voters. Predictably, those who once counted him as a reliable ally now competed to vilify him.

Jefferson's politics contrasted sharply with that of Lucinda's recently-appointed vice-president and running mate, Vada Potts-Jones – all they had in common was the color of their skin. Whereas he lamented the direction the country had taken, she encouraged it. A former congresswoman from California, she had famously posed for a campaign poster with an AK-47 cradled in her arms and the words "Burn, Baby, Burn" above her head. The first half of her name, "Potts," was from a former lover now serving a life sentence for bombing a synagogue. The second half, "Jones," was that of her father, Martin Luther Jones.

Lucinda had chosen her as a sop to the far reaches of her faction. A growing minority who commanded adoring media attention, they had never made their peace with Lucinda Trent Vere and the rest of their party. A white, blonde aristocrat from Boston, Lucinda was the end-product of the "racist" society they inveighed against so fiercely. For them, racism was not just the country's original sin, it was the basis for every inequity – wealth, education, social position – suffered by their partisans for 400 years. The president and her advisors believed that bringing Potts-Jones "inside the tent" would soften the hard edges, and add to their coalition, and so far they seemed to be right.

Access to the ballot was also a problem for the former president's campaign. The deadline to appear on the presidential ballot in all fifty states had passed months ago. Rumors regarding a fix – lawsuits against the states, a writ to the Supreme Court – swirled about the Capitol. The party's solution was revealed by its chairman on one of the Sunday morning talk shows:

"We've decided to do nothing," said the chairman.

"You're giving up?" said the host.

"Oh, no. Not at all. We plan to campaign vigorously right up to Election Day."

"For president?"

"Yes."

The host hesitated, puzzled. "I don't understand."

"We have a name at the top of the ticket. A man who's already won a presidential contest. We fully expect him to win again."

"But – he's dead."

"No matter. He's our candidate and, come Election Day, he'll be elected President of the United States."

This announcement was met with a few hours of silence while the mainstream pundits and social media gurus organized a response. Their initial salvo was ridicule. News readers for the major networks smiled and suggested, uniformly, that "perhaps the president's illness had addled more brains than his." The extremes on cable news laughed about "zombie presidents" and passed along rumors that the president wasn't really dead. The *Post* performed a "fact check" and found that his grave at Arlington was undisturbed.

After further thought, media and politicians condemned the plan as "interfering in the electoral process" and "stoking partisan tensions." Not long after that they began to address the real problem among themselves: If the former president's voters went to the polls, they might indeed "re-elect" him, and would certainly impact the rest of the ballot. And even if a dead man was unable to serve, could Lucinda Vere be president if he out-polled her? Would Jeremiah Jefferson lay claim to the office? After much harrumphing, a petition was filed with the Supreme Court of the United States seeking relief from this "cynical attempt to corrupt the nation's elections," but the Court, without comment, declined to participate.

Thereafter, the press reverted to its usual means of persuasion. What, they inquired, would happen after the election? Who would be inaugurated? Condescending voices in broadcast newsrooms and on editorial boards purported to instruct the public on the inevitable crisis. Every story assumed that its viewpoint was correct and therefore not open to question. A vote for the dead president meant chaos. The future of the republic hung in the balance.

In fact, the nature of the republic provided the argument, never fully articulated in the mainstream or social media, for the campaign. It was also downplayed, if not ignored altogether, by its proponents in order to keep their partisans fixated on their dead hero. I tried to fill the gap:

WHO REALLY ELECTS THE PRESIDENT?
Tommy Sawyer

Who elects the President of the United States? Most Americans believe they do but it's not really so. Yes, those millions of votes we see tallied on Election Night play an important role but they represent only an interim step. The president is actually chosen by a group of people most of us have never heard of.

The popular vote really elects "electors" from one party or the other who are determined, with minor exceptions, on a winner-take-all basis. That is, the candidate who wins a majority of a state's votes, even if only by a single vote, gets all the state's electors. Those electors, in turn, meet in mid-December to vote for a president and vice-president.

Nothing in the Constitution or federal law requires that they be bound by the popular vote but, in practice, they almost always abide by the will of the people. After those electoral votes are cast in each state – separate ballots for president and vice-president – they are sent on to the House of Representatives where they are counted during a joint session of Congress. The result is certified by the President of the Senate, and the inauguration takes place a few weeks later.

Legally speaking, then, when you pull that lever on Election Day you're not actually voting for the person whose name is on the ballot, which brings us to the current controversy: If the deceased president wins, who will be sworn in on Inauguration Day? The short answer, as always, is whoever the electors choose. But what are the restraints, if any, on that choice? And do those electors truly have the right to make that decision?

Taking the second question first, is an elector purporting to "stand-in" for a man everyone knows is dead and thus unable to serve, legitimate? Understandably, the Constitution is silent in this regard. All it requires is that each state appoints electors as it sees fit. Also, as noted, electors are not necessarily required to vote for the person who gets the most votes, so it might be argued that the candidate named on the ballot is irrelevant anyway.

With respect to the first question, it's unlikely an elector would vote for a dead man to become president. Absent some enforceable restriction on whom he might choose imposed by a state or political party, a limitation recently upheld by the Supreme Court, it seems likely he can pick from all those who meet the Constitution's eligibility requirements – a citizen over thirty-five years old and resident in the United States for fourteen years.

If that's the case, the potential for mischief seems high. Rather than seeking a mandate from 150 million voters, only a majority of the Electoral College – 270 of 538 votes – is necessary to elect a president. Perhaps more troubling in these tumultuous times is the prospect of a deadlock among the electors, or one where no candidate receives a majority. Under those circumstances, the vote is de-

cided by the institution deemed closest to the people, the House of Representatives. Since the House is also our most polarized arm of government, whatever its members decide might be unpredictable, to say the least.

FOUR

*We toiled not in the acquirement
or establishment of them – they
are a legacy bequeathed us, by a
once hardy, brave, and patriotic,
but now lamented and departed
race of ancestors –*
Abraham Lincoln, 1838

THE CAMPAIGN to re-elect the dead president began with a nation-wide advertising blitz
emphasizing his contempt for the political establishment, half of which now invoked his name to
justify its own preservation. His image was everywhere and, whether intentionally or not, the bizarre circumstances served to reinforce the notion,
among friend and foe alike, that he had been assassinated. To tamp down the increasingly acrimoni-
ous debate, and to limit its impact on her political
fortunes, President Vere determined to appoint a
committee to investigate.

She met the press this time in the Rose Garden. Rain threatened, and an awning had been
added to the platform to shelter the dignitaries.
Television cameras broadcast the proceedings to
the nation.

Before introducing the members of her commission – the three living former presidents, the
Chief Justice of the United States and the Speaker
of the House of Representatives – she said, "The
president died of a terrible disease after every possible effort to save him. The facts are indisputable.
However, because of irresponsible speculation to
the contrary, I've appointed this commission to
study the evidence and report back to the nation.
They will be given access to everything, classified
and unclassified. I've asked them to submit their
report six months from today."

After each member of the commission made
a few remarks, the president returned to the podium. "Questions?" she said.

I raised my hand without much hope given
our last encounter, but she surprised me. "Tommy?"

"What could possibly be classified about this
investigation?" I said.

"I don't know. But it always comes up. We'll
deal with it when it does."

I pushed my luck. "Why six months? Surely
it can be done faster than that."

She shook her head. "We'll leave no stone
unturned. I believe six months is the minimum we
should devote to it."

Actually, the proposed timing of the commission's report exposed it for the time-honored politics
it was – a holding action designed to quiet the controversy until after the election and well into the
next Vere administration. The media would flog
hundreds of "crises" in the interim, and there would
be delays and extensions of the commission's mandate so that when the report was finally issued,

maybe no one would remember what all the fuss was about.

And "classification" issues would certainly be raised. Armies of bureaucrats existed only to conceal even the most benign acts of government from the public eye. Depending on its political significance and whose ox was being gored, classified information was often "leaked" to the media, another means by which press and politicians manipulated public opinion. In order to ensure that only they could engage in this selective parsing, those same politicians had declared leaking a crime, but the criminals were never prosecuted.

Fully aware that her commission was only an exercise in political damage control, the reporters in the garden wanted to talk about other things. "The polls have you running neck-and-neck with a dead man," said the woman from the *Times.* "Would you like to comment on that?"

I rehearsed the rote reply in my head: "I don't pay any attention . . ."

"I don't pay any attention to the polls," said the president. "The only poll that matters is the one we'll conduct in a few weeks." She looked over the crowd and pointed. "Yes?"

"What about the protests in Oregon?" called another woman, this one the White House correspondent for the Associated Press. "What's the federal government doing?"

"We are coordinating with Governor Monroe and Oregon law enforcement, and I've directed the F.B.I. to investigate. We know exactly who they are. The so-called White Army will meet swift justice. We don't tolerate their brand of racism in this country."

I wanted to ask her about the "brands" of racism we *did* tolerate but restrained myself. "Race" was the great divide, despite the fact that, genetically speaking, all of humanity was virtually the same. Racism wasn't really about skin color, it was about ancestry, who your people were, and was thus far too complicated for the average reporter or politician to wrap his brain around. The great god "Science," in this case, just got in the way of the rhetoric.

A day earlier, a group calling themselves "Americans United" had gathered in front of the Oregon State Capitol to protest legislation allowing non-citizens to participate in local, state and federal elections. With cameras rolling and reporters hovering, another group, wearing masks and armed with clubs and tasers, waded into the protestors. Dubbed the "Red Brigade" by the press and lionized for their "diversity" – they famously refused to permit whites to join in their mayhem – they beat dozens of people to the ground and chased the rest away. A few policemen stood by, watching.

It had become a familiar scene on the nation's screens, but this time was different. As the reporters moved in to interview the Brigade's leaders, another swarm of people, carrying guns as well as clubs, appeared. There were no masks and the faces were all white, and they wore white caps with red and blue lettering: "The White Army." The police were quickly disarmed, and the Brigade surrounded and systematically beaten unconscious. There were no gunshots but two people were left dead – one a member of the Brigade, the other an elderly woman who had been part of Americans United. Two television reporters were injured.

The politicians in Salem and the media declared a national emergency, and demanded that the White Army be eradicated. The Oregon National Guard was activated, and President Vere placed regular Army units on stand-by. According to the social media, White Army cells were springing up all over the country. The caps were available on Amazon.

Their overarching goal was secession. Their politics spanned the spectrum from left to right, but they shared a common belief that the country had failed and they no longer wanted to be part of it. The various factions had put aside their differences and united under the White Army banner. They claimed that the name had been selected, not as a provocation, but to highlight the historical distinctions between "Red" and "White." Its leaders assumed *noms de guerre* from the Russian Revolution.

Calls for secession from several quarters had been ongoing for years. The Alaska Independent Party, the Northwest Kingdom of Cascadia and the New Republic of Texas had made several attempts to leave the United States "legally," always thwarted by courts and legislatures protecting the status quo. A bill of secession had been introduced in the Oregon Legislative Assembly, where it was promptly voted down by a large majority, leading to the militarization of the movement that ultimately became the White Army.

Legal secession had been abandoned in favor of the more militant kind. Many of its nominal participants objected to the violence, but tolerated it in order to preserve the "country" they were trying to create. The Red Brigade was intent on destroying that country – victory in the secession wars would be pyrrhic if the Brigade and its adherents were allowed to operate unchecked.

A light rain began to fall. "I understand the Sons of Liberty are coming to the White House," said a third lady from National Public Radio. "Is that right?"

"Yes," said the president. "We're still working out the details. There'll be a ceremonial surrender of arms on the South Lawn." She smiled. "I don't want them bringing guns into *my* house." Almost everyone laughed.

And so it went for another twenty minutes. Her first nationally televised appearance since assuming office, it was a love-in. She was the first woman president, not to mention the first woman vice-president and the first woman chief justice. More importantly, she was a member of their clan, and she believed all the things they believed, and they would do all they could to see that she was elected president in her own right.

One of her military aides stopped me on my way out. "Mr. Sawyer?"

"Yes."

"The president would like to speak to you," she said. "In the Oval Office."

I'd been there before, twice, but on those occasions I had entered the West Wing directly through a door off West Executive Avenue. This time we left the Rose Garden and walked past the Cabinet Room. Near the end of the corridor, we stopped outside the Oval Office where my escort announced me to the president's secretary, a man wearing the uniform and insignia of a Navy ensign. A few seconds later, Lucinda leaned into the hallway. "Tommy. Come in." She looked at her secretary. "I don't want to be disturbed," she said, and locked the door behind us.

THE PRESIDENT'S Commission on the Death of the President wasn't the only assassination story making news. Thousands of people across the country had confessed to killing him, and their numbers increased daily. They formed clubs and published blogs, and appeared on talk shows where they revealed the details of their "crimes." News segments on radio and television were devoted to the most creative murders. On-line forums asked participants to vote for the best scenarios. Novels, plays and movies were rushed into production.

Because they lacked media, cultural and government resources, those who mourned the president's death – or had sickened of the reaction to it – began turning off their radios and televisions. Newspaper subscriptions were cancelled. Citizens between the coasts drew ever closer to families and friends. Increasingly, they separated from the society that had already separated from them. Every scab was picked at relentlessly by one or the other faction and, inevitably, when something went wrong, it was the other side's fault.

Sales of guns and bullets exploded but, unlike such binges in the past, buyers were spread evenly across the country, and the usual furor over gun control had abated. The Ivy League schools announced that ten per cent of each freshman class had been reserved for the Sons of Liberty. "Protests" attributed to historic injustices roiled the nation's cities. Mega-churches multiplied, and street preachers raged on every corner.

For many on both sides of the divide, the alternative universe they once only visited had become real. Nothing and everything was true, and unrelieved hatred of the "other" was the new watchword. I was caught in the middle – a member of the media that was largely responsible for all the ill feeling, I didn't share its orthodoxies. Neither side wanted to talk to me and, as a consequence, my inquiry into the president's liver disease was stymied early on.

The relevant records seemed to confirm the official account of his death, though there were some odd coincidences that raised a few eyebrows. For instance, mushrooms had been served in the family dining room the evening before his first complaint. They weren't "death cap" mushrooms, of course, and other people, including his wife and children, ate them as well.

Also, the president was a long-time user of botox, and he kept a bottle of Tylenol on his bedside table. Blood tests had confirmed that neither was in his system in the hours leading up to his death but, again, those inclined to discount the idea that his disease was enigmatic found it hard not to speculate. The conspiracies they generated – plots among family, staff and a combination of the two –

competed with the assassination confessions for the media's attention.

Only the president's personal physician agreed to talk to me. We met at a bar in the Willard Hotel just around the corner from the White House. It was wet, windy and cold, and my umbrella, only part of which opened when I pressed the button, provided little protection from the blowing rain.

It took me a moment to locate him, slumped in a corner booth on the far side of the circular bar. Framed drawings of famous patrons loomed over him. Owing to the gloom outside, there was little light from the windows, and the electric globes on the walls had not yet been switched on. Aside from the bartender, we were alone.

I stood over him for a few seconds, but he didn't look up. He seemed shriveled somehow, smaller and more fragile since I last saw him. Swaddled in a black raincoat that was too big for him, his head extended from its upturned collar like a bloom from its leaves. Sunglasses and a matching rain hat completed the ensemble. Though it was not yet 11:00 AM, he had a drink in hand and it wasn't his first.

I sat down across from him. He raised his eyes. "I'm Tommy Sawyer, Doctor Cohen. From the *Star*. Thanks for coming." He continued to regard me in silence. "I watched you testify on the Hill the other day, and I read over the transcripts last night. I have a few –"

"I've been threatened," he whispered.

"By who?"

"By everybody." He lifted his hand for the bartender. "They claim I killed him. Thousands of them."

"Have you been to the police?"

He nodded. "Don't worry, they say. It's just Internet trolls." He paused. "What do I know? I'm worried."

I shook my head. His was a cohort in which idle threats had rarely been made. They were ubiquitous now, words wielded like weapons by anonymous cowards bent on inflicting pain at no risk to themselves. Yelling "Fire!" in a crowded theater was no longer a crime – it was encouraged by an endless chorus doing the same thing.

The bartender delivered his drink – he was drinking mint juleps for some reason – and I ordered a beer. "They're probably right," I said. "People do it because they can. It's just a bunch of blowhards."

"But – what kind of world is that? Strangers making threats. Calling me names." He lifted his glass. "It's barbaric."

"It's the world we live in." I paused. "Was it your decision to send the president to Walter Reed?"

He stared at me, blinking, as if trying to recall who I was. After a moment, he said, "Not really. He needed to go to the hospital. Somebody said 'Walter Reed' so that's what we did."

"Who was that?"

"I'm sorry. I don't remember."

For the next hour we discussed the facts and fantasies regarding the president's death. The only news was that Doctor Cohen himself had performed the botox injections, which theoretically made him a suspect in the president's death – botox was extremely lethal if misused – but there was no hint of guilt. "I told him it was silly," he said. "His father would've laughed at him. But he insisted."

As we rose to leave, he said, "I just remembered. It was the vice-president who first mentioned Walter Reed."

"The vice-president? She was there?" According to the press, Lucinda had been at a fund-raiser in New York when the president fell ill.

"Yes. I remember it now because of her voice. You know, that Boston 'I came over on the Mayflower' accent."

"Lucinda Vere was at the White House when the president got sick? In the same room?"

"That's right."

"Who else was there?"

"The chief of staff."

"That's all?"

He nodded.

We crossed the lobby together. I stopped at the newsstand. "Don't use my name," he said. "Please."

"I won't."

He turned toward the revolving door and exited onto Pennsylvania Avenue. I picked up a copy of the *Star,* hot off the press. The headline read, "Twelve Die in Crash at Reagan." The sub-head was "Former Presidential Aide Among the Dead." I scanned the story. The dead president's chief of staff had been killed that morning when a private jet crashed on takeoff at Reagan National Airport. There were no survivors.

I paused on the sidewalk, immersed in the story, and didn't notice the commotion in front of me. When I looked up from the paper, traffic in all directions had stopped, people were running past me, and a crowd had gathered in the street. A policewoman speaking on a cellphone pushed through them. A siren sounded in the distance.

Doctor Cohen lay sprawled in the crosswalk, sunglasses askew. At first glance, he appeared untouched, but blood seeped from beneath him and formed rivulets that reached the curb. The cop knelt and felt for a pulse. Shaking her head, she rose and said, "Did anybody see what happened?"

Several by-standers told the same story, and it didn't sound like an accident. The doctor was crossing with the light when a pickup truck, travelling at high speed on the wrong side of the street, struck him and, without so much as a pause, crossed into the proper lane and sped away. No one was able to describe the driver or remember the license number, though one witness said she thought the truck had no license plate at all. There was disagreement regarding the make of the truck – opinion was divided between Ford and Chevrolet – but everyone agreed it was black.

By that time an ambulance and more policemen had arrived. In minutes, the body was removed and the crowd dispersed. Only the blood remained, and it was already merging with the other stains on the pavement. I went back inside and ordered a mint julep.

New conspiracies were in the offing. The two people closest to the president in the run-up to his death had been killed within hours of each other.

When the details of the doctor's death became public knowledge, the plane crash would become sinister in the eyes of many, part of a plot to deny the "truth" of the president's demise. Others would argue that they were murdered by the Martyrs for Christ in retribution for not saving him. And, given the way Doctor Cohen died, there was more than a little evidence that one of the conspiracies was real.

According to him, a third person was on hand when the president got sick – the current President of the United States. Would she be the next victim? As I turned it over in my head, an equally disturbing possibility occurred – was she part of the plot? Or had I become delusional, too?

Still in a state of shock, I let my eyes wander down the rest of the front page. Things had changed elsewhere, seemingly for the better. Torrential rains had ended the drought in West Africa, paving the way for crop production not seen in decades. The tropical storm that once churned the mid-Atlantic, dubbed *Joan* by the National Hurricane Center, had become muddled, and was about to slip off the media radar. World-wide, the news was anodyne, for today anyway.

One of the paper's columnists, a recent graduate of Sweet Briar College, specialized in whimsy. She wrote vignettes about people who refused to go with the flow, most often those who resisted the ever-tightening grip of government bureaucracy. Her column always made me feel better.

Today's edition was a little different. It featured Alberto Sanchez, a plumber in New York City who, according to him, made a "good living" servicing the fancy apartment buildings that lined Central Park. The tenants' association at one of them, The Dakota, had advised him that his workforce was not sufficiently diverse and that, unless he added black and brown people of various genders, sexual outlooks and preferences, it would terminate his services.

Sanchez, a man of Mexican heritage, checked with his union steward and was advised that there were no plumbers of that description currently available and probably never would be. The Dakota was unmoved. Then Sanchez got mad. "As of five days ago, we stopped answering their calls," he told the *Star's* columnist. "I've talked to my competitors. They aren't going to The Dakota, either. They don't want to get caught up in that stuff. It's crazy."

BACK ISSUES of the *Star* and other newspapers barely mentioned Vice-President Vere in their coverage of the president's death, nor did I find much in the Internet archives. A few sources said she was in New York giving a speech to a group of bankers when news of his illness broke, and one reported that "she hurried back to Washington" with an augmented Secret Service detail. Her ultimate destination wasn't mentioned, and there was nothing to indicate she went to the White House. Her name hadn't come up during the hearings on Capitol Hill and, despite the saturation coverage, she never appeared in the narrative of his death.

Stranger still, a media obsessed with partisan politics had failed to comment on her absence from the story. She was their lodestar, the vessel into which they poured all their ideological ambitions. For her to go unmentioned when their dreams were about to become real seemed beyond happenstance.

I shook my head to clear the gathering accusations. Was Cohen wrong? His recollection of her voice was plausible, and what reason would he have to lie? The bankers' association confirmed that she had spoken to them for an hour and, uncharacteristically, left without taking questions. Her public itinerary for the day ended with the speech in New York. Her calendar for the following morning, when the president was moved to Walter Reed, was blank.

And what difference did it make? Whether she was there or not, nothing said she had anything to do with his death. A suggestion that he go to Walter Reed, the Army hospital where presidents often went for medical procedures, was unremarkable.

It was the unaccustomed reticence, the *failure* to report on her whereabouts, that gave rise to suspicion. In an age where nothing went unsaid, the situation of the woman who would become president was news, and its suppression – if that's what it was – was bigger news. Her absence from the story and the death of two people might generate a firestorm that would be hard to ignore.

I scrolled through my email. Marty Jones had left me on my own:

No prints on the envelopes and the DNA on the stamp is not in any database. I'll be in Seattle for the rest of the week. The ball's in your court.

Jones, an ardent capitalist, had not abandoned his real estate business when he bought the *Georgetown Star.* Early in his career, he had created a lucrative niche catering to "survivalists." In the beginning, he built his bunker communities in remote locations chosen for their isolation. Conceived as havens from nuclear fallout, pandemics and government overreach, the bogies now were global warming, terrorism and, most especially, the increasing hostility among the population. As a consequence, the sensibilities of his buyers had changed, and his most recent projects were situated near the cities on both coasts where they lived.

They were not the fallout shelters of the 1950s. Most of them came with amenities like tennis courts, hotels and polo fields. Lakes and beaches were carved from soil and rock to provide "waterfront views" for hundreds of dwellings built almost entirely underground. Armed security guards patrolled the walled compounds, and helipads allowed for ingress and egress. Sealed vaults were available to preserve DNA in the event cataclysm actually arrived. Prices began at $2 million, and they were selling like hotcakes.

According to Marty, buyers for his bunkers reflected the hierarchies where they were located. Hollywood types and sports stars, for instance, owned most of his West Coast community. New York's Upper East Side had bought out the compound on Long Island. Washington politicians could decamp for the mountains of the Maryland panhandle in case of trouble.

Golf courses planned for each community had been eliminated. Now firmly linked in the "progressive" mind to the dead president, pre-construction surveys revealed that most of Jones's potential buyers emphatically rejected any association with the game. Another survey demonstrated that they preferred communal gardens or arrays of solar panels though, to date, none had been built.

While unapologetic about his new clientele, Jones regretted their surprising lack of social conscience. "I believed all that preaching about diversity," he said. "But that's the last thing those people want."

"Maybe the price tag has something to do with the pale faces," I said.

He shook his head. "They say they're worried about property values. Personal safety. Crime, even." He paused. "Rich people come in all colors, but some are less desirable neighbors than others. It's a race thing. A stereotype."

The notion that diversity was a contrivance rejected by its champions made Jones wonder if it was likewise anathema to those they pandered to. His latest efforts were planned communities whose citizens were limited to a single race. Construction of the first village, for blacks only, was underway on the northwest coast of Washington. Plans for Hispanic and Asian enclaves were on the drawing board.

The Washington project was sold out. Unlike his bunkers, there were no physical barriers. It was designed to be an ordinary, middle-class community where everyone, from the mayor to the sanitation worker, was black. Their self-appointed guardians were horrified, and suits to stop it were pending, though the basis for the litigation was unclear.

Jones was also engaged in a running battle with the local chapter of "Boycott Racists Now," an organization seeking to ban commerce between "racist states," meaning those that voted for the former president the first time around, and "progressive states," meaning those that didn't. Their campaign had achieved some success – New York no longer "imported" guacamole from Texas and California had banned alligator hides from Florida – but had yet to acquire the momentum of previous boycott efforts. Lawsuits, of course, had been filed, injunctions issued, and the powers of the third branch of government further enhanced.

Manipulation of the markets was Marty's *bête noir.* His mantra was that people left to their own devices, without interference from the state, would create the most successful society, and he viewed those unable to thrive under such a régime as "eggs in the omelet." He was the founder of the Adam Smith Society, an organization that challenged any act of government – local, state or national – that infringed on the people's right to do business. His editorial page often served as his megaphone.

He and his friends were opposed by the entirety of the country's governmental, cultural and educational establishments, and much of the "woke" business community as well. Ironically, many of those same people had made a lot of money investing in his various enterprises. Defending unfettered capitalism sometimes made for strange, not to say repugnant, bedfellows, but as long as there were willing buyers and willing sellers, he argued on their behalf. Despite themselves, his foes sometimes agreed with him though for different reasons.

For instance, though theoretically opposed to abortion, Jones viewed it in terms of supply and demand, whereas for its proponents it was a blood sacrifice essential to their worldview. The country's abortionists were extremely profitable, a fact Marty found hard to ignore. Harvesting organs was also big business. Those who supported it ignored the money except when converted into campaign contributions, but the politics was far-reaching – impeachments were underway in dozens of jurisdictions for judges who failed to toe the line.

After a particularly unsympathetic editorial about the plight of workers in the sex industry, I confronted him: "Don't you think those people deserve a little compassion?" I said. "They don't choose to live like that."

"How do you know?"

"Because no one would."

"I disagree. There's a market for it, and someone will always supply that market."

"But – it's demeaning. It makes them less than human."

"That's your opinion. It's not mine and, I suspect, it's not theirs, either."

He used his wealth in other ways. Fascinated by the genetics revolution, he built a sprawling laboratory just outside Reno, Nevada, whose mission was to "improve" the species by manipulating human DNA. Over time, his lab had developed tools that helped eliminate birth defects and reduce the impact of certain genetic diseases. Recently, it had focused on humanity's minute differences in race and ethnicity in order to discover why those diseases only appeared in certain segments of the population.

A separate division was charged with investigating diseases not ordinarily considered genetic. He had a heart condition that his doctors said was heritable, and he wanted his geneticists to explain why and, if possible, do something about it.

Jones's disdain for government regulation did not preclude business *with* the government. He had raised public buildings all over the country, and was currently engaged in the construction of the largest such project ever conceived. Universally panned for its scale and grandiosity when proposed during the previous administration, criticism turned to praise when President Vere changed its name. Originally dedicated to the dead president, it was now called the People's Plaza.

Its mission had likewise changed. First imagined as a monument to capitalism, its millions of square feet and miles of corridors were initially dedicated to the business of America, from the smallest one-man entrepreneur to the largest corporations in the world. The Vere Administration had recently proclaimed that the People's Plaza would instead serve as the headquarters for its war on poverty, injustice and racism. A bill creating the Department of Equity was pending in the Congress.

Jones kept a rendering on the wall in his office. Made almost entirely of white marble, the central tower – embellished by gothic spires and arches – stood nearly 2,000 feet high. Dozens of massive temples in the Greek Revival style formed its stepping-stone base. Classical details from mankind's architectural past – arches, domes, pediments – were appended randomly like ornaments on a Christmas tree.

Criticism of the project wasn't limited to aesthetics. The former president was anxious to have it finished in time for his second inauguration, so it was conceived as a "design/build" project to be constructed on a "fast track" basis, and let for bids. Responsibility for the entire job, with only minimal oversight, was in the hands of the successful bidder, Mammoth Construction Company, whose Chief Executive Officer was Martin Luther Jones.

With an unrealistic deadline and only the barest guidance regarding the end result, educated engineering assumptions were made in order to get the project underway. One of those assumptions proved wildly false. The District of Columbia's seventy square miles sat atop two geographic provinces, the Piedmont and the Coastal Plain. The northwest third of the District was in the Piedmont where granite and other remnants of the Blue Ridge Mountains lay beneath the surface. The rest lay in the Coastal Plain whose underground geology consisted of sand, gravel and clay. The building site appeared to be easily within the Piedmont but, after construction was well under way, it was determined that the building's foundation was actually located in the weaker, looser soil of the Coastal Plain. The site's elevation, among the lowest in the city, added to the problem.

The critics howled. The ongoing construction of the building's foundation, designed for the Piedmont's solid rock, could not support the loads –

wind, the structure itself and the people and things inside it – that would be imposed when it was finished. The former president, faced with the loss of his monument, sent out his vice-president, Lucinda Trent Vere, to defend the project. She was accompanied by Marty Jones.

Lucinda's trust in big government extended to the infrastructure it occupied, and she had no trouble making the case for forging ahead. Marty, staring at losses in the millions, assured everyone that a "fix" was in the works. In the end the fix, though severely criticized by professionals as inadequate, was implemented and construction continued. Politicians and the media, mollified by Lucinda's endorsement, grumbled and moved on.

The Peace Plaza's most unusual, and most controversial, feature was the final 250 feet, a steel steeple plated with gold and topped by a solid gold medallion. Once seen as a "kick in the teeth" to low-income citizens barely able to get by, it was now hailed as the symbol of "the cornucopia of America, soon to be available to everyone." In the original design, the medallion was inscribed with the former president's monogram. After much discussion, it now featured a raised fist. Located in the heart of a once-thriving minority neighborhood in the nation's capital, Jones's forces were scrambling to complete the structure by Election Day. Criticism of the engineering was forgotten.

The leader of the boycott movement, Matilda Fleck, was also president of one of the local colleges. Rather than celebrate the culture that cossetted her and her colleagues, or at least treat it evenhandedly, she championed every new scheme devised to destroy it while pledging fealty to academic excellence. Naturally, she was the go-to "expert" for the networks and cable channels whenever the issue was "education."

Her most recent enthusiasm was "Open College," an aspirational construct whereby all requirements for college admission – grades, test scores, literacy, numeracy – were abolished. So long as a prospective student could pay the tuition, usually funded by the taxpayers, she could enroll. People who otherwise agreed with all of Fleck's ideas were divided. Some viewed a college diploma, at least from certain schools, as an obligatory credential for induction into the country's secular priesthood. Others saw it as the rankest form of racism, and argued that colleges should either be eliminated or degrees awarded to whoever wanted one.

Fleck, who wore a hood and academic robes whenever she appeared on television, possessed a single characteristic that separated her from the academic herd and made her invaluable to the media. She spoke in clear, concise sentences, without jargon. No one who heard her had any doubt about where she stood. A recent interview was a good example:

"With the president dead, Doctor Fleck," said the news anchor, "will you end your boycott?"

"Certainly not. He was only an indicator. The virus, of which he was the most prominent symptom, must be stamped out."

"Virus?"

"Yes. A plague of racism and ignorance." She paused. "Minds have to change. Those people need to do the right thing."

"And the mechanism for that is what?"

"We will stop doing business with them until they see things our way. Their wheat and their corn will rot in the fields. Their Frankenstein animals will die."

"Won't that have an impact on everyone else?"

"The rest of us will be fine. The economy's global now. Other countries are stepping up food production, and California's the breadbasket of the world." She stopped. "We can get whatever we need somewhere else."

Surprisingly, the benefits of a global economy were among the few things that Fleck and Jones agreed upon, Jones because it enabled a "dog eat dog" market economy that provided low costs and high profits, Fleck because it erased national boundaries and gave rise to an international elite. Globalization, in its broadest sense, had been ongoing since man emerged from the ooze, but its recent manifestations – unlimited immigration, free trade and global governance, all conducted in the same language – were intended to create a single, profane kingdom, signs of which were everywhere. Its weight had begun to settle over the world like lava from a great volcano.

MY CELLPHONE, seldom used, vibrated. Prepared to ignore it, I looked at the screen and punched the button. "Hi," I said.

"Hi," she said. "Where are you?"

"At the office. You?"

"At the office."

"Working late?"

"No. I moved in this morning."

"Oh."

"This place is – eerie. Dozens of people around and no one to talk to." She paused. "Can we have dinner tonight?"

"Sure. Where?"

"Here. It's impossible for me to go out."

"Okay. Shall I arrive at the North Portico?"

She laughed. "No. I'll have Wolf call you."

The White House complex stretched north and south from Lafayette Square to the Ellipse, and east and west from 15th Street to 17th Street. Within that grid were roadways – East and West Executive Avenues, State Place, part of E Street and two blocks of Pennsylvania Avenue – once open to the public, now closed "for reasons of national security" dating as far back as 1951.

The mansion itself was comprised of 6 stories, including basements, and 55,000 square feet of floor space. There were 132 rooms, eight staircases, twenty-eight fireplaces and three dozen bathrooms. Amenities included a tennis court, bowling alley, jogging track, movie theater, swimming pool and putting green. Five full-time chefs prepared meals for the president and her guests. All of this, of course, was funded by the taxpayers, but the President's House, where ordinary citizens once attended inaugurals and receptions on the Fourth of July, was now accessible by invitation only, and those invitations were hard to come by.

A slash of lightning illuminated the night as I stepped from my cab. Wolf Robinson, President Vere's favorite Secret Service agent, was waiting for me at the State Place gate. We walked past the

Eisenhower Executive Office Building – at one time the Department of State, now offices for various White House fiefdoms – and turned north onto West Executive Avenue. Both streets, converted into parking lots, were mostly deserted at this hour.

Robinson, half a head taller than my six feet, had been chief of Lucinda's Secret Service detail when she was vice-president. He had orchestrated our meetings in Georgetown Heights, and stood guard while we dallied. A former Marine, he was intensely loyal to the new president, and unlikely to reveal anything she didn't want known, but I tried anyway. "You were with her when the president got sick, weren't you? In New York?"

"Yes, sir."

"When you came back, did she go to the White House?"

He shifted his eyes toward me without turning his head. "Why?"

I told him part of the truth. "I'm working on a story about what happened that day. I can't find anything about her schedule after New York."

We'd reached the door into the West Wing. "You'd better ask her," he said.

I followed him down the corridors to the president's study adjacent to the Oval Office. After knocking on the door, he pushed it open. Lucinda was sitting behind the desk.

She rose. "Thank you, Wolf."

He left us, closing the door behind him. We shared a quick embrace. "Thanks for coming, Tommy. The first night here is a little intimidating." She paused. "I was just upstairs in the residence. Rooms, rooms and more rooms. All unoccupied."

"Lonesome?"

She sighed. "I'll get used to it, I guess."

"I could make you an honest woman. Keep you company."

She smiled. "If that's a proposal, I'll pass. For now."

We ate in the small dining room next to her study. The food was cold – shrimp salad, bread and cheesecake – and we served ourselves. I cleared the dishes while she poured a brandy for each of us, and we returned to her study. "Were you here when the president got sick? In the same room?" I said. She gazed at me, but didn't answer. "Doctor Cohen says you were." There was still no response. I watched her carefully. "He's dead, by the way. Run over by a pickup truck."

Her eyes widened. "When?"

"This afternoon. In front of the Willard Hotel." I stopped. "And I'm sure you've heard about the plane crash."

We sat in silence. Finally, she said, "I'll tell you what happened that day, but you have to promise to keep it to yourself." I frowned. "It's not about me. It's for the good of the country."

I frowned again. "Patriotism?" I said. "The last refuge of the scoundrel?"

She smiled. "Are you calling me a scoundrel?"

I smiled, too. "Everything's a secret now. And that's *not* good for the country."

"This is important. Believe me."

"Okay. Tell me."

"They hustled me back here because it was the safest place. They thought he might've been poisoned somehow. They didn't want me to be next."

"Who's they?"

"The Secret Service."

"Why did they think he'd been poisoned?"

"I – I'm not sure." She paused. "It's classified."

I raised my brows. "Really?" She nodded. "I thought all that classification BS wasn't going to get in the way." She didn't answer. After a moment, I said, "Do they still think he was poisoned?"

"No. The medical evidence seems pretty conclusive."

"If it's accurate." I hesitated. "Are you doing anything about it?"

"No. He died of liver failure. Even a hint of something else, something official, might start a civil war."

"Is that why none of your friends are reporting it?"

"Yes."

Further questions were met with silence. Finally, she said, "Please, Tommy. I can't talk about it."

We sat in silence. Reaching for my hand, she said, "I want to show you something."

We passed into the Oval Office and then into the hallway beyond. She pressed a wall panel that slid aside, revealing a staircase. At the bottom of the steps was a passageway that led to an elevator. "Wolf just showed me this today," she said. She pushed a button and we began to rise. At the top, the doors opened and we stepped into a tiny enclosure that turned out to be a closet in her bedroom. "It was installed in case of a terrorist attack," she said. "We can use it for something else."

I DECIDED to walk home. The rain had stopped and the weather had turned warm. A few storefronts along Pennsylvania Avenue gave way to monolithic office towers whose daytime occupants fled each evening to the Virginia and Maryland suburbs. The only people in the parks were homeless.

On the far side of Washington Circle, I crossed Rock Creek and turned north on 28th Street. As I climbed to Georgetown Heights, the houses became fewer and grander until, just beyond Q Street, there was only one. A palace surrounded by brick walls, perched on some of the richest real estate in the world, its opulence bordered on obscene. It was really a museum, and I its reluctant caretaker.

Inside, I poured some scotch and switched on the television. I had a story I couldn't write, not just because I'd given my word, but because Lucinda's intuition was correct. The country, already riven by rumors, couldn't risk their confirmation however improbable that might be. The truth, in this case, might be the last straw. Still, the events of the day nagged at me. And how long before someone else began asking questions?

No time at all, as it turned out. The picture on the screen, produced by a cellphone camera, was Doctor Cohen lying in the crosswalk. I turned up the volume. "The doctor's death," said the late-night anchor, "looks like murder. Combined with the crash at Reagan Airport this morning, which now appears to be the result of explosives on board, it raises concerns about how the late president died. Traffic on the Internet is unprecedented."

The only thing missing was Lucinda's presence at the White House and the reason for it. She had hushed it up with the help of a compliant press, but some elements, particularly among the social media, were beyond her control. Someone would leak the news, probably sooner rather than later, and the frenzy would accelerate.

FIVE

Theirs was the task (and nobly they performed it) to possess themselves, and through themselves, us, of this goodly land; and to uprear upon its hills and its valleys, a political edifice of liberty and equal rights; 'tis ours only to transmit these, the former, unprofaned by the foot of an invader; the latter, undecayed by the lapse of time and untorn by usurpation, to the latest generation that fate shall permit the world to know
– Abraham Lincoln, 1838

RELUCTANTLY, I decided to change course. Though I was convinced he'd died of liver disease, I would play the devil's advocate. Having begun my investigation on the assumption that the president had succumbed by way of natural, albeit unusual, causes, I took the opposite tack: He'd been murdered, perhaps in a manner already suggested, perhaps by way of something not yet disclosed. Every possibility under the sun was bouncing around in the media, but I would begin with the facts with which I was personally acquainted.

First were the letter to the *Star* and the hair in the envelope. I felt a twinge of disloyalty as I acknowledged that they were facts only because Marty Jones said so, but I had to start somewhere. Whoever had sent them was either just one of many or an actual assassin and, as far as I knew, none of the others had provided a lock of hair or any other evidence of access to the dead president.

Next were Doctor Cohen's revelations that Lucinda Vere had been present while the president's treatment was debated, and it was she who had proposed he be sent to Walter Reed. The doctor's apparent lack of motive to lie, combined with his probable murder, allowed me to accept his account as true. Plus, I had given her the chance to deny it, and she had declined to do so.

Finally, there were the things she *had* said: The Secret Service had spirited her back to the White House because they feared the president had been poisoned and she might be next, neither of which they believed any longer because the medical evidence "seemed" conclusive. Everyone was keeping it all a secret , supposedly for the good of the country. It seemed likely that some or all of that story was false and, if it was, the question was why.

Why suppress something as trivial as her whereabouts? Why conceal the poison narrative if the medical evidence was truly conclusive? And since when did her media partisans care about the good of the country? As I considered the next step, maybe the most important question popped into my head: Had *I* swallowed the Kool-Aid?

THE PRESIDENTIAL hair had been a media obsession from the beginning. Thousands of purportedly serious news outlets "analyzed" its style, length and color, always in an effort to demean and ridicule. It gave the chattering classes something else to sneer at, while providing further evidence of the media's increasing pettiness.

Predictably, the president's response was to provide more rope. He instituted a weekly ritual dubbed "The President's Salon" during which his personal barber set up shop in the Roosevelt Room and cut his hair. Invitations to each televised event, where the participants could "engage in informal and frank exchanges with the president," were issued to media executives and high-profile reporters. Each "salon" was limited to ten people and, at first, it was the hottest ticket in town.

In practice, the salons were conducted along the same lines as the gaggles. The regular furniture was moved out and a dark curtain used to cut the room in half. The president's armchair was placed on a platform in front of the fireplace. After panning the room to show the news people dutifully seated in undersized chairs around the perimeter of the president's "barber shop," the camera remained on him for the rest of the hour.

There was no conversation – only he and his barber had microphones. Questions from the attendees were submitted beforehand and, for those he chose to answer, read aloud by the barber. The end result was a typical presidential monologue broadcast without interruption to the country while his enemies, mute, served as props.

At the end of each session, the president and his barber discussed the highlights of his hairstyle. "You don't really have to color it yet, do you?" the president, smiling at the camera, might say.

"Oh no, sir," the barber might respond. "Just a touch here and there."

"Am I going bald?"

"A little thinner, maybe, Mr. President. That's all."

"So I've got more than they do?" the president would say, indicating his guests, at which point the camera would survey the bald or nearly bald ones.

"Absolutely, Mr. President."

The TV ratings were through the roof and, after each show, his poll numbers rose. His victims were a laughingstock – even the late-night comedians made fun of them – yet, such was the aphrodisiac of proximity to the president that it was six weeks before they finally stopping coming.

It would've been easy for one of those men to pick up a few clippings of his hair. Equally plausible was the possibility that the barber had retained what he cut. I looked him up on the Internet and called to make an appointment. A cancellation made room for me right after lunch.

The shop was in the basement of a building at 18th and K Streets. Except for the prices, it appeared to be an old-fashioned barber shop with three chairs, old magazines and no women. It looked much like the set for "The President's Salon."

After I settled into his chair, the proprietor – the name above the breast of his white Nehru jacket was "Francisco" – explained what he intended to do with my unruly mane of graying red hair, and I agreed. Directly in front of me was a huge color photograph of Francisco and the president taken in the White House barber shop. Only the president's head was visible above the striped cloth tied around his neck. Francisco stood behind him, comb and scissors at the ready.

"I used to watch that show all the time," I said.

"It was so wonderful," he said, sighing. "The best days of my life."

"Was he a good customer?"

"Oh, yes. He never quibbled about my work. Always a big tip."

He pulled a comb through my hair. "Did you have any help?" I said.

"No. It was just me."

"You cleaned up afterwards?"

"Yes. It was part of the deal."

"What do you mean?"

"His hair was part of the deal. I swept it up and sold it here and on the Internet. A hundred dollars a pop." He laughed. "He told me once he wanted ten per cent, but he was just joking."

"How much did you sell?"

"I don't know. Hundreds of clumps. Maybe a thousand."

"Do you have any left?"

He shook his head. "Every batch was sold out before I collected it."

"Do you still have the names of the people who bought it?"

"No."

I hesitated. "Did you, by any chance, notice one of the guests picking some up?"

"No."

We were quiet while he finished cutting my hair. I paid him with a credit card. "Has it helped your business?" I said.

"People come from all over the country now for me to cut their hair." He gestured toward an appointment book next to the telephone. "Six guys from Chicago are coming in tomorrow."

The presidential hair concession rendered the hair in our envelope almost beside the point. Any one of a thousand anonymous individuals might've sent it. I still had to check out the media people, but the president's locks looked like a dead end. Poison, whether by mushrooms, botox or Tylenol, was next on my list.

THE CEREMONIAL return to the fold by the Sons of Liberty was accompanied by all the pageantry that Washington could muster. The White House was decorated with flags and red, white and blue bunting, military bands marched back and forth on the South Lawn, and civilian dignitaries and military brass arranged themselves on a platform beneath the Truman Balcony. Contrails left by fighter jets crisscrossed a peculiar red sky, the product of haze and a blazing blood-red sun. Television cameras ringed the platform.

The blackened remains of the Washington Monument, visible from every vantage, had been partially concealed by scaffolding, though there were no plans to rebuild it. Replicating the great obelisk was never considered. It was, after all, a tribute to a dead white man whose sins were now deemed greater than his accomplishments. Instead, another government commission had been appointed to come up with something new. It was comprised of the politically influential and those who hoped to profit, whether by ego or money or both, from a more enlightened symbol of the nation's ideals.

The choices had been narrowed to three. The first was a gigantic statue – at 566 feet, one foot taller than the monument it would replace – of the country's most recent progressive president. The second was a replica of the Statue of Liberty enameled in rainbow colors, its torch replaced by a One World flag.

The last, my favorite, was the world's largest clock tower. It featured a carillon that played "Auld Lang Syne" on the hour. The clock face was a huge, fiery sun, and the interior of the building that served as its base had the trappings of a medieval church. The clock itself was set permanently at one minute to midnight.

Despite President Vere's assurances to the contrary, the White Army remained at large, ever more prominent in the public's imagination. Social media, pro and con, raged. One side saw it as a "virulent, fascist cancer at the heart of our democratic enterprise," the other, smaller but almost as loud, called it "the last, best hope" for mankind. The press touted the Red Brigade as a countervailing force.

Rumors of a potential attack during the ceremony had circulated for days and, as a consequence, the president had ordered troops placed along the entire perimeter of the White House complex, with tanks guarding every entrance. The fence around the mansion had been electrified for the occasion. Navy helicopters hovered, and the roof bristled with snipers, rifles pointed at the sky. Members of the public were not invited.

I was seated with the rest of the press corps at right angles to the president and her podium. She wore a dark blue sheath with matching heels and a red and white scarf. She never looked more beautiful. A light breeze lifted her hair, revealing ears she felt were less than perfect. They looked fine to me.

Vada Potts-Jones, likewise a very beautiful woman, sat next to her. Surprisingly, she had come out against the pardon, not because of the mayhem the Sons had committed – she was fully on board with that – but because of the "privilege" that she claimed led to their pardon. Despite the murderous attacks, she viewed them as inauthentic, white boys playing at war until their mama – President Vere – called them home for supper.

Having participated in several "protests" with the Red Brigade, she knew who the real revolutionaries were, and the Sons of Liberty weren't among them. She had not abandoned her own privilege – she availed herself of it, openly, all the time – but, because she was on the correct side of the other critical divides – age, race, gender, sexuality, politics – her wealth was overlooked. An iconoclast who didn't always hew to the party line, she was a throwback to the counterculture of the 1960s, and her partisans thrilled at the notion of her inside the White House.

She also liked to play golf. Having learned the game at her father's club in Atlanta, and captained the team at Berkeley, she scoffed at the idea she should quit playing just because it was the former president's favorite pastime. In fact, she'd played a few rounds with him at the height of the hysteria over his golf "habit," and it was a measure of her hold on the media's imagination that, instead of condemning her, they laughed at it and told jokes about "sleeping with the enemy." She was modern-day radical chic, an avatar of the *beau monde* they so desperately wanted to join.

The *Georgetown Star* tried to treat her like any other politician – only the truth, all the time – but it was hard. She was the boss's daughter and, though unhappy with her radical ways, it was obvious that he loved her very much. I had never met her, and never had occasion to write about her.

A representative sampling of the Sons of Liberty, perhaps fifty in all, stood before the podium. Each head was covered by a black balaclava mask, and guns were slung over every shoulder. The program for the event, entitled "America – United Again," explained that the masks were necessary to prevent "profiling" and "discrimination" when the Sons re-entered polite society. As for the guns, they had seldom used them during their attacks – their weapon of choice was a drone packed with explosives. The rifles they carried now looked suspiciously like standard-issue Army carbines.

The president began her remarks with a hoary quotation used by countless politicians to demand another chance: "My fellow Americans," she said, "our long national nightmare is over."

Those watching at home may have thought she was referring to the Sons' surrender, but I knew better. It was an inside joke intended for her partisans – the "nightmare" was the previous administration. The smirks and chortles around me signified a knowing assent.

The rest of her speech was election-year boilerplate designed to convince the public that the "country had never been stronger," that our "disagreements" were actually proof of that strength, and that we would "go forward together" to ever greater prosperity. If the people favored her and her party on Election Day, "fairness" would be restored – unrestrained capitalism would be banished and replaced by a kinder, gentler variety. Her hand-picked guests, even the admirals and generals, nodded in agreement. The gentlepeople of the press led each round of applause.

Turning to the business at hand, she unfurled a scroll and began to read the Proclamation of Amnesty. Early in the "whereas" clauses, she mentioned "felonies and misdemeanors" committed by the Sons of Liberty, but that was the only reference to their crimes. Most of its many words were devoted to an enumeration of the benefits now theirs because they were *ex*-Sons of Liberty. Thus was another class added to the rolls of the entitled – no doubt a caucus would emerge soon on Capitol Hill.

When she was finished with the Proclamation, she addressed the gathered Sons directly: "You will signify your assent to these terms by surrendering your arms." One by one, each masked man approached the podium and laid his weapon on the platform beside her. I imagined that one of them might shoot her instead, but, of course, there were no bullets in the guns. The combined bands played "The Star-Spangled Banner," after which she stepped down from the platform and grasped each hand with both of hers.

To call the event surreal was to give it more heft than it deserved. A made-for-television production that everyone knew was theater, it only widened the chasms among the people who picked up the tab for the entire extravaganza. The threat from the White Army never materialized, but attack from within was apparently still on the horizon. The fence remained electrified, the snipers and the military cordon around the White House became permanent, and the tanks stayed where they were.

AS EXPECTED, the Medical Examiner's report was classified, but copies had been circulating among press and politicians since the day it was issued. Nothing in it contradicted the official storyline, and the underlying information – physician's notes, test results and other hospital records, likewise deemed "top secret" – was still unavailable. The Medical Examiner herself wasn't taking questions. The doctors at Walter Reed and George Washington University Hospital declined to meet with me.

I considered a story about the implications of all that secrecy, and decided against it. Certainly, there was no *good* reason for it, but I was reluctant to add to the rampant paranoia. Thus, I was both pleased and irritated when the cable news channel most closely aligned with the former president took up the poison narrative. The most intriguing aspect of its campaign to reveal the "truth" about his death was an effort to have his body exhumed.

The first order of business was to convince his supporters that such a wrenching procedure was necessary. They were all-in on the assassination conspiracy, but many were squeamish about digging up their hero. The religious among them, according to polls, were almost unanimous in their opposition, citing its impact on the president's potential "resurrection." After a repetitive, week-long series about the secrecy failed to move the needle, the network's panels and commentators began to speculate openly about the reason for it, that is, was he poisoned and would his body confirm it?

For its part, the mainstream press opposed the exhumation on the surprising grounds that it was "sacrilegious" and "undignified." The social media busied itself with passing around cartoons about open tombs and grave robbers and corpses in various stages of decomposition. Whatever the state of the body – gaseous bloat, maggot-infested tissue, skeletal decay – the head was always his, perfectly preserved.

The "newspaper of record" finally provided the template for media uniformity. "What purpose would be served?" it said in a Sunday editorial. "The people who indulge this partisan fantasy will never be satisfied. Four medical experts testified that he died of liver failure. Science has spoken. Enough!"

Undeterred, the cable network hit upon a winning strategy – not only had the president been poisoned, his body wasn't at Arlington at all. Without a shred of evidence, they hyped the notion that his grave was empty or occupied by someone else. Elaborate schemes, beginning with the *closed* coffin taken from the Capitol Rotunda, were debated, and rumors that he was still alive grew more fervid. Momentum built for the exhumation.

The Request for Disinterment, signed by the CEO of the network, outlined why it was necessary. After listing dozens of incidents nationwide stemming from "uncertainty over the president's death," wherein citizens had clashed with law enforcement or other citizens, the notarized affidavit concluded with a startling disclosure:

Finally, two people with direct knowledge of the president's death have died recently under questionable circumstances. Investigations commissioned by this network have revealed that one, his personal physician, and the other, his chief of staff, may both have been secret operatives of the Chinese Communist Party. Our sources in the intelligence community have refused to comment. The implications for the country are clear.

It seemed inconceivable that the government's vast security apparatus had overlooked such a malign association. More and more, its surveillance was directed inward rather than at the country's foreign adversaries, and it was entirely possible the spooks knew of the Chinese connection and chose to keep it to themselves. But the word "may" left a lot of room to maneuver in search of the "news" – Doctor Cohen, certainly, was an unlikely spy.

As it was, the media went crazy – reactions ranged from euphoric to infuriated, judged almost entirely by its supposed impact on the dead president's legacy. Speculation about *his* association with the Chinese Communists arose. Damage to the country was barely mentioned. Everyone clamored to see the reports, and opposition to the exhumation vanished.

But an unexpected roadblock stood in the way. According to the rules of the National Cemetery Association, every member of the president's immediate family had to agree to the disinterment of his body. His adult children, long accustomed to celebrity, missed it, and his widow, traumatized by the past four years, just wanted it over. Their signatures were easy to obtain.

His youngest child, however, a girl just beginning her senior year in high school, balked. Despite being savaged by the media and both sides of the partisan divide – she was routinely mocked for her resemblance to her father, particularly her hair – she stood her ground. The cable network turned to the courts, ensuring that the fever generated by the turmoil would continue to rise.

THE CAMPAIGNS for president had shifted into high gear. The old president's party resurrected videos of past rallies and replayed them on huge screens all over the country. It was standing room only at every venue. Because they were so good for ratings, and thus advertising revenue, the broadcast and cable channels covered them from start to finish. It was not unusual for three or four to be played simultaneously, and it was often easy to forget that he was dead.

The print media ridiculed these "warmed over polemics," just as they had done the first time around. What was striking, however, was how thorough the coverage was. Initially, they scoffed at the idea that a presidential campaign could be sustained by electronic images rather than a live human being, while failing to recognize that the country's electioneering had been conducted via radio, television and computers for almost a century. When it became apparent that their readers were taking the late president's "virtual" campaign seriously, they reverted to type.

The manipulation of words was their most powerful weapon. Once upon a time, the people reading them were looking for a story or information or maybe just a laugh and, by and large, they were unaware of the subtle and not-so-subtle propaganda directed at them. Those days were long past – the media existed now only to validate its own prejudices and those of its audience, and everyone knew it. The civic responsibilities implied by the Constitution in exchange for unfettered intercourse with the public were ignored, and every iteration of the mainstream press was greeted with disbelief and resentment by half the country.

However, the press was unable to concede its corruption. Instead, newspapers and newsrooms cloaked their bias in words intended to convey the message to the faithful without admitting their lack of candor. Marty Jones had laughed at the notion of "journalism," but it was this intentional exploitation of the language that set it apart from other forms of communication.

The national magazines had the techniques down pat. First and foremost, remarks that proved inaccurate by someone's measure were always "lies" when made by opponents and "misstatements" or "a slip of the tongue" when spoken by those they agreed with. If a fabrication was so egregious as to cast doubt on the veracity of a friendly source, it was explained away, often at great length – sometimes even attributed to "a confused state of mind" caused by the enemy's outrageous disregard for the truth. Unnamed, unaccountable informants were the norm. Political jeremiads posing as book reviews were universal.

Every story assumed that all previous stories were accurate even if they'd been thoroughly discredited. This, despite the fact that it was often other media who grudgingly disclosed the errors in their reports. If history interfered with the story, they changed the history. Their readers, cloistered inside a few zip codes on the coasts, were impervious to the fraud.

Even so, their "facts" were never allowed to speak for themselves. Each new piece required that their readers be freshly conditioned. They beatified their friends – "a loving mother of three" who "advocated for the poor" – and vilified their enemies – "a serial adulterer" who "cared only about money." They juxtaposed unrelated facts to diminish the validity of others, while at the same time omitting those that argued against the narrative they wanted to create. Quotations were paraphrased or bowdlerized to twist their meaning. Motives were pure or self-serving, depending on whose they were. The only hypocrites were those who disagreed with them.

Another tactic was to take a figure from history that everyone loathed and point out his purported similarities to their chosen target. Usually citing Hitler, sometimes Genghis Khan or Caligula, never Stalin or Mao, the characteristics they complained of – vanity, exaggeration, mendacity – were ordinary human traits that seldom led to death for millions, but the reader was left with the impression that genocide was just around the corner. It was guilt by association where no association existed.

The media operated in lockstep. Every new theme was quickly adopted by others and passed around among themselves until the message, and the words used to convey it, was identical. Without exception, they tried to counter this suffocating provincialism with a token European whose views were the same as theirs, only more so. When their enemy did something they had urged him to do, they condemned him for not doing enough.

The attacks were relentless. All the world's deficiencies – poverty, plagues, natural disasters – were laid at the feet of their opponents. Every failure, disappointment and inconvenience suffered by their readers resulted, not from any fault of their own, but from malicious circumstances orchestrated by the "other." They looked for conspiracies everywhere but where they really were – inside the febrile hothouses they called newsrooms.

Even the words themselves were chosen to persuade rather than inform. During the previous administration, adjectives and adverbs loaded with negative connotations were always appended to every sentence. With Lucinda Vere in the White House, they had been replaced by smiling phrases reflecting the euphoria they felt. The parsing of near-synonyms to put the worst possible spin on the most mundane event – "justify" instead of "explain," for instance, and "smirk" rather than "smile" – stopped. The new president's staff were "officials," not "commissars," "progressives" instead of "fascists."

Talk radio, which often skewed the news as badly as the rest of the media, added to the daily drumbeat of discord. Some states had passed "fairness" legislation in an effort to shut it down, and still the country was inundated by an ever-increasing number of "talkers" on radio, television and the Internet. No arena was spared. Sports, game shows, even the Sunday morning religious services, featured toxic partisan talk. Outrage was always front and center.

In keeping with the need to indulge their patrons, a few outlets made no effort to disguise the loathing they harbored for the country and its citizens, and their number was growing. They had festered unnoticed for years until the advent of the perpetual media machine, enabled by the Internet, allowed their views to go mainstream. A daily outpouring of emails and blogs ensured that the rants were only a click away. Increasingly, theirs was the commanding voice.

As a result of the rampant misinformation, all fifty states were considering restrictions on the freedoms traditionally enjoyed by the media. Each

one was carefully contrived to target only those organizations with which that particular legislature
disagreed, but the premise for all of them was that
the press was no longer entitled to the protections
of the First Amendment. Similar legislation was
directed at the social media. As always, the courts,
in all their lumbering glory, would be the final
word.

FOR HER part, President Vere held a few
rallies in New York and Chicago and San Francisco
before returning to traditional means – scripted
speeches, canned television interviews, negative
advertising and Q & A's with friendly audiences –
to get her message out. Her rallies were well-
attended, polite and utterly soulless, and she had
long ago lost touch with any semblance of an ordinary voter. To her great bewilderment and the increasing fury of her supporters, the few honest polls
were all within the margin of error – she remained
neck and neck with a dead man.

Convinced that his people would stay home
on Election Day if they could be made to
acknowledge that he was truly dead, her partisans
urged her to participate in the single presidential
debate, scheduled for months but widely presumed
to be abandoned, on nationwide television. The idea
was to pit a flesh-and-blood woman of great accom-
plishment against a vacant podium. The sponsor of
the debate, one of the networks, fell in with the
scheme enthusiastically – promotions for it aired
constantly in the lead-up.

The presidential debates had long since become just another demonstration of media persua-

sion. The questions were leaked to the favored candidate, and the moderators participated in her preparation. Breathless speculation regarding who would "win" or "lose," seemingly ludicrous under the circumstances, issued from every news outlet. Objections about fairness, always before the most pressing concern, were ignored.

In the event, President Vere "lost" the debate. She answered each question put to her in the traditional way – glittering generalities designed to pander to the largest group of voters. The first time the cameras turned to the other podium for a response, the studio audience laughed, but it was a joke that only worked once. The laughter quickly gave way to an uneasy silence and, midway through the event, questions directed at the dead president stopped. After a hurried consultation during a commercial break, the debate was abruptly terminated.

Of the country's 130 million households, fewer than five per cent tuned in, and those who did tuned out during the first ten minutes of the broadcast. Subsequent polling revealed that the great majority of the people found the idea of a one-person debate patronizing, and resented the notion that it would influence their vote. When queried about their support for the former president, the response was the same as it was four years earlier: "What choice do we have?" with a caveat – "He did what he said he would." Ideas, not the relative worth of a man or woman, were the issue.

Thus might the election become a referendum, not on the current president or even the dead one, but on the nature of our compact. Were we all created equal, or were some more equal than others? Was ours really a rigid hierarchy where a lesser citizen tugged his forelock and knew his place, or a republic where people were free to pursue their own interests without fear of condemnation? And, if there was disagreement on that score, how long would we last?

Unfortunately, the politicians never got the message. Their politics was like Marty's commerce — savage competition aimed at the lowest common denominator. The media's enormous reach, having increased exponentially over the last few decades, guaranteed that only the loudest voices would be heard.

SIX

This task of gratitude to our fathers, justice to ourselves, duty to posterity, and love for our species in general, all imperatively require us to perform – Abraham Lincoln, 1838

THE OTHER election news was the tinkering with the Electoral College underway in some of the state legislatures. Proposals varied, but all had the same purpose – to shift the electoral power of each state from its voters to its politicians. Florida's plan was typical: The people's vote on Election Day would be deemed advisory only, and the governor would actually choose the state's electors and tell them who to vote for. "Winner take all" might or might not still be the case, but the deadlock anticipated by the country's founders would be more likely. "Faithless" electors, those who defied the state's mandate, would be subject to removal, fines and imprisonment.

Alberto Sanchez's "strike" in New York City had escalated into a real one. Sanchez's other buildings – The San Remo, The Ansonia, The Apthorp and The Beresford – had sided with The Dakota even though a majority of the residents in each building opposed it. The woke members of the tenant associations criticized their fellows and refused to back down. All five buildings were now without plumbing services, and the dispute threatened to spread throughout Manhattan and beyond.

The relative calm in place since the president's death was giving way. Skirmishes between the White Army and the Red Brigade were reported up and down the West Coast. Political spokesmen for each group had emerged. Celebrities, politicians and media scrambled to glorify the Brigade and denigrate the Army, while ignoring the vast mass of the country altogether.

Equally troubling, clashes among citizens unaffiliated with either group were on the rise, leading to lockdowns and curfews. Businesses were closed and boarded up. Historic statues and monuments that offended anyone were destroyed. The grievances supposedly giving rise to all the unrest were quickly overridden by new ones.

Citing a lack of official support for their efforts to keep the peace, the police in several cities were on strike with predictable results. Other public unions – firefighters, sanitation workers, maintenance personnel – refused to cross their picket lines, and utilized "slow-downs" and "sick-outs" in their own work to show sympathy with the cops. Still other workforces – teachers, healthcare workers, ambulance drivers – stayed home because of their now "unsafe" work spaces.

Because much of his movement depended on labor support, the turmoil had resulted in greater visibility for Earnest Pogue and his Martyrs for Christ. He was now cited by newspaper columnists

– still scornful, but aware of his increasing rele-
vance – and featured on the cable channels, sometimes as "news," sometimes as one of their talking
heads. He had added a white Panama hat to his
costume.

The *Star's* front-page headline announced
another airplane crash, this one clearly the result
of a bomb planted on board. Given the layers of security imposed on air travel, officials were at a loss
to explain how it happened. President Vere signed
an executive order shutting the airlines down until
the puzzle was solved. Business leaders warned
that large swathes of the economy were at risk as a
result of the tumult.

On the other side of the world, things had
taken a turn for the worse. Heavy rains in West Africa had indeed ended a years-long drought while,
at the same time, creating conditions for another
plague: locusts. The additional moisture and resulting vegetation had caused an increase in the grasshopper population not seen for decades, leading to
crowding by the insects and competition for food.
As a consequence, they had become "gregarious,"
and begun to "swarm" to avoid starvation. Swarm-
ing grasshoppers were called "locusts."

According to the news accounts, crowded females laid eggs that hatched into nymphs, also
called "hoppers." The hoppers shed their skins multiple times, changed colors, became adults and
grew wings. The new females would begin to lay
eggs in four weeks. Over two inches long with a
wingspan of more than five, the mature locust in
flight could achieve altitudes as high as a mile.

The sheer numbers were mind-boggling. A swarm might contain *billions* of insects, a plague hundreds of swarms. Each locust consumed the equivalent of its own body weight in vegetation every day. Always acting as a group, they formed and re-formed as they landed, fed and returned to the sky. All crops were at risk – one reporter described past devastation as a "living fire."

At one time or another, locusts had swarmed on every continent except Antarctica, but outbreaks over the past 100 years had been confined to Africa and other areas bordering the Red Sea. Their version of the pest was called the desert locust. Despite the occasional outbreak, the developed world had defeated the plague, primarily by avoiding or changing the conditions that allowed it to emerge. Geography, poverty and a lack of interest, within and without, had condemned Africans and Arabs alike to periodic deadly infestations for centuries. Mass starvation followed each plague.

The victims seemed inured to their fate – visited upon them by their god, perhaps, as in biblical times – while the rest of the world dabbled in solutions – chemical, mechanical, genetic – that never bore fruit. Science said that trying to control the swarm was useless, that the insects had to be attacked in the egg stage, but a real effort at eradication was never attempted. As a result, the already poverty-stricken people of Africa and the Middle East were left to defend themselves with brooms and shovels, or pesticides delivered from the back of a truck.

MY INVESTIGATION was again at a stand-still. It seemed pointless to continue if there was even the slightest chance that the former president wasn't dead and buried at Arlington. His exhuma-tion, now in the hands of the Circuit Court for Ar-lington County, Virginia, was stalled indefinitely.

Marty Jones beckoned from his doorway. "How's it going?" he said, after closing the door be-hind me.

I described the various dead-ends encoun-tered so far, omitting any mention of President Vere's potential involvement. Nodding, he said, "Let's put it on the back burner for now. If they dig him up and he's not there, it's a different story al-together. If he *is* there, we can discuss our options."

"Okay."

"There's something else I want you to do."

"Yes?"

He hesitated. "Things are getting dicey on the West Coast."

"How do you mean?"

"The violence is much worse than you know. It's being under-reported."

"How much worse can it be?"

"A lot. Believe me."

"Why's it not being reported?"

He grinned. "Your lady friend says that America is 'united again.' A pitched battle in the newspapers every day wouldn't be good for her campaign. But the people are choosing sides."

"They've been doing that for years."

"Yes, but it used to be just talk. Not any-more." He paused. "Anyway, I want you to check it out. I've got a list of names you can start with."

The prospect of a trip across the country, especially when the airlines weren't operating, wasn't very appetizing. "Can't the West Coast papers handle it?"

He shook his head. "They're doing what they can, but this is a big national story, and I want it covered by our best people." I lifted my brows. "You've developed a significant following. Serious people listen to what you say."

"Can I have a raise?"

He laughed. "Come see me after you get this story." He drew an envelope from his pocket and handed it to me. "Trains are the best way to go now. You leave tomorrow."

It was a short walk from the office on R Street to the mansion on 28th. Washington's miserable summer weather had returned, and my clothes were damp with sweat by the time I got home. Her limousine, hidden by the trees, was parked in the courtyard at the top of the driveway. Watchful eyes followed me as I approached the house, but only Wolf Robinson allowed me to see him, and then only for an instant.

My everyday journey up the hill became something more. The parallax resulting from each step seemed exaggerated, and I felt an unaccountable menace, as if the malice emanating from the rest of the country had materialized here. The air was thick and hard to breathe, the hair on the back of my neck stood up, and colors dissolved to black-and-white. It was like a scene from a Frankenheimer movie. I tried to dial back my imagination.

She was in a bedroom at the back of the house, the one I'd used since my wife's death. Naked, she stood with her back to me, gazing into the garden. The only light was the failing afternoon sun. She looked over her shoulder, but didn't speak. I scooped her from the floor and laid her on the bed.

She was ruthless in her sex. Not selfish – she was generous in her desire to please, but she had needs of her own that had to be satisfied first. Every touch, every spasm, was squeezed for the last tranche of pleasure. The confines of her sexuality were expansive, its expression joyful. While I often fell asleep when we were sated, she seemed always refreshed.

I attributed her impatience to her father who, unbeknownst to her, was not the man who raised her in the red-brick Victorian on Boston's Exeter Street. She had been conceived during the brutal rape of her mother by a man who would one day become her own lover, facts now known only to me. His suicide had paved the way for our liaison, a real love affair though neither of us ever said the words.

Her expression, melancholy, was new. "Forget what I told you about the president's death," she said. "Please don't write anything." She paused. "I should never have mentioned it."

"Why?"

"Certain – people are – interested. I don't want anything to happen to you."

"What are you talking about?"

"Tommy, please. Just forget it."

Had the drama conjured an hour before been justified? Were her guardians – or captors – coming for me now? Suddenly, a few days out of town didn't seem so bad.

UNION STATION'S street address was 50 Massachusetts Avenue, but entry into the massive train station was by way of Columbus Circle. Built in the early 1900s and larger than the Capitol Building a few blocks away, the ceiling of its vaulted entrance was gilded in 23-karat gold. Floors and staircases were rendered in red and black marble. The barrel-vault over the Main Concourse, eight hundred feet long, was made of wire glass and hundreds of cast plaster coffers. Originally conceived by the federal government to remove train traffic from the National Mall and to accommodate the operations of two railroad companies, it was now much more than a train station.

It was a transportation hub and retail colossus. Buses, taxi-cabs and subway cars shuttled in and out continuously, and restaurants, shops and kiosks served patrons who never set foot on a train. Museums, theaters and a concert hall added to the mix, and plans for more of the same were on the drawing board. Ostensibly a manifestation of the economic innovations so dear to Marty Jones's heart, it nevertheless owed its existence, and now its operation, to the government even though the vast majority of the American people had never laid eyes on it, much less used any of its services.

The *Capitol Limited* was departing from a platform on Concourse A at 4:05 PM. Its "consist" that day was composed of two electric locomotives, two coaches, three sleeping cars, a dining car, a lounge and a baggage car. The trip to Chicago covered 764 miles. Total elapsed time was just over seventeen hours, and it would stop fourteen times along the way.

I boarded via the first sleeping coach. After leaving briefcase and laptop in my roomette, I made my way to the lounge and ordered scotch. After the second drink was delivered, I sat back, contemplating this, the first leg of my cross-country journey to San Francisco.

At the close of the Revolutionary War, the United States covered more than 512 million acres of land. Seventy-seven years later, at the beginning of the Civil War, the land within its borders had increased by 1.4 *billion* acres, most of it west of the Mississippi River. Rather than allow it to remain fallow, or in the hands of Native Americans or European invaders, the government – with lots of help from Yankee industrialists, New York intellectuals and newspaper publishers – set out to create "flyover country." The principal means by which this was achieved were the railroads and land grant legislation, primarily the Homestead Act of 1862.

On May 10, 1869, tracks laid from the east by the Union Pacific Railroad, and from the west by the Central Pacific, were joined at Promontory Point, Utah Territory, by a one-pound, 17.6-karat golden spike, thus creating the first transcontinental railroad. The land on which the tracks lay, 128 million acres, was donated by the federal government. By the end of the century, there were four such lines in operation, and every advancing mile drew settlers to the Midwest and the Great Plains. There were "booms" in the Dakotas and Oklahoma driven not just by poor Americans, but by equally impoverished immigrants from Ireland, Germany and Scandinavia. Altogether, some 2 million people filed 4 million claims under the Homestead Act, resulting in land grants of almost 280 million acres.

Freight and passenger lines shared the same tracks, but the freight industry was still thriving today, whereas passenger trains had fallen on hard times, leading to a takeover by the government. The *Capitol Limited* operated within a network of 21,000 miles of track on forty-plus interconnecting routes, including more than 500 stations. Passengers might be delivered to as many as forty-six states, but travel time, especially on the longer routes, was measured in days, not hours. If everything went perfectly, my time on two different trains would be just under three days.

My seat in the lounge, called the Sightseer, was on the top deck looking over the outskirts of Washington. The coach was full of people, mostly military men and women in various uniforms making do with the train in the absence of airplanes. Washington, of course, was teeming with generals and admirals, but there was no brass in this crowd – the highest rank in evidence was a black Marine Corps sergeant dressed in camouflage fatigues. The name etched into his uniform blouse was "Smith." He was studying a thick notebook which he closed when I sat down beside him.

Gesturing at the people around us, I said, "Is there a war somewhere I don't know about?"

He stared for a moment. "There's always a war somewhere," he said, finally.

He was right, and it was men like him and the young people sitting with us who fought them. War was no longer a national obligation – it was now left to blue collar volunteers, not unlike policemen and fireman, whose job it was to fight and die for those who wouldn't. Their leaders were careerists, as privileged and partisan as the rest of the vast, unfathomable government bureaucracy. A state of affairs in place for fifty years, it had enabled me – to my secret shame – to avoid serving myself. "How long have you been in?" I said.

"Nineteen years."

"Retirement coming up?"

He shook his head and smiled. "I'm a lifer."

After a quick stop in Rockville, Maryland, we shed the D.C. suburbs at Germantown, crossed the Potomac River into West Virginia and entered Harper's Ferry in the twilight. Most of the small town was part of the country's largest national park – a stretch of land reaching 186 miles from Georgetown to Cumberland, Maryland – occupied by remnants of the Chesapeake and Ohio Canal. The late autumn foliage was stunning.

As the *Limited* pulled into the station, my companion rose and left the car, taking two soldiers and two sailors with him. They reappeared on the platform a minute later. After shaking hands with the others, Sergeant Smith re-boarded the train and resumed his seat next to me. The same scene, this time with three more soldiers and another Marine, played out at the next station in Martinsburg.

When he returned the second time, I said, "What are you guys doing? Some sort of interservice exercise?"

"Yes," he said. "You could call it that."

BECAUSE I had a sleeper coach ticket, I had a reserved seat in the dining car. I sat down just as we entered a long tunnel whose entrance and exit were located in West Virginia, but whose length was mostly in Maryland. Beyond the tunnel, we re-entered Maryland and stopped at the station in Cumberland. The town's winding waterways and rolling hills, plus a skyline punctuated by rising spires, were barely visible in the increasing darkness. A waiter delivered the menu.

Despite periodic infusions of cash from the government, the passenger train business was dying. Dozens of destinations had been discontinued recently and more were planned, leaving many small towns and rural communities stranded without train stations, airports or interstate highways. A loss of the long-distance lines to the West Coast, like the one I would board tomorrow, would be particularly devastating. For those trains that remained, austerity was the order of the day – food service was downgraded, lounge cars abolished, maintenance unperformed.

Perhaps because of its lineage – it had once been the pride of the nation's oldest railroad, the Baltimore & Ohio – the *Capitol Limited* had avoided that fate for now. The dining car and lounge were spacious with large windows and skylights. Seating in the dining car was arranged in back-to-back booths along both sides, all set with white linen and flatware for four people. The menu provided several options and I chose the steak, but decided to wait for my dinner companions if there were any.

They arrived in short order: First, a young man wearing a White Army cap, probably in his twenties, introduced himself as "Roy," then a middle-aged couple, "George" and "Veronica." Roy removed his cap and rose as they joined us and, after a moment's hesitation, I stood up as well. Veronica was puzzled, then embarrassed. "Please," she said, in an accent I couldn't place. "Please. Sit down."

Roy, sallow but still sunburned, was balding and a little overweight. He wore jeans and a red flannel shirt. His blue eyes, which never quite looked at anyone, seemed cloudy, and a vivid white scar, slashed across his forehead, added to an already unhealthy appearance. Drink of some kind, bourbon maybe, was on his breath.

George and Veronica, by contrast, were in the pink, likely the result of hours in the gym and careful diet, both of which were confirmed during our dinner conversation. He was also dressed in jeans and flannel, but his shirt was blue. Her clothes looked like pajamas, and she wore a long string of pearls around her neck. Both displayed tell-tale signs of indifferent plastic surgery, and they passed out business cards, a ritual of their class. There was a "Ph.D." beside each name.

I prodded Roy with the usual question. "Where you from?"

"Nebraska," he said. "Zion."

"Where's that?" said Veronica.

"The southeastern part of the state." Roy paused. "Where Kool-Aid was invented."

"Really?" said George. Roy nodded.

"Going home?" I said. He nodded again. "What do you do?"

"I work on my dad's farm."

"You're a farmer?" said George. "I've never met a farmer. What's it like?"

Roy stared at him. "It's not very exciting. Not very profitable, either. Not anymore."

The waiter arrived with more menus and paused to take drink orders. I asked for scotch and Roy requested bourbon. George and Veronica ordered some kind of flavored seltzer water I'd never heard of. "We're not teetotalers," said Veronica when I inquired. "There's a little alcohol in it, but it's low calorie and gluten-free. I like the cherry banana best."

George re-started the earlier conversation. "It's interesting that you're in agriculture," he said. "We are, too, in a way."

"You farm?" said Roy.

"Oh, no. I teach business at George Washington. She's a consultant with the Agriculture Department."

Veronica chimed in. "We have a grant from the Department to study the – um, the decline of the American farmer. We're going to Chicago for a conference."

"Of farmers?" said Roy.

"No. Mostly academics and government people, I think. It's sponsored by the University of Chicago."

The waiter arrived to take our orders. Roy and I ordered steak. After much back-and-forth with the waiter about "fiber" and "organics," George and Veronica each settled for the spinach and arugula salad with chile-lime dressing. George turned to me. "What about you, Tommy? What do you do?"

"I'm a reporter."

He brightened. "For whom?" he said, smiling.

"The *Georgetown Star.*"

The smile faded. "Oh," he said. "That must be – interesting."

Any reference to the dead president or politics, undoubtedly frequent topics in their respective camps, was scrupulously avoided. After a few more fruitless attempts at conversation, we sat without speaking until the food was brought to the table. Roy ordered another bourbon. "A double," he said. We ate in silence.

While we waited for our checks, George addressed Roy again: "You said you work on your father's farm. Do you, by any chance, still live with your parents?"

"Yes, sir. Why?"

"Our son and his new husband are moving in with us next week. It's not quite the same thing, I guess, but –"

Veronica broke in. "They're both still in graduate school. At Georgetown."

"Anyway," said George, "I was wondering how everyone copes." He waited and, when he realized he would get no response, signed his check and stood up. Veronica joined him. They turned away.

Roy remained in his chair as they left the table. Not quite drunk, he said, "What did he mean 'our son and his new husband?'"

"I guess their son is married to another fellow. It's legal now."

"Two guys?"

"Yes."

He sat very still, blinking. Finally, he said, "I *do* something for this country. My dad and me feed people. What do *they* do?"

"Well –"

"They go to conferences and write reports. They do nothing for nobody but themselves. And get rich doing it." He stopped. "It's *bullshit.*"

"I suppose somebody has to do it."

"No they don't," he almost screamed. Conversation in the dining car stopped. After it resumed a moment later, he spoke in a softer voice. "No, they don't. That grant of theirs is my tax money. They're going to use it to study *me.* Again."

The American farmer that George and Veronica were delving into had been on the ropes for years. Farming itself was doing fine, but the family farm had given way to large conglomerates, many of them foreign, another manifestation of the global economy. "You said things were tough on the farm," I said. "Maybe their work will help."

He shook his head. "The government's been studying us for as long as I can remember. Nothing good ever comes of it. Rules and regulations *we* end up paying for." He paused. "I'm tired of being – *examined* like some goddam bug, and being told what to do by *experts* –" he spat the word out "– who've never done an honest day's work in their life."

I searched for a way to redeem George and Veronica. "He's a college professor, too, you know."

"More bullshit. They're not learning anything at those schools. It's all about who you know and what some buddy of yours can do for you." He stood up. "*I'm* what this country used to be. *They're* what it is now." He clapped his cap on his head and staggered out the door.

I considered his last remarks. They reflected a lingering myth, that "rugged individualists" and "yeoman farmers" were the "backbone" of the country. To the extent such people ever existed in fact, rather than in the imaginations of artists and poets, their time had come and gone long ago, and even then they were hardly masters of their own fate. They were, in truth, grist for the great capitalist mill, and they had been ground into dust and left behind. Abandoned by the poets, their descendants were a drag on the business of America who now endured the same unhappy slog as the rest of the underclass.

I saw him again a few minutes later, nestled in a seat in one of the regular coaches. A leather-covered flask lay open beside him. Wrapped in a blanket, he was asleep, the side of his face pressed against the window, drool easing down his chin. Most of the other seats were taken by the military people. Sergeant Smith slept next to the far door.

The conductor's voice announced our arrival in Connellsville, Maryland. Smith rose, shook several of his colleagues awake, and led them to the door. A moment later, the train stopped and the door opened. They disappeared into the darkness. I continued on to my roomette.

WHILE I slept, the *Capitol Limited* passed through several small towns in Pennsylvania and stopped in Pittsburgh for twenty minutes. After that, according to the schedule, we would travel the breadth of Ohio and Indiana, stopping eight more times before arriving in Chicago at 8:45 AM. By the time I awoke, the train was still, but the sign at the station said "Cleveland," which was more than 200 miles short of our destination.

I leaned into the corridor and caught the conductor. "What's up?" I said. "Why aren't we in Chicago?"

"We had to stop here to speak to the authorities. Make a report."

"About what?"

"Death on board." He paused. "Well, not on board exactly. He jumped into the Allegheny River last night."

"Who did?"

He shook his head and pushed through the door. I was left with the uneasy feeling that I knew who the jumper was, a suspicion confirmed a few minutes later.

Two women approached me in the dining car. One introduced herself as "railroad superintendent for this region," the other was a detective for the Cleveland Division of Police. "We're investigating a possible suicide on board," said the railroad lady. "Roy Miller. I understand you had dinner with him last night?"

I nodded. "I didn't know his last name. He was just Roy."

The detective consulted a small notebook. "From Zion, Nebraska?" she said.

"That's him."

We spent the next thirty minutes discussing my dinner with Roy and George and Veronica. They wanted to know if Roy had seemed suicidal and, of course, he had, at least in hindsight, but I was unable to convey the emotions behind his words. Some farmer complaining about government and experts and college professors wasn't very compelling. It's the way it was.

"If that was enough to commit suicide over," said the woman from the railroad, "there'd be a lot more dead farmers."

Five hours and six stops later, the *Capitol Limited* pulled into Chicago. Sergeant Smith and I stood side-by-side to collect our luggage. "Where's the rest of your crew?" I said.

He didn't answer.

SEVEN

How then shall we perform it? –
At what point shall we expect
the approach of danger? By what
means shall we fortify against it?
– Shall we expect some transat-
lantic military giant, to step the
Ocean, and crush us at a blow?
Never! – Abraham Lincoln, 1838

I BOARDED the *California Zephyr* with just minutes to spare, and then only because the *Zephyr* itself was three hours late leaving Chicago. The delay was occasioned by the logistics involved in adding a private car to the end of the train. I watched from the observation deck as railroad employees moved the old-fashioned Pullman back and forth before finally coupling it to the baggage car.

It was the same size as the *Zephyr's* regular sleeping cars, but looked nothing like them. Instead of a silver "bullet" with serrated sides, the Pullman – with its many windows, green siding and red mansard roof – looked like a shotgun house on wheels. Its name, the "Prairie Star," was inscribed on the side along with the registration number: "MLJX – 1000."

My sleeping car on the *California Zephyr* likewise had a name: the "Isle Royale." It was one of three such cars which, along with engines and regular coaches, and baggage, lounge and dining cars, made the *Zephyr* twice as long as the *Capitol Limited.* This part of my journey, from Chicago to San Francisco, would cover almost 2,500 miles and stop at thirty-three stations along the way. It was scheduled to arrive in just more than two days, meaning I would spend two nights on board.

My roomette, located on the car's upper level, looked much like the one on the *Limited.* About forty feet square, it featured two upholstered benches – which would be converted into a bed later that evening – facing each other, and hooks and shelves for carry-ons and sleepwear. A giant window showed the urban expanse of greater Chicago receding into the distance as the *Zephyr* slowed to make its first stop in Naperville. Minutes later, we passed through the shuttered station in Aurora and, as the train gradually achieved its average speed of fifty-five miles per hour, began our odyssey into America's heartland.

The people who settled this vast wilderness had been lured by promises of free land, abundant water and trees necessary for fuel, fences and the construction of a homestead. As it turned out, most of the property fitting that description had been acquired by speculators before they arrived. The "free" soil was thin and arid, and the effort to make it suitable for farming often heroic. They lived in dugouts or sod houses. They toted water for miles, or dug wells as deep as 300 feet. They burned manure and hay to keep warm.

Each season brought its own burdens – prairie fires in autumn, ice and snow in winter, spring floods and summer heat and drought. People and animals often shared the same space. Periodic invasions of locusts like those in Africa destroyed crops. Despite it all, they persevered and ultimately created an abundance – grain, vegetables, meat – the likes of which had never before been seen. The nation and the world fed on the harvest of their labor.

That American bounty still fed a lot of people – the recent harvest of wheat, corn and soybeans was the largest on record – but fewer and fewer Americans participated in its creation. As a consequence, whatever influence they once had had waned and, as we crossed the Mississippi River into Iowa, chasing the sun, it showed. Every third station was closed, rusty tractors and combines grazed in the fields, and the ruins of rambling farmhouses languished at the end of dusty lanes. Their villages and towns were notable only for their neglect.

The late edition of the *Star* reported that Matilda Fleck and her boycotters had achieved a significant victory. The states from Maryland north to Maine had formed a compact called the "Yankee Coalition" whose citizens would no longer purchase anything from the states who had voted for the former president. "This will bring them to their knees," said Fleck. "They'll rue the day they elected that racist bastard."

Other boycotts were under way. An organization called "Stop the Crap" encouraged its adherents to quit "subsidizing" the "so-called culture spewing from New York and Hollywood," leading to a noticeable decline in the purchase of books, recorded music and movie tickets. Television viewing in all its variations, and the advertising revenue it generated, was down twenty-five per cent. Media celebrities fell out of favor. Attendance at sporting events, usually fueled by players in the same media thrall, had dropped dramatically.

A Broadway sensation once acclaimed by the hip and even the woke had also fallen into disfavor. A play that loosely depicted the country's founding, the tickets were expensive and hard to come by, and each presentation was sold out months in advance. Vada Potts-Jones had recently denounced it because "the founding and everything it produced" was racist. As a consequence, it now played to empty houses and was scheduled to close in a few days.

The latest polls showed the new president ahead of the old one. Marty's editorial explained in great detail why those polls were unreliable. "In short," he concluded, "polling for this election is like everything else. It is *not* designed to reflect the attitudes and opinions of the people. It *is* designed to manipulate those attitudes and opinions."

In other news, Florida had become the first state to revise its laws regarding the Electoral College. Passed with no debate, it was presented to the citizens as a *fait accompli.* After paragraphs of legalese extolling the "nobility" of the state's voters, it came down to this: Its governor would choose Florida's presidential electors subject to an override by three-quarters of both houses of the legislature. Candidates for president would still be on the ballot and their votes tallied, but the outcome would have no impact on the election. To compensate the people for the loss of their franchise, Election Day was declared a state holiday, and a printout of every ballot was good for a happy meal at McDonald's.

Legal challenges to this defrocking of Florida's voters were being considered, but the pundits were unanimous that the new arrangement complied with the Constitution's mandate: "Each State shall appoint, in such Manner as the Legislature thereof may direct, [its] Electors." Otherwise, the change received little attention beyond its borders. States considering similar legislation were waiting to gauge the response of Florida's citizens as the election drew nearer.

The locust plague in Africa was gathering momentum. Despite evidence of such attacks down through the ages, man-made climate change had, inevitably, been blamed for the coming disaster. Likewise, a "consensus" had emerged among the experts to the effect that global warming led to more and faster winds, thereby enabling the spread of the insects.

That wind was now a greater factor in the world's weather was undeniable. All the oceans and every continent had recorded increases in the volume, intensity and speed of the winds circulating above them. Gales, hurricanes and typhoons were ongoing events all over the world. Hailed as wondrous news by the green industry – higher wind speeds had raised the output of electricity generated by wind turbines by more than a third – a few bugs on the African coast were little cause for concern. Climate change, it turned out, might be a good thing.

In a related matter, the president had signed off on the replacement for the Washington Monument. "The Climate Clock Tower," she said in her announcement, "reflects our belief in man as the final arbiter of his own destiny. It is both historical and aspirational. Our past refusal to accept responsibility for the destruction of the planet has brought us to the verge of extinction. If we allow the clock to strike midnight, we are doomed to oblivion." She stopped. "Auld Lang Syne will become the national anthem." A vote among the citizenry was planned in order to give the clock tower a suitable name.

Dominating all the news, however, was the carnage that was now impossible to suppress. Mobs roamed the country's largest cities. Faneuil Hall in Boston had been ransacked and burned to the ground. Twenty-two people died when firebombs destroyed a wing of the Metropolitan Museum of Art. San Francisco's Conservatory of Flowers lay in smoldering ruins, and bombs were discovered in the bowels of the Capitol and the Supreme Court building. My visit to the West Coast seemed more pointless by the day.

I found a new page on the laptop:

THE AMERICAN PROJECT
Tommy Sawyer

Is it time to "cancel" the American project? Is there any reason to believe we can still achieve a more perfect Union? Answers to both questions are hard to divine because we no longer tell each other the truth. Do we riot because of history? Do we steal because we're entitled? Do we kill because we can? Most importantly, are we committing suicide because we no longer care what the answers are?

Contradictions abound. The founding document of the American project is the Declaration of Independence. It enshrines the "truths" of liberty, equality and human rights bestowed by a "Creator" who sounds a lot like God. Much of the violence and discord today is excused on the grounds that those fundamental privileges have been disregarded from the beginning. But God is dead in much of the country – the new myth is that He never existed at all – so how could rights "granted" by a non-existent deity be the source of such unrest? Without some higher authority, "equality" is absurd on its face. "Liberty" is a political ideal, though not for everyone. "Democracy" is whatever some demagogue says it is.

Rather than blame men for their troubles, some hold that a single man, recently deceased, is responsible, though the more thoughtful acknowledge that no human being has the power to create or enforce the rights in question. The prevailing view among those capable of broadcasting it is that we are only genes and hormones, flesh and blood, and there's no such thing as "judgment." Ethics, principles, and values are up for grabs. Each of us is free to adopt his own personal "religion."

But that's not the worst of it. Too many of us have concluded that none of it matters. Only a few months ago, if we witnessed a crime without protest, or stood by while our fellows were beaten, or heeded obvious lies, we were complicit. Now, we have no responsibility for anything, not even our-selves. Now, it's all "relevant."

Have we finally reached the end of Western culture, as Hegel predicted 100 years ago? Do we truly give a damn about anything? Is there a single principle to which we adhere beyond our own self-interest? When everything's relevant, nothing is. Unless something changes, suicide, the signs of which are all around us, appears to be the only an-swer.

I WOKE up early the next morning. Accord-ing to the *Zephyr's* timetable plus the three hours we had lost in Chicago, we would stop in Zion, Ne-braska, at 7:40 AM. I wanted to see the place Roy Miller called home. I had my pick of seats on the upper deck of the lounge and settled in as we pulled out of Hastings, the last stop before Zion, fifty miles down the line. A light snow was falling.

The timetable included a short blurb describ-ing the highlights of each stop along the way. Zion's claim to fame, besides Kool-Aid, was the Home-stead National Monument of America, "a memorial to the spirit and achievements of the American set-tler." I checked for more information on the Inter-net – the monument had been the least-visited memorial of its kind in the country, and it had shut down six months earlier due to a lack of funds. The gloom from yesterday returned.

As the train slowed, I could see Zion in the distance. It looked like all the other small towns we had passed through – a Central Business District of two- and 3-story brick buildings surrounded by smaller, lower wooden structures in need of paint.

Chain-link fences weaved in and out, and cars were parked haphazardly along a few narrow roads leading to a single highway running north and south. Silos and grain elevators sprouted in the surrounding countryside. Nothing moved.

Just before we reached the station, a two-story brick building came into view. I could see a dozen windows from my vantage, each with twenty-four panes, all broken. A large blue and white sign dangled from the roof: "WHIRLPOOL."

I rose and moved toward the door as the conductor entered the other end of the car. Rather than stop at the platform, the *Zephyr* began to pick up speed. Startled, I peered out the window as a prospective passenger, suitcase in hand, waved and shouted, to no avail. In seconds, he was gone from sight.

The conductor was beside me. "The company dropped this station a couple of days ago," he said. "That fellow must not've gotten the message." He handed me an envelope, and passed through the other door. What would've happened, I wondered, if Roy Miller had made it this far?

I studied the envelope. Made of fine vanilla linen, it bore my name – "Mr. Sawyer" – in a flowing script of blue ink written with a fountain pen. The invitation on the matching stationary inside, folded once, was also hand-written: *"The Prairie Star requests the pleasure of your company for cocktails and dinner on Saturday, October 10, 2020, at seven o'clock PM."* The usual request for some kind of response was omitted, and there was no signature.

Over breakfast in the dining car, I looked at the invitation again. According to my watch, today was Saturday, October 10, 2020. *Who* aboard the Prairie Star requested the pleasure of my company?

A few minutes later, we crossed into Colorado and began the spectacular journey through the Rocky Mountains. The last stop in Nebraska, McCook, sat 2,500 feet above sea level, and the first stop in Colorado, Fort Morgan, was situated at an elevation of 4,330 feet. From there it was another eighty miles to Denver, elevation 5,167 feet, and then the climb really began. Between Denver and Winter Park, a distance of some sixty miles, we rose to a height of 8,573 feet, the highest station on the line. The descent from there to the Utah border, elevation 4,250, was not quite as steep.

On the way we passed through tunnels too numerous to count, the longest of which was more than six miles. The gorges between the rocks were dark, narrow defiles, and the track beds were often cut into the vertical cliffs. Just before crossing the Continental Divide at 9,000 feet, we encountered a series of "hanging valleys" – shallow valleys carved by small glaciers that "hung" above the floor of larger valleys created by larger glaciers – where animals of all sorts – cattle, bison, yaks – grazed. Elk, moose and bald eagles were also prominent. Snow covered the peaks and valleys, and there were no roads, no cars and no power lines. Except for the *Zephyr*, an undertaking now hard to imagine, evidence of man's presence was minimal.

THE STOP at Grand Junction, the last station in Colorado, allowed me to make my way to the rear of the Prairie Star just after 7 PM. Huge snowflakes fell in the darkness illuminated by a single light that arced over the platform. I pulled the chain on a brass bell that hung beside the door. She opened it immediately. "Hi, Tommy," she said. "Can I call you Tommy?"

"Sure."

"Good. Come in."

I followed her into a compartment with a domed glass ceiling that allowed the light from a full moon inside. About 150 feet square, dark walnut paneling covered the walls, and brass sconces and lamps added light. The windows along both sides of the car were covered with silk shades. Elaborate moldings outlined the ceiling and the oak floor, and the furniture was heavy wood with leather and plush upholstery. A fire burned in the marble fireplace in the corner.

"Nice place," I said.

"It's Daddy's. He lets me use it." She stepped behind a mahogany bar that lowered from one of the walls on hinges. "Look around while I fix you a drink. Scotch, isn't it? And ice?"

"Yes. Thanks."

I mulled her knowledge of my drinking habits as I passed into the next compartment, a kitchen on one side, a dining room on the other. Something was cooking in the oven, and the table was set for two. Next was a billiard room, then two small bedrooms with full baths. The last compartment was a master suite, which included a large bathroom and a paneled office. All were as richly-decorated as the lounge. Improbably, Vada Potts-Jones and I were alone on the Prairie Star.

The *Zephyr* began to move as I returned to the lounge. Seated in a red leather armchair, martini in hand, she gestured toward a tumbler full of scotch on the bar. Never married, she was in her mid-thirties, but didn't look that old. Dressed in a white silk jumpsuit that tied behind her neck, the straight black hair fell to her shoulders. Blood-red lipstick and fingernails, green eyes shadowed in gray, and a gold rope around her neck added accents of color to the white clothing against the black skin. Her bare feet were drawn up beneath her.

"Don't you have a Secret Service detail?" I said.

She nodded. "They're easy to avoid. They'll shed no tears at the White House if something happens to me."

"Aren't you part of the campaign?"

"No. They know I'll say something their precious voters won't like."

Though it was no longer polite to say so, her features had an oriental cast, probably because her mother was from Singapore. Early on, the press had relegated her to the black delegation on Capitol Hill, a designation she resisted because she had bigger fish to fry. Rather than allow herself to be typecast, she refused to join any of the congressional caucuses or participate in their countless campaigns for special treatment. She had studied microbiology in college and, before running for Congress, had been in charge of her father's DNA lab, circumstances that may have added to her reluctance to be categorized.

None of that had stopped her from making use of the Colored Caucus and its subsidiaries when necessary. There was a lot of grousing among those whose influence was determined by skin pigment but, in time, her defiance of the accepted order of things became yet another aspect of the persona so zealously championed by the media. Their newsrooms were primarily white and male, and her skin and sex provided cover for the gushing adulation. She was a renegade who lived a life they could only imagine, and they competed among themselves for her favor.

Despite her refusal to become a part of the great, unwashed masses that her colleagues embraced, she shared with them the idea that the country was partitioned between whites and everybody else. Ignoring the everyday evidence otherwise, she spoke and acted like apartheid was the law of the land. Her opponents weren't men and women, they were the "white race" or the "Caucasian majority." She possessed many attributes of the demagogue, especially the ability to seem reasonable when the occasion called for it.

When queried about her refusal to recognize that the country was, in fact, a crucible of people who interacted with one another, including the white ones, on a daily basis, she cited the usual pieties – "privilege," "inequality," etc. – and never failed to mention something now willfully ignored by her progressive friends: eugenics. Unlike the banal abstractions now used to excoriate white people, eugenics was real, it was imposed mostly on poor blacks, and its history – and the refusal to acknowledge it – seemed to enrage her.

During the first third of the 20th century, great swathes of earnest white people had subscribed to the belief that "imbeciles" and the "feeble-minded" should be sterilized to prevent them from having children. It was intended to do what "Nature" had done before civilization, human sympathy and charity interfered with Nature's plans. Once only the fittest had survived to maturity, to produce and raise the next generation, but the feeble and defective had begun to live long enough to breed, resulting in terrible burdens on them and others. The feeble-minded among us had to be saved from themselves, and the offspring of such people had to be forestalled.

Politicians, academics, men in the learned professions, all accepted the idea that neutering imbeciles, usually defined as "childlike" individuals with low IQs, was best for everybody, including those most immediately affected. Every college in the country taught the "science," churches and civic organizations supported it, and the Federation of Women's Clubs and the League of Women Voters sponsored approving legislation. Public intellectuals allied themselves to the cause. No thinking individual, certainly none of those whose wealth or influence assured that neither they nor theirs would ever be targeted, raised an objection.

Only Nazi Germany practiced eugenics more enthusiastically than the United States. That association began to pall when the extent of Nazi experiments became widely known, but blacks were still being sterilized into the 1970s. Some of the laws were still on the books. It was a crusade, one in which the enlightened crusaders were overwhelmingly white and the enfeebled infidels overwhelmingly black, and the cadre responsible for it had never apologized, an omission Vada never failed to mention.

For her, "party" was just a logo. While her politics had grown increasingly radical, she was hard to place on the ideological spectrum. Though clearly "down for the struggle," she sometimes differed with her colleagues on how to achieve victory. Those who usually denounced her occasionally found themselves in agreement, while those who counted her as an ally puzzled over her contradictions. Her public attitude was often extreme though she was alleged to be more circumspect in private. She had kept a surprisingly low profile since becoming Lucinda's vice-president.

"By the way," she said, "this is all off the record."

"Off the record" meant that I couldn't report whatever she said. Its purpose was to shape events without disclosing who was saying what, another example of press and politicians conspiring to conceal the news from the public. That news might be trivial or monumental, but its non-disclosure added to a poorly informed citizenry, which seemed to be the goal. What the people didn't know couldn't hurt those who did.

We sat quietly, contemplating each other. She moved first: "How long have you known my father?"

"Oh – twenty years, I guess."

"He thinks you're a great writer."

"He's too kind."

"I've read some of your stuff."

We were quiet again. "He told me you were going to San Francisco on the *Zephyr*," she said. I nodded. "I decided to take the opportunity to meet you."

"Why?"

"Lots of reasons." She paused. "I wondered what kind of man could put up with that bitch in the White House." I didn't respond. "Well? What kind of man are you?"

"The kind who stays out of cat fights."

She laughed. Rising, she poured another drink. After resuming her seat, she said, "Change is coming. Soon. Lucinda Vere will be right in the middle of it." She smiled. "She may not be who you think she is."

"What are you talking about?"

She smiled again. "You read the papers, don't yu?"

"Yes. But we've had riots and – and rebellions off and on from the beginning. Nothing ever really *changed*."

"This time's different."

Her father had said the same thing. I didn't want to agree with them, but I worried. Always before, there were people who stood up to the opportunists and the anarchists and the criminals and, in the end, the country pulled itself together and moved on. Those people, if they existed, were silent now. "So – the rioters and the looters are taking over?"

"Not necessarily."

"What's that mean?"

"They aren't the only ones out there."

"Who else? You? Your dad?"

"Maybe."

Weary of the cat-and-mouse, I said, "What do you want from me?"

She stared into the fire. "Every crusade requires a chronicler," she said, finally. "I want you to be mine."

I RETURNED to the *Zephyr* when it reached Provo, half-way across the Utah desert. This part of the journey was a magnificent desolation. Black and white – stone and snow – plateaus, mesas and canyons were forbidding in the moonlight, and other, isolated formations – arches, pinnacles, bridges – looked like ruins from a lost world. People were scarce, to say the least. There were only four stations across Utah's broad expanse and one of those, Helper, had suffered the same fate as Zion. I planned to be sound asleep when we stopped at the last one, Salt Lake City.

My visit aboard the Prairie Star had been, for lack of a better word, tantalizing. Each time Vada Potts-Jones seemed on the verge of saying something meaningful, she backed off. When I pressed her about what was coming all she would say was that events beyond President Vere's control were on the horizon. Her "crusade" was one of them.

The idea that Lucinda might not be who I thought she was was troubling because I had entertained the same notion myself. There was never any doubt about her politics but, since becoming president, she seemed even more rigid in her beliefs. Now that she was able to put her policies into practice, there was less room for compromise. A full term in office, or maybe two, might render our relationship too parlous to maintain.

The give and take grew more serious over dinner. The country's way of life – its "reason for being," as she called it – had reached a tipping point. The white race was losing control, the Caucasian majority going soft, the self-hatred rampant. The old ways were no longer sufficient, and she planned to be in the vanguard of what was coming. And, despite my race, I could be, too, if I played my cards right.

She refused to elaborate. Other than vague allusions to "change," the crusade went unexplained. But, as her chronicler, she promised that I would be "in the loop" as long as I agreed not to publish anything without her permission. I would be her undisclosed mouthpiece, a state of affairs I had studiously avoided with others. My relationship with the President of the United States, for instance, was strictly personal, and I was happy to keep it that way.

The country had a surfeit of demagogues now, of every persuasion, none of whom I took very seriously, but this time the elixir – the heady draught of *knowing* and access to the powerful – proved too much. I told myself that even if I was wrong, and she proved to be just another politician on the make, it would help me keep tabs on Lucinda, and I could back out whenever I chose.

Despite her physical charms, Vada Potts-Jones was no temptress. She had hinted broadly that I was welcome to remain on the Prairie Star until it reached San Francisco, and I had declined without actually saying so. In her mind, I imagined, sex would cement our deal, and the chance to humiliate Lucinda, even without her knowing it, was too good to pass up. For my part, it was enough that I could be bought without actually engaging in the act itself.

While contemplating her unspoken offer, I realized that she was indifferent to any sort of intimacy. A true convert to her ideology, she saw only groups, never individuals, and was without the ability to focus on a single person, much less have meaningful sex with him. Race, sex and gender were important, not to the makeup of an actual man or woman, but as labels in the service of political gain.

She wavered between practical enterprise and political zealotry. She was her father's child, and she was still nominally the chief of his genetics lab. Wildly successful, her experience as a businesswoman was never far from the surface. On the other hand, she spoke in slogans, and proffered dramatically flawed reasoning she would never have accepted at the lab. Sometimes, she just seemed out-of-control.

We had agreed to meet again in San Francisco two days hence. There was a "conclave" she wanted me to attend. "Don't tell anyone what you're doing," she said.

"Not even your dad?"

"*Especially* my dad."

It all seemed a little melodramatic, but I resisted the urge to smile. She was a wealthy, charismatic woman who had acquired a lot of power in a short period of time, and wanted more. I was a newspaperman who worked for her "daddy," from whom she apparently kept secrets. The least I could do was watch her crusade play out.

My roomette was now a bed looking out onto a rolling lunar landscape highlighted by the moon itself. Propped up against the window, I switched on the laptop and found the front page of the *Georgetown Star.*

The news was mostly small potatoes. Marty's alternative to the Internet, the Grapevine, was up and running, and its ad-free format was garnering a lot of attention. On-line gurus predicted that it would divert a substantial number of users from the traditional Internet. The congressional committees investigating the former president's death had reached no conclusion in their reports, but mentioned all the possibilities raised at the hearings, and added a few more. The governor of Idaho was being sued by the governors of Oregon and Washington because of her fence.

The courts had been busy. Marty Jones's single-race villages were declared unconstitutional. The validity of the presidential ballot featuring a dead man at the top of one ticket was affirmed and denied by two different judges. The pardon for Earnest Pogue was deemed invalid. Appeals were promised by all the losers.

Most important to me was the ruling by the Circuit Court for Arlington County, Virginia, that the exhumation of the dead president could proceed. My story about the former president's death was on hold, but that didn't mean it was forgotten. According to the court, and dozens of "friends of the

court," the rules of the National Cemetery Association had to give way for reasons of national security. Attorneys for the dead president's daughter
vowed to "take it all the way to the Supreme
Court."

Judges were the new kings. From the lowli-
est magistrate in Bessemer City, Alabama, to the
marble palace at One First Street in Washington,
D.C., they were importuned from all sides. The
people no longer relied on those they elected to
oversee the country. Anything that was even slightly controversial – laws, monuments, pipelines –
was immediately judged not for its worth, but for
its chances of getting through the courts intact.
Judges were people, too, and – more and more fre-
quently – the opportunity to right a perceived
wrong, rather than do what the law required, was
the path they followed. For many, their motivations
– true belief versus cynical politics – were questionable.

Individuals with actual grievances participated in the process, but it was political interest
groups – the American Union of Civil Libertarians,
say, or the Poor People's Justice Center, plus those
at the other end of the spectrum – who were responsible for most of the judicial abuse. Rather
than win elections, they opted for lawsuits. Their
policy goals were impossible to achieve without a
"win" in the courts.

Sometimes, "winning" was defined as forcing
an opponent to withdraw from the contest. Lawyers
were expensive, and ordinary people were often
priced out of the fight. Others, like Marty Jones,
had staying power, and the litigation over his race-

based communities *would* reach the Supreme Court if necessary.

The Court itself was mired in controversy. For almost a century, President Vere's faction had relied upon the Supreme Court to backstop its agenda. The previous president had threatened that prerogative and Lucinda, while serving as Chief Justice, cut a deal with him: She and her colleagues would resign one at a time and he could fill each seat, but only with candidates who were acceptable to all 100 of the senators who would vote on their confirmations.

The media, whose stock-in-trade was conflict, panned the idea but, after six months of the worst sort of horse trading, a brand new Court was in place. Usually the most intensely hypocritical undertaking in a town whose mother's milk was hypocrisy, the vetting and seating of nine new justices was reduced to a search for those who took their oath seriously – to do equal and impartial justice for all.

The Court's refusal to intervene in the election on their behalf a few weeks earlier had reminded Lucinda and her friends of the advantage they had given up. Now that there was no danger of the other side "tampering" with the Court, they would do it themselves. Bills had been introduced to double its size plus one, to limit its jurisdiction and to impose race, gender and sexual quotas on its membership, all for the purpose of insuring that whatever they wrote into law would remain there. Immediate passage had been stymied by a procedural vote in the Senate, but that obstacle would be gone after the election.

EIGHT

*All the armies of Europe, Asia
and Africa combined, with all the
treasure of the earth (our own ex-
cepted) in their military chest;
with a Bonaparte for a commander, could not by force, take a
drink from the Ohio, or make a
track on the Blue Ridge, in a trial
of a thousand years.* – Abraham
Lincoln, 1838

I SLEPT through most of Nevada. The next
morning, after an exchange of emails with Marty
Jones, I prepared to exit the *Zephyr* in Sacramento,
eighty-five miles short of San Francisco. The governor was holding a news conference that afternoon
to address the most recent "unrest" in her state. As
an extra-added attraction, the spokesman for the
Red Brigade would also be in attendance.

"It's a good thing you're getting off in Sacramento," the conductor said when I told him my
plans. "You weren't going to make it to San Francisco anyway."

"Why not?"

"The crew's leaving the train at the next-to-last stop. Richmond. Nobody's going to replace them."

"What's the trouble?"

"The union's called for a walk-out. Every passenger train in the country will stop at the next-to-last station on its route."

I puzzled over that. "I'm in the newspaper business," I said. "I haven't heard a word about problems between the unions and the railroad."

He sighed. "Neither have I. But – it's what the leadership wants." He looked at his watch. "We'll be the last train running. So, in about six hours, the country will be totally without passenger service."

I opened the laptop. Sure enough, trains all over the country were shutting down and no one seemed to know why. The president, apparently blindsided by the news, was meeting with railroad officials later that day. Transportation in the Northeast Corridor, which relied heavily on the trains, was at a standstill.

As I scrolled through the news, a "Special Alert" popped up: Earnest Pogue was about to begin a press conference that, he said, would "explain the reasons for the railroad work stoppage." I clicked on the link and smiled at an image I recognized immediately – Pogue's front porch in Bessemer City. It was the site of an earlier presser convened a few years before when federal agents converged on the house to arrest him.

The porch was empty. Several people, presumably reporters, hovered on the perimeter. A local television personality filled the dead time with background on Pogue and the Martyrs for Christ, of which he was apparently a member. The minutes dragged on.

Finally, Pogue and his wife emerged from the house. Holding hands, they approached a microphone that looked like it was left over from a 1940s radio program. The questions started immediately.

Pogue held up his hand. "Please," he said, "let me read a brief statement first." His accent was more pronounced than ever. He slipped on a pair of tortoise shell cheaters and drew a folded sheet of paper from his inside coat pocket:

"Godless communists and anarchists, aided and abetted by the Vere Administration, are taking over this country. We've all seen the pictures on TV. An especially vir – viru – vile strain of this contagion, located in the northeast, is waging economic war on the states where many of our martyrs reside. As a result, we have consulted with our friends in the railroad industry, and they have agreed to suspend passenger rail service for the entire country until further notice."

He looked up. "We didn't start this fight," he said, "but, by God, we'll finish it."

"Earnest," called one of the reporters, "the president says she's going to order them back to work."

Pogue shook his head. "She can do all the ordering she wants, but the trains will stay shut down until I say different."

"Is this a union action?" said another reporter. Pogue nodded. "Why did they agree to do this? What's in it for them?"

"They're Americans. They're tired of being treated like – like peasants. They – we can vote for whoever we want." He paused. "If some communist jackass like Matilda Fleck can punish us for it, what's going to happen the next time we do something she doesn't like?"

As usual, all the press cared about was the "horse race" – who was going to win this fight? – and their questions reflected that mindset. The futility of Earnest Pogue and the Martyrs for Christ, even the railroad unions, taking on the federal government was the theme. Pogue seemed unconcerned. "We are not without friends," he said, finally.

"What if she calls in the military?" said a reporter.

"Like I said, we are not without friends."

Depending on how long it lasted, the lack of passenger train service would be an inconvenience for most of the country. Without air travel, though, it was more serious. And for the big hitters in the big cities – Washington, New York, Boston – who used the trains to commute, it meant that the business of America would be harder to do.

THE *ZEPHYR* came to a stop outside Reno. Passenger trains were required by law to give way to freight trains, and a string of closed cars was being shuttled from a complex of low-lying buildings to the eastbound tracks alongside us. Each car was marked, in large white letters: "MLJ Laboratories, Reno, Nevada." It took me a minute to recall that MLJ Laboratories was the genetics lab owned by Marty Jones.

It was Marty's nod to non-profit enterprise. The scientists there worked to eradicate previously incurable genetic diseases, and each time they developed something new it was distributed to clinics and hospitals world-wide free of charge. When I asked him why he had relinquished such a lucrative stream of cash, he muttered something about "tax breaks" and changed the subject. It was an unusual deviation from his capitalist orthodoxy.

Unlike most of his businesses, he was not hands on where the lab was concerned. Once it was up and going, he put Vada in charge and then basked in the praise that issued after each success. MLJ Laboratories was very much his daughter's work and, after she went into politics, the people who ran it were her people, not his. She maintained her place as Chairman of the Board, and still kept an office at the Reno facility.

According to recent reports, it had shifted its attention from specific diseases to the genetic characteristics that allowed those diseases to attack one population and not another. Why were people of African heritage, for example, more susceptible to sickle cell disease, while cystic fibrosis was mostly limited to white people? Despite her instincts, Vada had refused to buy into the notion that disease, like everything else, was the product of racism.

Minutes later, we crossed into California just beyond Reno and climbed into the Sierra Nevada Mountains. Though not as broad or high as the Rockies, they were every bit as intimidating, certainly for those once called upon to construct that first transcontinental railroad. Tunnels driven through the granite, blasted with dynamite, were measured in inches per day, and Donner Pass, where the line crested the mountains, was more than 7,000 feet above sea level. Snowfalls of 500 inches per year and winds exceeding 100 miles per hour were not uncommon. It was snowing now, hard. Everything was white, as if nothing existed beyond my perch in the *Zephyr's* lounge.

The Tahoe National Forest occupied much of the northern portion of the mountain range. The east side of the forest was arid with little vegetation. As we approached the crest, the *Zephyr* passed under a series of concrete snow sheds designed to keep the tracks clear during heavy weather. The west side of the mountains featured steep, rugged canyons dense with firs and pines. A grove of giant sequoias grew in the watershed of the nearby American River.

The descent from the heights of the Sierra Nevadas to Sacramento, 150 miles away, was startling in its climatic, topographical and biological variety. The snow stopped between Truckee and Colfax, the surface flattened and then dipped, and plants and animals of every sort, including man and his many enterprises, were everywhere. Unlike most of the journey, a highway – Interstate 80 – ran beside us. We had entered California's Great Central Valley, of which Sacramento, only thirty feet above sea level, was the capital.

Sacramento was California's first city. Gold had been discovered nearby in 1848, and immigration from the United States, barely a trickle before the "Gold Rush," exploded. Construction of the first cross-country railroad, begun in Sacramento in 1864, added to the influx of Americans, not to mention natives of other countries, including the 12,000 Chinese who actually laid the tracks. The Valley itself, more than 21,000 square miles in the middle of the state, was bounded by three mountain ranges – the Cascades, the Sierra Nevadas and the Tehachapis – and San Francisco Bay. It was a prime example of the global economy at work and the increasing distance between the haves and the have-nots.

Agricultural development, massive altera-tions to hydrologic regimes – diversions, channels, dams – and urban expansion had combined to total-ly eliminate the original habitat. Energy producers, greens and fossil fuels, littered the landscape, and dozens of high-tech companies sprouted along its maze of highways. The ever-growing population generated thousands of retail and service sector jobs.

But, although it had diversified in recent years, it was agriculture and the industries it spawned that dominated the Valley's economy. More than 250 crops were grown year-round. With less than one per cent of the country's farmland, it produced twenty-five per cent of the nation's food, and sent more to foreign countries. The Valley was the world's sole source for certain fruits, vegetables and nuts. It also produced more milk than any oth-er area of the country, and manufacturing facilities that processed the Valley's raw products were ubiquitous.

All it lacked was water. Rainfall was only twenty inches a year and, despite the frantic engi-neering of lakes and rivers, drought was always a threat. The area had fallen into a mild dry spell the year before, a condition that was still ongoing. Schemes to shift water from lesser localities were pending in the Assembly. Water was politics in the Valley, and vice versa.

The temperature was in the 60s and the sky overcast when I stepped off the train. Waiting to check my luggage with the station agent, I noticed that something was missing: Sometime during the night, the Prairie Star and Vada Potts-Jones had uncoupled from the *California Zephyr* and gone their separate ways.

The agent handed me a claim check. "How far's the capitol?" I said.

"About ten blocks." He pointed. "Turn left on I Street then right on 5th. When you reach the Capitol Mall, turn left again. You can't miss it."

"Thanks."

Sacramento was busy. Not only was it the hub of the Central Valley, with all that entailed, it was also an educational center, tourist destination, and major healthcare provider. Museums abounded, and the old waterfront district along the Sacramento River was only one of dozens of attractions that drew new residents and visitors every year. As the capital of the most heavily populated state in the Union, it was home to thousands of government bureaucrats, and young people flocked to the area to fill science and engineering jobs.

Plus, though nearly 100 miles from the coast, Sacramento was trendy. Named California's most "hipster" city by those in the know, it had also been deemed "America's Most Diverse City" by *Time* magazine. "Hip" and "diverse" signaled "tolerant" and "virtuous" to people without values of their own and, as a consequence, Sacramento was the state's fastest-growing city as well. It was a bubble of cosmopolitanism in a sea of provincials.

The Capitol Mall was lined with upscale shops and office buildings. Los Angeles and San Francisco had seen fires and looting the night before, much of it in fashionable areas previously untouched. Nothing seemed amiss here – Sacramento had apparently been spared for the time being.

I approached the State Capitol Building from the east. Framed by elms and oaks that had lost most of their leaves, it was almost a replica of its counterpart in Washington, D.C. It didn't have the House and Senate appendages at either end, and its cast-iron dome was unpainted. There were no steps – entry was by way of doors inside granite arches at ground level.

The Mall ended with a roundabout just before it reached the building. Pausing for the traffic on 10th Street, I noticed some workmen struggling to load a large white statue onto a truck. It was covered in red paint, and the head was missing. According to the plinth, which still stood, it was a tribute to Mexican-American veterans.

"What happened?" I said to the man nearest me.

"They tore it down last night." He gestured. "Just like the rest of them."

"Rest of them?"

"Every statue in the park has been pushed over or mutilated or both. Look behind you."

I looked over my shoulder. A huge bronze relief sculpture stood about fifteen yards away. Closer inspection revealed that it was a memorial to po-

lice officers killed in the line of duty. It featured
three men in law enforcement attire from different
time periods, a woman on a bench hugging a little
girl and a folded American flag. Plaques listed the
names of the fallen. Everything was drenched in
red paint.

The forty-acre park surrounded the Capitol
Building. I had an hour to kill before the press conference, so I decided to inspect the rest of the damage. A large "you are here" sign was posted on the
far side of the building. It listed 155 memorials and
other points of interest, ranging from the Apollo 14
Moon Tree to the ship's bell from the U.S.S. California. Some were gardens or groves of trees, but
most were man-made tributes to people and recog-
nition of significant events.

Not everything had been destroyed. The
lawns, gardens and walkways, with one exception,
were pristine, and minor installations – the Great
Seal of California, for instance, and the September
11 Memorial – had been by-passed by the maraud-
ers. Other, larger memorials were not so lucky.
Toppled and beheaded when possible, covered in
paint and graffiti when not, monuments to firefighters, Purple Heart recipients, Catholic nuns, a
Catholic missionary, and veterans – of all wars as
well as specific tributes to those from the Spanish-
American and Vietnam conflicts – had been vandalized.

The Civil War Memorial Grove, located just
west of the building, was the first monument in
Capitol Park. Planted in 1897, its trees came from
dozens of Civil War battlefields, including a "tree of
peace" from Appomattox. The plaque on the stone

marker indicated that it was "dedicated to the memory of Union veterans of the Civil War." The marker, covered in paint, now stood by itself – the trees had been burned to the ground.

THE MAN I was looking for stepped from the shadows of one of the granite arches. "Tommy," he said. We shook hands. "I was afraid you weren't going to make it."

"And risk the wrath of Marty Jones?" I said. "Never."

A long-time newspaperman of the old school, Mike Beach was the chief political reporter for one of Marty's papers, the *San Francisco Press.* He was a native Californian, one of the few Marty employed, and his beat was state and local politics. He was a good reporter, but news beyond the bounds of the Golden State held little interest for him.

We pushed through the ground-floor doors, presented our press credentials to a uniformed Highway Patrolman, and passed into the building's rotunda. It was an open, circular room about fifty feet across. The floor was black and white marble laid in a checkerboard pattern, and the ceiling arched from all sides to a wide opening into the structure's inner dome whose highest point, the oculus, was 130 feet over our heads. The walls on the lower level were murals depicting urns, foliage and griffins interspersed with niches containing real urns with fresh-cut flowers. Cast-iron grizzly bears, and plaster columns, swags, and cornucopias, decorated the dome.

Light from sixteen large windows in the dome, plus dozens of high-intensity bulbs, illuminated our space. It was like standing under a great, golden bowl turned upside-down. The room was crowded with reporters and television cameras, but the governor and her guest had not yet made an appearance.

A podium with teleprompters had been placed on a large platform in the middle of the floor. A marble tablet was attached to one side of the platform. I pushed through the crowd to read it: "Columbus' Last Appeal to Queen Isabella." I turned to Mike. "What's this?"

"It *used* to be a big statue of Columbus and Isabella. Been there for more than 100 years. They hacked it apart and carried it out of here this morning."

"Was it vandalized?"

He nodded. "Not in the usual sense, but it *was* vandalism. It was removed by order of the governor. The act of a vandal if there ever was one." He paused. "I guess they didn't have time to move the base."

"Have you walked through the park?" I said.

"Yes."

"What's the point?"

"It's the grievance industry on steroids. The statues are just stand-ins for you and me. The losers have convinced the winners to surrender without a shot." He smiled. "Jacobins without guillotines. So far."

The room fell silent as two women, surrounded by a squadron of armed Highway Patrolmen, entered the room and climbed onto the platform. One was easy to recognize – the governor of California, Victoria St. John, née Annabelle Smith.

A former Hollywood starlet, with the face and figure typical of the breed, she had abandoned a mediocre movie career and turned to politics, winning the race for governor on her first try. Another media darling, she was rumored to have her eye on the White House.

I assumed her companion was a woman because of her size, shape and the way she walked, but it wasn't confirmed until a few minutes later when she began to speak. Dressed in black from head to toe – leggings, long-sleeved turtleneck and full face mask – she was shorter and heavier than the governor. Only her hands – brown skin, prominent veins and short, ragged nails – were exposed. Governor St. John wore an identical outfit minus the mask, and she had opted for three-inch heels instead of the combat boots chosen by the Red Brigade's spokeswoman.

The governor tapped on the microphone. "Let's get started," she said. "I have an announcement, then I'll turn it over to my friend here. After that we'll take questions."

Looking first at one teleprompter, then the other, she began:

"As you know, last night there were more demonstrations in our cities, including San Francisco, Los Angeles and here in Sacramento. The right of the people to gather and express themselves in public is protected by the First Amendment, and yet certain elements in this state have demanded that they stop. Some have gone so far as to say that if I don't stop them, they will. I take those threats seriously.

"Accordingly, I have declared a state of emergency. I signed an executive order this morning calling on the citizens of California to turn their guns over to local authorities. The protocols to accomplish the disarming of our population will be posted in the courthouses of all fifty-eight counties and on the Internet. If the authorities have reason to believe that someone is not in compliance, they are empowered to search homes, businesses and all other places, and confiscate any weapons they discover. Non-compliance will subject the perpetrator to criminal penalties.

"It is unfortunate that a few hotheads have forced me to take this action. On the other hand, it's no secret that guns are the most immediate threat to our democracy, so perhaps it's a blessing in disguise. We can no longer allow right-wing lunatics to hide behind the Second Amendment."

She looked directly at her stunned audience. "We live in a profoundly unjust society." She gestured. "This woman and her fellow patriots are fighting to change it. I stand with them. It's long past time for the underdogs in this country to have a seat at the table." She backed up and urged the other woman forward.

After a pause, the masked woman identified herself. "I am John Brown and Martin Luther King. Matthew Shepard and Tyler Clement. Trayvon Martin and George Floyd . . ."

The names continued for ten minutes. As far as I could tell, she was every victim, martyr and icon in the progressive pantheon. After concluding her recitation, she said, "For the past four centuries, you have stigmatized, marginalized and exploited us. You have hoarded resources that should be available to all. Our grievances are legion. And just." She paused. "We're tired of seeking equality. It's no longer enough. We want what you have. And we're going to get it. "

You could hear a pin drop. The governor joined her at the podium. "Questions?" she said.

Incredibly, no one said a word, including me. "Very well," said the governor, smiling. "Thanks for coming." They left the podium. A few reporters finally shouted questions at their backs, but it was too late.

We were quiet during the ride to San Francisco. As we crossed the Golden Gate Bridge, Mike said, "None of that gun control stuff will ever happen, of course. The courts won't permit it, and it would be impossible to enforce." He stopped. "Political grandstanding from a clueless politician."

"What about the Brigade's declaration of war?"

"I think it was a mistake. The folks who've been treating all this as just another minor eruption may look at it differently now. That part about confiscating the wealth will certainly get their attention."

We passed between two ornate lampposts and stopped in the circular, red-brick courtyard at One Nob Hill, otherwise known as the Mark Hopkins Hotel. "How about lunch tomorrow?" said Mike.

"I can't. I'm running all over town tomorrow. Courtesy of Marty Jones."

"Dinner?"

I shook my head. "I've got an — appointment."

"Okay. Let me know if you need anything."

"Thanks. I will."

I stepped gingerly through a small collection of tents and other makeshift dwellings. The hotel rose nineteen stories above the highest point in San Francisco on land once owned by Mark Hopkins, one of the founders of the Central Pacific Railroad. The mansion he built there had been destroyed in the Great Fire after the 1906 earthquake. The hotel, with its French and Spanish Renaissance façade and terracotta ornaments, opened in 1926.

Three canopies stood over red-carpeted steps leading into the hotel. At the top of the steps, I stopped and looked back. San Francisco was the nation's homeless capital and its denizens, with the encouragement of the city's Board of Supervisors, had gradually taken over the sidewalks, parks and other open spaces. Their drug use, public sex and lack of hygiene, plus the increasingly venomous verbal harassment and panhandling, had forced the city's hard-pressed taxpayers — who had acquiesced, more or less, in the usurpation — to forego the amenities they paid so dearly for and remain besieged in their homes. The invasion had now reached San Francisco's most storied heights, in the courtyard of the Mark Hopkins Hotel, and it probably wouldn't be long before they pitched their tents in the lobby.

Two uniformed doormen held the middle doors open and I passed through. Enormous crystal chandeliers, plush furniture and tasseled pillows recalled the ostentatious trappings of the city's

Barbary Coast days, when the 49ers came to town flush with gold. My room, though ordinary enough, was palatial compared to my accommodations for the past few days. The view was spectacular – across San Francisco Bay to the Golden Gate Strait, the bridge that spanned it, and beyond to the Pacific Ocean.

I re-boarded the elevator and climbed to the 19th floor. Originally a penthouse with eleven rooms, the Top of the Mark was now a lounge with a 360-degree view of the city and the rest of the Bay Area. The Art Deco décor was dark wood and iron balustrades, and the vaulted ceiling and split-level floor added to the uncluttered vista. The room was crowded. I found a seat at the bar and ordered a martini.

I spread my notes on the bar. I was scheduled to meet with five people tomorrow: a member of the Board of Supervisors, the Chief of Police, the Executive Director of the San Francisco Labor Council, the chairman of the local funeral home association, and the Director of San Francisco General Hospital. The idea was to look beyond the well-publicized clashes between the Red Brigade and the White Army to the everyday violence perpetrated by otherwise ordinary citizens. Marty's last instructions were, "I want to know what's *really* going on in this country, not what the media choose to report."

A television over the bar, which no one was watching, was tuned to the late president's favorite channel. It showed endless replays of last night's riots, only blocks away. People were beaten, windows broken and stores stripped bare. The Cable

Car Museum down the street had been gutted by fire. The chyron at the bottom of the screen screamed, "CITIES BURN WHILE VERE FIDDLES!"

The bartender changed channels to the local news. The lead story was the governor's executive order, lauded by a variety of San Francisco officials, followed by a police investigation of "right-wing vigilantes." The message from the Red Brigade's spokeswoman wasn't mentioned.

NINE

At what point then is the ap-
proach of danger to be expected?
I answer, if it ever reach us, it
must spring up among ourselves
. . . If destruction be our lot, we
must ourselves be its author and
finisher. As a nation of freemen,
we must live through all times,
or die by suicide –
Abraham Lincoln, 1838

THE CONSENSUS of the people I spoke to the next day was that there *might* be more violence in their city than ever before though they were re- luctant to say so, and if there was, it was due to "policies" instituted by the former president. When asked for examples, they never mentioned laws or orders or rules, of which there were many during his administration. Instead, they responded with media buzzwords associated with the president like "division" and "lies" and "racism."

The hospital director, after recounting the 100 per cent increase in admissions as a result of street violence, hastened to assure me that he ex- pected a sharp decline now that the president was dead.

"He's been gone for over a month," I said. "Any dip in the numbers?"

"No. They've gone up slightly. But they typically lag a week or two."

It was the same story with the woman from the Board of Supervisors. "How can you expect the population to remain under control," she said, "with a man like that in the White House?" The labor leader was even more direct. "He was a pig who deserved to die. If he was assassinated, whoever it was did the country a favor. I support those kids in the streets."

Only the police chief, perhaps because he was just a few weeks from retirement, told a different story on condition of anonymity. "We've been building up to this for years," he said. "Decades. This city tolerates violence as policy."

"What do you mean?"

"Many of the people who put these politicians in office year after year are the same ones who organize and perpetrate the violence. It sort of simmers under the surface for a while and then, when someone's 'program' or 'contract' is in jeopardy, they take to the streets." He paused. "The politicos and criminals are part of the same gang."

"Is it worse now?"

"Yes."

"Why?"

"Because the system is coming apart. The money's running out. The supervisors, the judges, even the police, can no longer bribe the thugs to be good, and there's no will to actually clean the place up." He stopped. "It's going to get worse, and it may never get better."

The funeral home director, a small, impeccably-dressed black man, brooked no levity about his profession. When I asked him if business was better than usual, he said, "If by that you mean have we had an increase in the number of funerals, the answer is yes. But we are not a business, as you call it. We are a service. The final, most important one our patrons will ever experience."

"Of course. I'm sorry."

"Our members have embalmed, cremated and buried hundreds of bodies recently without compensation. We are all God's children." He paused. "Except him, of course."

"Him?"

"Our late, unlamented president. *He* was the devil."

I SLIPPED on a jacket and, turning, checked my reflection in the mirror. Satisfied, I descended to the first floor and crossed the lobby. Vada Potts-Jones had chosen the California Suite at the Mark Hopkins for her meeting. Situated on the 18th floor, the rate for its 2,300 square feet was over $5,000 per day. Entry was via a special secure elevator that opened into the suite's service entrance. It was decorated like 1926 with furnishings from 2020.

The other participants were there when I arrived, and it was obvious from the cups and saucers, and the stack of dirty dishes, that they had been there for some time. I recognized them all: Vada, of course, the Red Brigade woman from yesterday's news conference – still in the same outfit, including the mask – and the man who led the

White Army. He called himself "Anton" after a general from the Russian Revolution.

The fourth member of the party was Earnest Pogue. I'd seen him on his front porch yesterday morning. "How'd you get here?" I said, grasping the outstretched hand.

"By air," he said, nodding in Vada's direction.

"He came on Daddy's plane," she said.

I raised my eyebrows. "Daddy's in on this?"

She shook her head. "I told him I needed it to get back to D.C. Which I do." She turned toward the others. "You can all speak freely. Tommy has agreed this is off the record." She looked back at me. "Right?"

Our "off the record" agreement had expanded. "Right."

It wasn't exactly Yalta – they were, after all, nominally enemies – but the meeting in the California Suite served the same purpose. The Red Brigade, the White Army and the Martyrs for Christ, at the urging of Vada Potts-Jones, had gathered to "re-organize" the United States of America. That the country was already organized, with governments at every level plus the most powerful military in the history of the world, was never mentioned. The idea that these four people and their rag-tag followers could take control of the United States was silly.

That, however, was the plan. It was clear that whatever haggling there was had taken place before my arrival – this part of the meeting was for my benefit. Their partisans had distinct agendas – to lavish the property of others on themselves, for instance, or to escape a suffocating governmental and cultural elite, or to simply be left alone. Race defined them all to one degree or another. The territory claimed by each group – urban, rural, a mixture of the two – reflected the battlegrounds already in play.

I had a good idea where Pogue and the Brigade stood, so I concentrated on Anton. He was a small, white man, soft-spoken to a fault. As a consequence, it was necessary to pay close attention to what he said. Plainly unmoved by the victim culture embraced by the Red Brigade, he had no time for Pogue's tirades against the federal government either, though he certainly agreed with the sentiment. Unlike the others, he was unhappy about what they were doing.

We had a quiet conversation at the coffee urn. "I'm not leaving the country," he said. "The country left me a long time ago." I nodded. "I'm not sure when it changed. Maybe it's always been this way. I just didn't know it."

He seemed more sober than the others. "What makes you think you can pull this off?" I said. "I mean, they have more divisions than you have soldiers."

He stared at me, blinking. "There'll be no battlefields," he said, finally. "If she pulls the trigger, they'll give up without firing a shot."

"If?"

"I don't think Vada's made up her mind."

"Why's it up to her?"

He grinned. "She's got the hammer."

"Which is?"

He shook his head. "That's not for me to say. You'll have to ask her."

The balance of the conference was devoted to the logistics of a future event that went unex-plained. "Is everyone ready to go?" Vada asked Pogue.

He nodded. "All the railroad teams have been delivered, and the unions are on the alert." He paused. "The non-coms are on board."

"What are you talking about?" I said.

"You're my chronicler, Tommy," said Vada. "I want you to report what happens when it happens. I'll let you know when you need to know."

"Are the tanks in place?" said Anton.

"Yes," she said. "The last ones left yester-day."

"And the pills?" She nodded.

The meeting broke up a few minutes later. Vada stood by the door as the others took their leave. "I'll let you know when the chaos starts," she said.

"What's the chaos?" I said when we were alone.

"It's a surprise."

"Is there some chance it won't happen at all?" She didn't answer. "What's your place in all this?"

"That's part of the surprise." She smiled. "Need a ride home?"

"Yes."

"Meet me in the lobby in fifteen minutes. The plane leaves in an hour."

WASHINGTON WAS in an uproar. While Vada and I flew across the country, someone finally leaked the "poison" narrative. The dead president's supporters were in a frenzy, not just because it gave weight to the conspiracy they had built around his death, but also because it had been covered up by the new president and the mainstream media. Despite blanket denials and ever more desperate citations to the medical evidence, the press and the administration were shouted down.

The plane crash at Reagan National and Doctor Cohen's death were scrutinized again. Potential assassins were considered, and President Vere voted the clear favorite despite the fact – now deemed part of the cover-up – that she might have been in danger, too. The most recent appeal of the president's exhumation was now lodged in the Supreme Court of Virginia, and there was much dark muttering about the consequences if it was not allowed. A round-the-clock guard was set on the gravesite at Arlington to counter threats from self-described "grave-digger vigilantes."

Meanwhile, the rest of the country had slowed to a crawl. The lack of transportation, strikes by private and public workers and boycotts in all sectors of the economy had brought business to a halt. Despite having no answer to the explosions on earlier flights, President Vere ordered the airlines back in the air, only to have flight crews balk because they might be blown from the sky. Another order, directed at passenger train personnel, was ignored. There was widespread speculation that the military would be called in to operate "essential" industries.

The "demonstrations" had finally reached the streets of the nation's capital, but the violence was oddly circumscribed. The former president had owned several properties – two hotels, a restaurant and an apartment building – within walking distance of the White House. They now belonged to his heirs, currently being sorted out in the District of Columbia Probate Court. The plate-glass exterior of the restaurant and the apartment building's storefronts were smashed on the first night of "unrest," and the hotels firebombed on the second. Nothing else in Washington, with its 200 years of "privileged" history and the shrines to it, was touched. The Speaker of the House of Representatives, caught on camera high-fiving another spectator outside one of the burning buildings, refused to comment.

We still had a paper to get out. The California Suite "summit" was "off the record," and I had no problem keeping it that way. The truth was, I didn't take Vada and her friends seriously – it was inconceivable to me that they might succeed, surprise or no surprise.

The "railroad teams" that Pogue had mentioned might well be military men and women like those Sergeant Smith had sprinkled between Washington and Chicago, perhaps to enforce the railroad strike if necessary. "Tanks," if not fanciful, would have to be deployed on an unimaginable scale, and I had no idea what role "pills" might play in their scheme.

That "the non-coms were on board" was more sinister. When the Vietnam War was winding down fifty years earlier, the country was in the process of ending the draft and converting to an all-volunteer military. At the same time, labor unions sought to recruit enlisted military personnel to their rolls, an effort welcomed enthusiastically by the rank-and-file. The Congress, the military leadership and public opinion all lined up against it, emphasizing the then-plausible notion that service to one's country was a more honorable calling than a mere "occupation," and that unionization – with its collective bargaining, picket lines and strikes – would inevitably turn "service" into "job." The idea lost momentum and faded into history.

It was entirely possible that today's soldiers, sailors and Marines, especially the non-commissioned officers charged with their everyday care and feeding, would not see their service the same way now. Endless wars the public barely noticed, superiors who sent them into harm's way from thousands of miles away and, above all, civilian leaders who neither knew nor cared about military service, might have led them to believe it was just a job after all, and a thankless one at that. They could very well be open to some kind of deal with Earnest Pogue and the Martyrs for Christ, but an actual mutiny seemed farfetched.

I wrote the story I'd been assigned, with just a hint of the future Vada envisioned:

AMERICAN AS CHERRY PIE
Tommy Sawyer

On July 27, 1967, H. Rap Brown, then Chairman of the Student Nonviolent Coordinating Committee, declared that "violence is as American as cherry pie." As if to affirm the power of that prescription, Brown is currently serving a life sentence for murdering a sheriff's deputy, but his assess-

ment seems as accurate today as it was fifty-three years ago. Indeed, some argue that violence has been part of our DNA from the beginning of the republic.

Since Brown uttered those words, countless people with a cause have tried to claim a slice of the "pie" – "gun" violence, "racial" violence, "domestic" violence, etc. – and, by and large, those folks have found a sympathetic ear among the press and those they shill for. But there's one form of violence that begets only silence or, worse, obfuscation – the "political" violence that Brown was actually speaking of, specifically the left-wing variety. To say the media turns a deaf ear as well as a blind eye to the depredations of their political soulmates is to seriously understate the reality.

The violence currently roiling our cities is a case in point. During a recent visit to a large West Coast city, the authorities there could barely acknowledge the mayhem evident to all and the resulting death and destruction. When they could bring themselves to discuss it, they blamed the former president, much as the ancient Greeks condemned Pandora for all the world's ills. The local press was silent.

More troubling, the Governor of California blamed the riots on those who were not rioting, and plans to take their guns away. If that process is actually carried out, it seems likely that Brown's "cherry pie" violence will raise its unlovely head once again.

One official from that aforementioned West Coast city told a different story. Once upon a time we had Boss Tweed and James Michael Curley *running "political machines" in our cities. Today's elected officials are, if not anonymous, less colorful, but it is the symbiotic relationship between them and their "activist" constituents that allows the violence to fester and spread. One-party rule, slush funds masquerading as government programs, and "plantations" where votes are harvested like cotton, all add to the rot that never sees the light of day. Mayors and governors aren't doing anything about it and, so far, neither is the president.*

All of which might seem to bode well for the dead president's re-election, but there's so much going on now that the mayhem, "as American as cherry pie," may be overlooked. If that's the case, the country could well be on the verge of dissolving into parts "governed" by the factions we're now so familiar with. H. Rap Brown's paean to violence was spoken in support of revolution and, fifty-three years later, it looks like he was on to something.

WE HAD agreed that she would initiate any contact between us, but by the time I returned to Washington I hadn't heard from Lucinda for five days. I dialed her cell and waited – nothing. No ring, no leave-a-message, nothing except a void in the communications cosmos reputed to be inescapable. I tried again, with the same result.

Willfully ignorant of cellphone technology, I considered the possibilities: Did she have a new number? A new phone? Could she just turn it off so that an incoming call wouldn't even register? Why would she do that?

Darker thoughts intruded. She had seemed fearful when we last met. I attributed it to concern for me, but what if she was in some kind of danger? What sorts of danger might threaten the President of the United States? And what could I do about it?

She was enveloped, smothered even, in security, human and mechanical. Sophisticated devices were deployed to protect her. From Wolf Robinson to the Joint Chiefs of Staff, everyone's brief included insuring her survival. Might those same arrangements be utilized to hold her prisoner, or worse?

My phone vibrated. Relieved, I pushed the button. "Hi."

"Hi," she said. "How was your trip?"

"Eventful. I'll tell you about it next time I see you." I paused. "Which will be when?"

"I don't know. We're in lockdown. I'm not going anywhere, and I'm not sure Wolf would let you in here."

"Isn't that for you to decide?"

"Tommy. I have to listen to the experts. It would be irresponsible not to."

An image of Roy Miller, railing against the "experts," appeared behind my eyes. "Are you sure?" I said.

"Of course, I'm sure. What are you talking about?"

There was no point in suggesting that experts and their edicts were not the panacea she imagined. She had to believe in something. "Experts" and "science" were the gods she worshipped, and "Man" – by which she meant the people in charge – always had the last word. That the scheme she embraced was more akin to feudalism than the equality her creed demanded was unthinkable.

The experts had no scorekeepers. Their friends in the media celebrated their few successes and ignored their many failures. It took years, sometimes decades, to acknowledge they were wrong, and even then it was a new generation of experts, eager to pontificate, who made excuses for them and continued the cycle. They were parasites who added nothing to the country's prosperity and, as Roy had noted, made an excellent living pretending that they did.

"Is something wrong with your phone?" I said.

"Not that I know of. I'm using it right now."

We signed off a few minutes later. Still uneasy about her cellphone, I tapped the "recent calls" icon on my own device. Hers was at the top of the list: "Lucinda – 202-455-1013." Satisfied, I laid it aside, then picked it up again. The final digit, "3," should've been "2." What did that mean? I tapped her number, the one with the "2" at the end, and was greeted again with silence.

"Tommy?" Marty stood next to my desk. "I just read your story," he said. "It doesn't sound pretty." I nodded. "Still – we've been through worse." I nodded again. "Have you talked to the president lately?"

"I just got off the phone with her."

"Did you know she's activated the National Guard?"

"No."

"And word has it that regular Army troops and a Marine battalion are being mustered."

"For what?"

"To protect this town, I guess."

"That seems a little over-the-top."

"Her people claim there's evidence of a possible – um, insurrection."

Did this have anything to do with Vada's plans? "Insurrection? By who?" I said.

"They won't say, of course. It's classified." He paused. "The Peace Plaza's basically finished. I'm going over there now to look around." He smiled. "Why don't you come with me? You might find something to write about."

We walked down to M Street and caught a cab. My brain was in turmoil – I felt like one of Vada's conspirators – but, as we negotiated Washington Circle and turned right on L Street, I saw evidence of "insurrection" all around me: Streets closed by sawhorses and police cars, store windows covered with plywood, and contingents of men and women wearing fatigues and carrying rifles. At 11th Street, we turned north past the ruins of one of the former president's hotels, then east on Rhode Island past the other one. It looked like the troops would have plenty to do right here.

As soon as we made the turn on Rhode Island Avenue, the People's Plaza rose in the distance like a great white phallus. The Shaw neighborhood, less than a mile from the White House, was one of the few black enclaves in the northwest quadrant of the city. The site on which the Plaza stood, the equivalent of more than three city blocks, had formerly been occupied by a "seniors dwelling," itself once a historic school built in 1902. Its destruction, not to mention the symbolic menace of the "orange" president among them, had convulsed the neighborhood for months. Several attempts to blow up the building while it was being constructed had failed.

With the advent of the Vere Administration, the community had simmered down but pickets, kept at a distance by D.C. police, still marched in front of one of the many porticos. Security had already been set up in the lobby. Marty led the way through the metal detector. "Let's go straight to the top," he said. "You won't believe the view."

The single express elevator, unmarked, was tucked away at the end of a short, narrow corridor. I felt the tug of gravity as we rose but, despite the speed of our ascent, it took almost two minutes to reach the top. We emerged into a round space, open to the air, about 100 feet across. It was empty except for the golden steeple rising from the middle of the deck.

The view was indeed spectacular. Mountains, rivers and forests, interspersed with man's puny constructs, spun outward from the city in all directions. I could just make out the White House, and the Capitol looked like a doll's overturned teacup. The Atlantic Ocean was a gray boundary fading to black in the east.

Marty stepped through an opening at the base of the steeple. "Look at this," he called. "They've finished the steps." A circular iron stairway wound above us. "It leads to the platform holding the medallion. I've never been up there." He started to climb.

I couldn't see the top. "How far is it?" I said.

"Exactly 145 feet, six inches. Two hundred thirty-two steps."

I followed him, reluctantly. We stopped to rest every thirty steps or so. Halfway up, we sat down side-by-side. He looked a little gray, and I was winded. "Sure you want to keep going?" I said.

He nodded. "I'm fine. Just give me a minute."

We rested more often as we continued to climb. The temperature was in the 50s, but both of us were sweating freely when we reached the top. Marty had regained his color. He pointed. "That thing's made of 22-carat gold. It's worth millions of dollars."

"It's obscene," I said. "I mean, it's a *government* building."

He laughed. "You don't think government's entitled to a little bling? A little veneration?" I shook my head. "Well – *government* obviously disagrees with you." He laughed again.

The round medallion, framed by golden olive branches, was about eight feet wide and four inches thick. A large black bird, so still I thought it might be part of the arrangement, perched on top of it. The surface was unmarked. "I thought it was supposed to have some kind of engraving on it," I said.

"It was." I lifted my brows. "I think a blank slate's more appropriate for the time being." He paused. "Let the winners decide what to write on it."

He turned toward the stairs and stumbled, clutching his chest. I caught him and eased him to the deck. "Marty?"

He didn't answer.

It took a helicopter, finally, to remove his body. I watched the chopper disappear into the twilight, then began the downward spiral cautiously. The bird was gone.

Surprisingly, I was near tears. I had worn a skeptic's armor for many years, and few events in my life had penetrated it. Despite his unthinking reverence for ruthless commerce, I would miss the small black man who had accomplished so much, always on his own terms.

I considered his daughter as I lurched down the stairs. She had lived her life exactly as she pleased, but always with the knowledge that, however much her father disapproved, he had her back. That was no longer the case – Vada Potts-Jones was on her own now. Martin Luther Jones had leavened her evolution from the merely outrageous to the truly radical, and her revolt had been arranged but not yet carried out. Would his death tip the scales?

TEN

I hope I am over wary; but if I am not, there is, even now, something of ill-omen, amongst us – Abraham Lincoln, 1838

THE MEDIA used Marty's death as a final opportunity to criticize his life. His obituary in the "paper of record" was a litany of "crimes" committed in the name of capitalism, followed by assurances that we would not see his like again: "There's no place in today's America for his sort of 'up by the bootstraps' ethic. And no need for it, either." His only saving grace was his daughter, an heiress now, who had acquired her wealth in the approved manner. There was no mention of MLJ Laboratories.

His billions went to Vada with one exception – the *Georgetown Star* and its assorted subsidiaries were placed in a trust for the benefit of the Adam Smith Society. I was one of the trustees. A letter, written months before he died, accompanied his will:

Tommy,
I'm sure it comes as no surprise to you that I can't trust Vada with the newspaper. I acknowledge my responsibility for who

she is. She had serious health problems when she was a kid and I spoiled her rotten, but that's no excuse for all this wild-eyed radicalism. For some reason, the "culture" she grew up in is hell-bent on self-destruction. I've made my peace with it, but I can't allow her to take the *Star* down with her. Help her if you can.

Remember: "And the truth shall make you free."

Marty

My fellow trustees happily turned over operation of the *Star* and its sister newspapers to me. After assuring everyone that things would continue as they were, I tried to revert to reporter/columnist status with limited success. I conducted the papers' business in Marty's office. The effort to find a real publisher began.

For some unknown corporate reason, oversight of the *Star* included keeping tabs on the Grapevine. Though still much smaller than the traditional Internet, it was gaining ground, primarily because it wasn't free. Its cash flow came from membership fees rather than advertising and its single search engine, "Navigator," contained algorithms that discouraged the rampant fraud that pervaded the Internet.

Marty had ordered up the most potent of these, deemed "the jury" by his subscribers. If a member believed a web posting to be untrue, she could explain her reasoning and immediately call for a "verdict" from a random, anonymous jury of 100 people. If a majority found in favor of the accuser, various levels of punishment might be imposed on the wrongdoer depending on the severity of the falsehood, the worst of which was loss of membership.

If the accused prevailed, the membership of the accuser was automatically revoked. The whole thing played out in front of all the Grapevine members who chose to participate. The number of complaints decreased daily. It wasn't perfect but, when combined with the membership fee that might be forfeited, the jury kept a lid on the spread of lies and misinformation.

EXPEDITED APPEALS for all sorts of controversies had been accepted by the Supreme Court, as if the Court was trying to clear the decks before the election. The presidential ballot with a dead man at the top was blessed, largely on the grounds that it was electors, not voters, who chose the president. In the unlikely event they elected a dead man, that was a question for another day.

Marty Jones's blacks-only community was revived because those complaining about it, the usual stew of social justice warriors, had no standing to do so. "It is worth noting," the Chief Justice wrote, "that Appellees have a long history of arguing for the rights of our black citizens to live *with* whites should they choose to do so. Here, they take it a step further. They argue that blacks cannot be allowed to live *without* whites because various social disabilities imposed by others have left them unable to reliably govern themselves. Though never stated so baldly, their real argument is that blacks cannot be trusted to live among themselves only, more of the 'soft bigotry' that mars race relations in this country. It is a concept with which we do not agree."

Earnest Pogue's pardon was reinstated because the president's pardon power was absolute. At the end of the one-paragraph opinion, the Court took the opportunity to complain about "baseless, partisan litigation." The press cited all three cases as further evidence of an "out of control" Court that required "meaningful reform."

A decision on the president's exhumation was expected any day. The alternatives were debated breathlessly. If he wasn't in his grave, where was he? Was he dead or alive? Was he still president? Who had orchestrated such a dangerous charade? Why? The media consensus was that the president himself had planned it in order to boost his sagging re-election effort, though how that might happen was never explained.

If he was still buried at Arlington, a different question arose: How did he die? Plans for competing autopsies – one arranged by his family, the other by Congress – had already been laid. Botox was the clear choice among the social media, while liver failure was barely mentioned. Another question was whether or not Lucinda Trent Vere could serve as president from prison, or would Vada Potts-Jones take over? And, of course, if the dead president won the election, who would actually move into the White House?

That last question had focused everyone's attention on the Electoral College. The Texas legislature, concerned that Florida's governor now had too much political clout and might control the outcome, had also given its governor the power to choose electors, and the inevitable political maneuvering had started. Because Texas had nine more votes than Florida, it was seen as the bigger prize. Both governors had made clear their willingness to deal, and the bidding between the opposing factions had escalated.

The contest to name the Climate Clock Tower had degenerated into a political food fight. In addition to multiple environmental icons, dozens of interest groups had backed their own champions – abortion activists, sexual pioneers, gun controllers – while the Martyrs for Christ had organized their supporters behind a single candidate, Alfred E. Neuman. As a consequence, Neuman won in a landslide. "What, Me Worry?" was the headline over the story. The president and leaders on Capitol Hill were said to be considering a re-vote with a limited number of approved nominees.

The African locust outbreak was finally garnering some attention. A report from the *Star's* news bureau in Addis Ababa likened it to a dark blizzard in the desert:

> *In the beginning, they looked like isolated flakes of snow, but soon they began to come faster and thicker in vast clouds that collided with dwellings and fell on the fields. Within minutes, every bush and tree, fences, fields and roads, everything, was black with grasshoppers.*

Having reached the swarm stage, only pesticides could control the plague, but the most effective chemicals were not allowed because of potential harm to the environment. Spraying from airplanes was banned for the same reason, so desperate villagers were forced to use ineffective insecticides delivered by backpacks and pickup trucks in an effort to salvage their crops. They failed to make a dent in the advancing horde, and the insects, their breeding cycle undiminished, increased in numbers never seen before.

THE SANITATION workers in Manhattan, in sympathy with the police and firefighters, went on strike, followed quickly by the longshoremen, cab drivers and subway workers. The mayor, once the darling of the city's unionists, had sided with the criminals and now found herself presiding over a city in tumult. As the garbage piled up, the murder rate rose and businesses shut down, she called upon her fellow partisan, the Governor of New York, for help.

The governor dispatched the state's National Guard to perform the most critical tasks, but the effort fell short due to a lack of participation by the troops. Thousands resigned while others chose to simply "remain in their barracks." The press howled "treason," and demanded trials, imprisonment and death. A few half-hearted attempts were made to impose military justice but, because the no-shows were so widespread, the system broke down and the effort petered out. Earnest Pogue, who was believed to be behind the "strike," had dropped out of sight.

The governor threw up her hands and turned to her partisan-in-chief, the President of the United

States. She was greeted with silence from the White House. Wild rumors circulated to the effect that President Vere had lost control of the nation's military. I tried to call her, without success.

Though reluctant to follow his instructions, I could hear Marty Jones calling from his grave: "Go to New York! It's the greatest city in the world, and it's falling apart. It's where the news is. Go!"

The first question was how to get there. No airplanes and no trains left helicopters, buses, automobiles and boats. Helicopters to Manhattan were booked solid, I didn't have a car and didn't want to rent one, and buses made me nauseous. A friend owned a forty-eight foot trawler he kept berthed in Annapolis, thirty miles to the east. The weather forecast was good, so we could make the trip in less than a day.

We left mid-afternoon with the goal of reaching New York before noon the following day. Starting from Back Creek, we motored north up Chesapeake Bay to the Elk River, which led into the Chesapeake & Delaware Canal. Once through the canal, we turned southeast into Delaware Bay. By the time we reached Cape May at the bottom of the bay it was dark.

From there it was north again in the Atlantic Ocean along the Jersey shore. We passed Sandy Hook at 10 AM, crossed under the Verrazzano-Narrows Bridge and entered the waters that defined the boroughs of the city of New York. With Staten Island to the left and Brooklyn on the right, we sailed past Governor's Island, whereupon the skyscrapers of Lower Manhattan, long visible on the horizon, rose like pinnacles from the sea. "Let's sail around the island before we park," I said.

Manhattan Island, bounded by the Hudson, Harlem and East Rivers, was the most densely populated place in the country. Its twenty-three square miles were home to almost 2 million people, which more than doubled Monday through Friday when over 2 million more crossed the rivers to go to work. Seventy million tourists added to the throng each year. Due to the mania over "identity," its citizens were classified by race, the largest of which, at sixty-five per cent, was "white."

In ordinary times, most of those entering and leaving Manhattan used the trains. When the strikes began, people were forced to drive and, despite emergency carpooling, remote parking efforts and lane reversals, the island's infrastructure was unable to handle the load. Traffic on the first bridge we went under, the Brooklyn Bridge, was at a dead stop at eleven o'clock in the morning. Likewise, further up the East River, the Manhattan, Williamsburg and Queensboro Bridges were all jammed.

At the northern extreme of the island's 13-mile length, the Broadway Bridge was shut down for some reason, and all fourteen lanes of the George Washington Bridge over the Hudson River – the world's busiest motor vehicle crossing in normal times – were at a standstill. It seemed likely that the tunnels and footbridges into Manhattan were in the same shape. We tied the boat up at a marina in the shadow of the World Trade Center, and I set out on my trek through the urban jungle.

Seven hours later, we were back on the water, heading south. Manhattan was dirtier, slower and even less civil than usual, and everyday life was harder, but it was still Manhattan, the center of the "civilized" world. Its accretions of enormous wealth, power and influence – in finance, technology, education, the arts and the media in all its endless varieties – still dictated events, large and small, around the world. To the degree its operations were hampered by the turmoil, the effects were felt wherever human beings accumulated – when Manhattan sneezed, the rest of the globe caught cold.

Its influence over every aspect of life in the United States couldn't be overstated. Without Manhattan, the banks would close, business would cease and the screens go blank. This stranglehold on the pulse of America had given rise to an arrogance toward the rest of the country that added much to the general malaise. It was Sodom and Gomorrah to the Roy Millers of the world.

During my walk around the island, I had again marveled at the regularity of the grid upon which all these enterprises were imposed. The twelve wide avenues ran north and south parallel to the Hudson River, and the narrower streets – the highest number was West 220th Street in the northernmost corner of the island – ran east and west. The major anomaly was Broadway, built at a diagonal from Lower Manhattan to the northern tip of the island, creating a series of squares – Times, Herald, Madison, Union – plus Columbus Circle at 8th Avenue and 59th Street. The squares, circles and sidewalks lining the roadways were always packed with people.

Few of Manhattan's citizens owned automobiles. Most travel of any length was via public transportation – otherwise, people used their legs to get around. There were dozens of neighborhoods, each with its own distinctions, and hundreds of parks and playgrounds, the largest of which, Central Park – stretching more than two miles long and a half-mile wide – covered 843 acres. Despite its population density, a consequence of the highrise architecture in Lower Manhattan and Midtown, the island had lots of open space.

The news was that there *was* no news. Despite the chaos, the tumult impacted only the "little people." The corporate and cultural aristocrats, safely apart from everyone else, lived as they had always lived, Marie Antoinettes in their eyries above the fray. Secure in their certainty, they looked down on the mob and smiled.

I HAD an email from Vada when I returned to the office:

> *Tommy, we need a secure method to communicate. We may be scrutinized very carefully in the next few days. There's a note in Daddy's middle desk drawer. Destroy it after you know what to do. Delete this email.*
>
> V

The note, in her handwriting, contained instructions on how to use the Grapevine via Marty's

computer. Computer literacy was not my strong
suit. When I had asked him what made the Grapevine different from the Internet, he said, "We've
removed all the intermediaries. The routers and
servers and so forth."

"Which does what?"

"It allows our subscribers to communicate
with others without going through some Internet
provider. That makes it very difficult for the government, say, or ordinary hackers, to gain access."
He paused. "Plus, we've eliminated human intervention, which makes the Grapevine even more secure."

The function Vada was trying to teach me
was called "Interface," which allowed two or more
individuals to see and hear one another as if they
were sitting in the same room. It involved one
password, a few buttons and one click. I mastered it
easily, but planted reminders of the password and
buttons around the room just in case. Vada wasn't
available, but she had left a message:

*"Tommy – Today is October 31. I'll
call you tonight at 7 PM."*

I switched over to the front page of the
Georgetown Star. The headline, in the largest font
I'd ever seen the paper use, read:

COURT ORDERS EXHUMATION

The order had been issued at 10 AM that
morning. After securing an agreement from the
dead president's daughter that no further legal

maneuvers would be forthcoming, Arlington National Cemetery scheduled the televised exhumation for 1 PM the following day. The competing autopsies, featuring the foremost forensic pathologists in the world, would begin shortly thereafter. Both sides promised public announcements as soon as the results were known.

If his death was not as the Vere Administration said it was, the reaction would undoubtedly be explosive but, because the partisan divide was now so bitter, the exhumation would probably have little effect on the people's vote. How one voted was now every citizen's perceived identity – politics was everything – and a failure to formally choose sides by casting that vote would be viewed as a serious character flaw, or worse. Nevertheless, the final margin in the Electoral College was in the hands of politicians from Florida and Texas. Contrary to the usual practice, the ongoing negotiations for their favor had not been leaked to the media.

The consensus among the political gurus was that Texas would ultimately go to the former president while the current president would win Florida. Assuming the rest of the country split evenly, President Vere would lose the election because Texas had thirty-eight electoral votes while Florida had only twenty-nine. However, both governors were still seeking every political concession possible – offices in the new administration, chairmanships in the new Congress, every bridge and road on their respective wish lists – so the outcome was still in doubt.

Life in these United States was approaching a crescendo:

AMERICA
Tommy Sawyer

Tomorrow, as the world looks on, we will dig up the body of the 45th President of the United States, an act unimaginable only a few months ago, now sanctioned by the highest court in the land. The ostensible purpose for this indignity is to sort out the media-inspired uncertainties surrounding his death. The real reason is to give impetus to one side or the other in the war we are waging amongst ourselves.

The battles are fought on many fronts but, at its core, the war is between those for whom equality and personal freedom are all that matter, and those who believe that something less absolute is necessary for human beings to co-exist in freedom. On the one side, "rights" – especially the personal kind – are the Holy Grail. On the other, "responsibilities" are necessary to temper the inevitable extremes of unfettered license. For hundreds of years, America has acknowledged responsibility while pursuing ever-expanding rights for its citizens. Today, responsibility is cast aside, while rights multiply at an alarming pace.

For most of our history, rights were exercised in deference to the rights of others. Loud music would be lowered so that neighbors might sleep, coarse language foresworn in the presence of children, opposing views at least heard if not considered. Now, we turn the radio to full volume, swear at will, and drown out everyone who disagrees with us. It is our "right" to do so, and woe be unto those who object.

What is the cause of this overweening self-absorption? Until recently, we have been a people who tried to figure out things for ourselves. We accepted no man's word for anything, while adhering to traditional beliefs built up over millennia. The opposite is now true. We are quick to latch on to the nostrums of the latest demagogue while jettisoning the wisdom of our ancestors. Rational thought and argument have disappeared, replaced by prejudice and passion. Why? Because most of us no longer think for ourselves. The media does it for us.

The modern media, including the Internet, is ubiquitous, as are the devices it uses to disseminate its content. Blogs, websites, and platforms compete with "traditional" media for hearts and minds. It takes a concerted effort, every day, to avoid them, and those few who do so risk alienation from the world, not to mention family and friends. One need only stand on a busy street corner, or wander through a shopping mall, to see its impact. No one raises her eyes from the screen she holds in her hand.

Those same people would be quick to deny they are programmed by the media. They still view themselves as free, autonomous individuals, fully capable of independent thought, more discerning even than their predecessors. They ignore the creeping authoritarianism in themselves, their government and their culture, while they acquiesce in the steady usurpation of their lives by a partisan media.

Which brings us to our 45th president. A prominent user of the media who despised him, he was at the same time the catalyst for what we have today, "a nation divided against itself." With its deranged and unrelenting criticism of him and, by extension, his voters – coupled with his instinctive response – the press has created the infernal region we now occupy. It is a place where the lunatic fringe receives fawning attention, a place where the maddest scenario is given credence, a place from which many of our citizens would like to escape. And a place where the former President of the United States is rousted from his grave to satisfy fantasies generated by an out-of-control media. In short, America has become the world's largest insane asylum, and the inmates are restless.

I FLIPPED a switch, turned a few knobs and clicked on the link.

"Hi, Tommy," said Vada Potts-Jones.

"Hi."

"It's almost time," she said. "I want you to be my go-between with your girlfriend."

"Go-between for what?"

"I'm going to create a crises that the president will be forced to react to. The price for resolving it will be her agreement to do a few things I want done. I can't deal with her directly for obvious reasons." She stopped. "She'll trust you to tell her the truth."

"Is this about divvying up the country?"

"Yes. Among other things."

"I don't see how you and your friends can do that. You're way outgunned. It's crazy."

"Well – I don't know. Look at the country now. Look what we've accomplished without any large-scale violence."

"What about blowing up those buildings?"

"We didn't do that. That was somebody else. We *did* engage in some strategic attacks."

"What? The airplanes?"

She hesitated. "We're still off the record?"

I considered. The journalist's "off the record" construct, whereby he withholds information from the public in exchange for insider knowledge, was approaching its useful end. Blowing up airplanes was a crime and, if law enforcement came calling, my promise to keep it to myself might not hold up. Still, I wanted to know.

"Yes," I said. "Did you blow up the planes?"

She nodded.

"What about Doctor Cohen?"

"He was already viral. His death put the conspiracy theories over the top." She paused. "Anyway, the partition's not that important to me. It's what the others want."

"You're just in it for the chaos?"

She smiled. "You might say that."

"What's the crisis?"

"I can't say until it starts. Election Day." She smiled again. "I'm going to give you white people a taste of your own medicine."

"Which is?"

"My version of slavery."

"Slavery? What're you talking about?"

"Helplessness. Impotence. All the pathologies that never go away. We'll see how you like it."

"That's nuts. How can you do that?"

"You'll find out pretty soon."

"But white people *ended* slavery. Some white people."

"No, they didn't. They co-opted it."

"What do you mean?"

"The people who profited from slaves 200 years ago are still profiting today. Generations owe their wealth to slavery. We're no better off now than we were then."

"You seem to be doing okay."

"There are always exceptions, then and now." She paused. "But the truth is, they treated Daddy like a slave, too. They tolerated him because he made money for them. That's what slaves do."

We sat without speaking. Capitalism was "slavery" now because that made it easier, more fashionable, to attack.

"Aren't whites helping you?" I said. "I mean, all the marches and protests. The media. That's mostly white people."

She shook her head. "They talk a good game but, at the end of the day, nothing changes. They're still the masters, and we're still the slaves. They have the power and we don't."

"And your crusade's going to fix that?"

"Maybe. Maybe not. It's a start. But this is about payback. I think you'll appreciate the – irony." She paused. "There's an envelope in the middle drawer." I removed it from the drawer and found a large white pill inside. "That'll protect you from what's coming," she said. "Go ahead and take it."

"Now?"

"Now."

"What is it?"

"Something that will keep you safe when the chaos begins."

"Oh." I hesitated. "I've got a bottle of water on my desk. Back in a minute." When I returned, I said, "Am I safe now?"

She smiled. "Yes. I'll be in touch." The screen went blank.

The crusade was coming into focus. If she had ever entertained any doubts about it, they had clearly been overcome. Perhaps Marty's death had liberated her, though she seemed oddly indifferent to the outcome. Her colleagues and their plans were no longer important, if they ever were – they had served their purpose by creating the circumstances necessary for her "crisis" to proceed.

My role as chronicler was a sham – I'd really been recruited to be the "go-between." The partition was still on, and white people were going to be turned into slaves beginning on Tuesday. The slave narrative was harder to swallow than the partition. Was she crazy or just pulling my leg? Had she confessed to the airplane bombings? And killing Doctor Cohen? I rolled the tape back and listened.

I looked at the pill in my hand. I had no idea what it was, and swallowing an unknown substance at Vada's insistence required trust I didn't have. I was *white,* after all. Maybe whatever was coming would change my mind.

ELEVEN

I mean the increasing disregard for law which pervades the country; the growing disposition to substitute the wild and furious passions, in lieu of the sober judgments of Courts; and the worse than savage mobs, for the executive ministers of justice – Abraham Lincoln, 1838

THE BACKHOE slipped off the truck and approached us. The press, family members, cemetery officials and Members of Congress cleared a path to the gravesite. An enormous marble plinth, ten feet high and five feet wide, was topped by a huge bronze bust depicting a smiling president, tie knotted to the throat. Not yet tarnished, the bust shone brightly in the early afternoon sun. He had chosen the inscription: "It was an incredible life. Maybe the best ever!"

Fortunately, the plinth and bust were situated so they didn't have to be moved, and the surrounding granite stones had already been pushed to the side. Within minutes, the backhoe had uncovered the steel coffin. It took longer for men and machine to lift the casket to the surface but it was done at last. There had been much back-and-forth about whether to open the coffin at the cemetery, or wait until it was delivered to the facility where the autopsies would be performed, but the widow finally gave in to the pressure of a world-wide television audience and the imperative of proving to the public that he was there. The seals were broken and the lid lifted.

He looked exactly like he did the day he died, right down to the aggressive golden cowlick and red tie firmly in place. The illusion of life was startling. It was hard to look away but, after a long moment, the press retreated to allow the cameras an unobstructed view. His widow, who had refused to look at first, fainted. Later that day, the autopsies reached the same conclusion: The president had died of complications stemming from acute liver failure.

Without missing a beat, the media, including the cable channel that had started it all, moved on to the next big news – the approaching election. Reports of the exhumation and autopsies were perfunctory. A few editorial pages said "I told you so," but none reflected upon the circus they had created. Unexpectedly, they had done the opposite of what they intended – rather than add to the bedlam, they had rendered a serious bone of contention moot.

The dead president's supporters, whipsawed by the alternative realities, vowed to back him more fervently than ever. The hardliners among them refused to give up on assassination, and a few suggested he wasn't dead at all, just catatonic. The rest of the country moved on.

Despite the lockdown, Lucinda managed to get me into the White House for dinner that evening. We met again in her private dining room. "You've been hard to reach lately," I said.

"It's been pandemonium around here. One thing after another. I'm hoping the assassination news will begin to settle things down." She touched my hand. "It's already made my life easier. Things should get back to normal pretty soon."

"What's normal?"

"No more Code Red. No more double security details. No more suspicion of everyone, including you." She paused. "People here can start going home at night."

"They suspected me?"

She nodded. "They suspected everybody. If you'd written a story about me and the Secret Service, we might've had to fish you out of the Potomac River. I now know every detail of your checkered past." She passed me the salad bowl. "They made me get a new phone because the old one wasn't 'secure,' and I can't take incoming calls. I have a food taster." She took a bite. "I'm hoping this – Praetorian Guard around me can at least be reduced. But maybe not."

"I guess the country's still pretty jacked up."

"Yes, but it's not as bad as it was. We're making progress with the unions." She smiled. "Plus, we've been trying to run a campaign."

I considered telling her about Vada's crusade and decided against it. What, exactly, would I say? I didn't know what the crisis was, and the "payback" seemed ridiculous. If I told her that her vice-president was responsible for Doctor Cohen's death, she'd think I was making a bad joke. I settled for trying to ease into my role as go-between without mentioning Vada who, after all, had an office right down the hall. "How about an interview after the election?" I said.

She nodded. "I'll be pretty busy for a couple of days. Let's do it Friday. One o'clock?"

If there was really a crisis in store, it would be well underway by then. "Great. Thanks."

"I'll tell Wolf."

ON THE eve of the election, the state of Washington was, surprisingly, still too close to call. Late that afternoon, its House of Representatives passed a law granting the governor the power to appoint the state's presidential electors. The Senate followed suit a few minutes later and the governor, without fanfare, immediately signed the bill into law. He was a member of her faction and, if things went as expected, the addition of Washington's twelve electoral votes would give President Vere exactly 270, the minimum number she needed for re-election.

Leaders in Congress, nervous about the reaction to such a naked power grab, had cast about for a way to control it. They finally decided to move the voting by the states' electors from mid-December to the Friday after the election, thereby allowing the people little time to consider what had happened. The bill sailed through both houses on a voice vote, and was ratified by President Vere later that evening.

Election Day dawned bright and cold. Rioting in the nation's capital had been suspended for the time being, and there were indications it was winding down in the rest of the country. Americans went to the polls, unaware that the fix was in. Exit polls confirmed that the country was evenly divided, making a Vere victory likely.

The returns from Washington, Texas and Florida were carefully scrutinized by the media, not because the results mattered, but because they might give rise to more serious unrest. To everyone's surprise, all three went for the dead president by narrow margins. The country, mostly unaware of the electoral changes, went to bed assuming he had been "re-elected." The pundits, unwilling to explain why that was not so, remained mum.

As the news of President Vere's re-election leaked out, the outrage that had almost died down was rekindled. The last-minute manipulation of Washington's vote was especially infuriating, and the former president's supporters, led by Jeremiah Jefferson, took to the streets. The current president's backers needed no excuse to join in. Guns moved from closets to kitchen tables. Unions ceased negotiations. The *status quo ante,* rioting and bloodshed in cities across the country, resumed.

Jefferson, with the election almost in his grasp, had become a committed, "born again," politician. He had already mounted a successful campaign to win all the dead president's electors when they convened on Friday. His appearances on television were increasingly frenzied but, unless something changed, when the final tally was announced he would be two votes short. He was canvassing the other side, hoping to turn up two more votes by any means possible, while the media exposed all the skeletons in his closet, real and imagined.

The president, about to be duly elected according to law, began preparations for her inauguration and beyond. Plans for a "New New Deal" in addition to those already in the legislative hopper were announced. Vice-President Vada Potts-Jones, nearly invisible since her nomination, made a few appearances, including one with the president in the Oval Office.

Beginning on Election Day, I checked the Interface site periodically, waiting for something to happen. Late Wednesday night, I clicked on the link again and found a message from Vada:

"I'll call you tomorrow at 10 PM."

Apparently the revolution had been postponed.

HURRICANE JOAN, once removed from the meteorological charts altogether, was making a comeback. Now situated again off the southwest coast of Africa, she had merged with other tropical storms and regained hurricane strength. Almost stationary, her winds were still in the lowest category, but those in the weather business were sure they would strengthen over the next several days. The models describing her future path generally agreed that at some point she would strike the East Coast of the United States.

Joan wasn't the globe's only violent storm. In a singular convergence of gale-force winds, more hurricanes were brewing in the northern and eastern Pacific Ocean, tropical cyclones were churning the South Pacific, and Typhoon Bess was roiling the waters off the coast of Japan. A world-wide weather phenomenon, it went virtually unreported by the domestic media.

As Mike had predicted, gun confiscation in California wasn't going well. Coastal residents refused to hand over their weapons and turned to the courts, though there was no guarantee they would abide by a negative decision. A few deputies in Los Angeles had been fired upon. Law enforcement in the rest of the state flatly refused to carry out the governor's mandate. Governor St. John, speaking from the remains of a gutted Coit Tower in San Francisco, condemned "right-wing gun nuts" in the strongest possible terms.

Marty's black village northwest of Seattle had chosen a name for itself: Jonesboro. "He offered something rare," said the newly-elected mayor. "A chance for self-respect. We may put up a statue someday." His Hispanic and Asian communities, presumably at Vada's direction, had broken ground.

And his People's Plaza was also in the news. President Vere herself attended its dedication, and made a few remarks:

"The building behind me is an engineering marvel that stands as a symbol of the greatness of this nation. And while it does, indeed, reach into the heavens, it was man himself, not some mythological deity, who put it there. Recently, our citizens have been talking past one another, leading to strife and confusion, but this People's Plaza proves that, when we all speak the same language, we can accomplish anything."

Her lack of religion was a point of pride, and she never missed an opportunity to express it. Many of her fellow citizens still believed in God, but surveys indicated that her disbelief didn't affect her poll numbers. In truth, her politics was actually an ersatz religion and she one of its most heartfelt evangelists. Had she ever dissented from it, of course, she would've been excommunicated from the rest of her church.

The new Secretary for the Department of Equity had just been confirmed. When queried about its mission, she said, "Every citizen must have access to the same things on the same level – health, wealth, opportunity. Outcomes will no longer be determined by race or hierarchy. True equity will be delivered at the point of a gun, if necessary."

From her office on the top floor of the People's Plaza, she introduced her undersecretaries – lifelong bureaucrats and politicians of many colors, sexes and outlooks, all graduates of Yale – and proclaimed them the most diverse group of "public servants" in governmental history. Each one, she said, was dedicated to the notion that all races, genders and sexes, "whether created in the womb or elsewhere," were equal in the eyes of government, and anyone who doubted it would soon learn the error of his ways. "Absolute equity is the goal," she said. "Disparities of any kind in the lives of our citizens will not be tolerated."

Matilda Fleck's Yankee Coalition, though hindered at first by the lack of air and rail transportation, had shifted all its agricultural commerce from the Midwest to California. Farmers in Iowa, Nebraska and Minnesota had been forced to warehouse their current crops while cutting back dramatically on next year's planting. Furious legislation and litigation were ongoing, but so far Fleck seemed to have the upper hand. Appeals to her "humanity" fell on deaf ears.

The strikes in Manhattan had caused the everyday population of The Citadel, Marty's bunker community on Long Island, to swell. Its 500 units, accessible only by helicopter, had filled up mostly with nannies and children removed from school for the duration of the turmoil. Parents commuted by chopper or remained in town. Elderly residents imposed an unanticipated strain on the medical facilities.

VADA'S IMAGE appeared on the screen. "What happened?" I said. "I thought the revolution was supposed to start on Election Day."

"It did."

"Really? I didn't notice."

"You weren't supposed to. Everything had to be in place before you meet with the president. Otherwise, she might've tried to stop it."

"What is *it*, exactly? Can you tell me now?"

"It's a virus that only attacks white people." I smiled. "Don't laugh. We can create new pathogens in the lab now, and they can target specific ethnic and racial populations. Mine's aimed at white people." She stopped. "It's only a short genetic step from disease prevention to disease creation, and the variations you can build into it are endless."

Her ideology had finally gone off the rails. If what she said was true, her answer to the racial divide was genocide. "How could you even consider something like that?" I said.

"Because, otherwise, things will never change. It's the only solution."

Was she crazy? Could I stop it? "How's it work?"

"It's an invisible, odorless aerosol that was stored in tanks, then driven to the target areas. It was released into the air in Manhattan at noon on Election Day. People inhale it. They pass it along by breathing. It's highly infectious and highly contagious, and there's no vaccine except the one I have. The one I gave you the other day."

"Is it just Manhattan? Or do you plan to kill all the white people in the country?"

She shook her head. "I don't plan to kill anybody. This virus will produce a certain condition. The aerosol becomes inactive after twenty-four hours. Those infected remain contagious for forty-eight more." She paused. "The symptoms – fever, headache, loss of taste and smell – show up after three days. If the vaccine isn't taken, the long-term effects begin to appear a day or so later, depending on the health of the person infected. Within days, it's irreversible."

We spent the next twenty minutes discussing the technical aspects of her virus and the vaccine that would stop it. Manhattan wasn't the only target – the virus was being kept in reserve in other cities. "It will disable the white race here forever unless it's stopped," she said.

"What am I supposed to tell Lucinda? I'm meeting her tomorrow at one o'clock."

"Tell her what I've just told you. That white people are doomed unless she meets my demands."

"Why should she believe me?"

She smiled. "I released the aerosol in the Oval Office Tuesday morning. She and the people around her are all infected. The white ones." She leaned back in her chair. "Her three days are up tomorrow morning. It'll get her attention."

It seemed impossibly evil, and I still didn't believe it, but I would know one way or the other pretty soon – according to her timetable, the symptoms would start showing up tomorrow. "I can't catch it from her?"

She shook her head. "You're immune now, and she won't be contagious by the time you get to the White House. There's another envelope in the drawer." A moment later, I held another white pill and a few sheets of paper. "That's a list of our demands," she said. "The pill is for the president. She needs to be able to deal with this. She'll be cured and immune once she takes it." She disappeared.

I switched off Marty's machines and sat behind his desk for a long time. Regardless of the truth of her scheme, that it could even be seriously imagined was a sign of the treacherous reality that was modern-day America. The hatred was irrational, all-consuming. How long before someone invented a virus to attack blacks? Or Asians? And why stop there? Surely it was only another "genetic step" to the destruction of the whole human race.

The "demands" – composed in three different hands, none of them hers – were obviously a wish list compiled by Pogue, Anton and the woman from the Red Brigade. The many lines, taken together, reflected their overarching goal – a transfer of wealth and power from those who had it to those who didn't. Vada promised to make the vaccine available once their demands were met. If that didn't happen, other cities would be poisoned.

Vada had not contributed to the list because if the vaccine worked as anticipated her goal had already been achieved. The "disabling" of the white race, or maybe just a few million of its members, was an end in itself. Even if Lucinda gave in to the demands and managed to stop the advance of the virus, it seemed inevitable that many of those already infected would succumb to the "condition" it imposed.

What could I do? If what she said was true, a terrible crime had already been committed. To whom would I report it? Who would believe me? Unsure what I would say, I dialed Lucinda's number. As expected, there was no answer.

I walked home. The television was tuned to one of the networks and a late-night comedy show, taped earlier that day at a Manhattan theater, was playing. If Vada's virus was real, the aerosol had been absorbed by thousands, or hundreds of thousands, of people before it became inactive. Those people had spread it – were spreading it – to many thousands more. Each newly-infected person would be contagious for forty-eight hours, at which point the symptoms would appear.

The comedian I was watching and most of his live audience, probably infected without knowing it, might be out in the streets right now, passing it along to others. The first victims would begin to feel the symptoms tomorrow at noon. After that it would be a whirlwind of disease among the millions of white people who lived or worked on Manhattan Island, as well as the tourists temporarily in residence.

Equally distressing, those going to and from the island undoubtedly carried the virus with them. Connecticut, New Jersey and the other boroughs were infected by now, the spread of contagion limited only by the speed and mobility of the unsuspecting victims. The lack of trains and airplanes, which meant that travel was limited to smaller, perhaps fewer, groups of people, might now be perceived as a godsend. The Citadel, conceived as a sanctuary against those outside its walls, was instead a kind of lazaretto whose inmates would soon feel the lash of the disease.

If Vada had really poisoned all those thousands of people, what could I do about it? The virus couldn't be recalled. The only cure was the vaccine, and the two doses in my possession weren't enough for a million victims. I called the president again, to no avail.

The comedian's guest was a highly esteemed playwright with a long string of successes on Broadway. Distracted, I barely heard their patter until the dead president's name entered the conversation. "Did you see the pictures of him in that coffin?" said the playwright.

"Yeah," said the host.

"He looked like a vampire, didn't he?"

"Yeah. All he needed was a pair of fangs."

"He's the inspiration for my next play. A modern-day version of *Dracula.* He'll be the star."

The host grinned. "Nobody else ever sucked the country so dry. I see many Tonys in your future." They laughed.

The screen changed abruptly, and one of the network's news anchors appeared behind a desk. "We have a report," he said, "that Erwin Muckenfuss, governor of the state of Washington, has died in an automobile crash. He was returning to the Governor's Mansion after hosting a reception for the state's presidential electors who are meeting tomorrow to cast their votes for president. Governor Muckenfuss was himself one of the electors." He stopped. "The state's lieutenant governor likewise perished in the crash."

TWELVE

*This disposition is awfully fearful
in any community; and that it now
exists in ours, though grating to
our feelings to admit, it would be a
violation of truth, and an insult to
our intelligence, to deny —*
                    Abraham Lincoln, 1838

THE LEGAL and political dust didn't settle
until late the following day. Governor Muckenfuss
and his lieutenant weren't yet at room temperature
before the lawsuits began. After Washington's secretary of state — a thirty-five-year-old woman
named Susannah Lemon who was *not* of the late
governor's political persuasion — was sworn in as
governor, she immediately advised citizens and
party leaders, including the President of the United
States, that she planned to appoint twelve new
electors before the vote took place.

Because those electors were unlikely to vote
for Lucinda Trent Vere, a veritable wake of the
president's lawyers descended upon the state's capital, Olympia, to seize the process. Jeremiah Jefferson provided a like number of legal scavengers in
support of the new governor. One reporter estimat-

ed that the total fees generated were more than $1 million per hour.

The governor claimed that the clear language of the state's new law allowed her to appoint electors up to the day "designated by Congress for the College of Electors to meet." The president's lawyers said that was rubbish, that the old governor's vote could be cast *in absentia*, and there was no need for the new governor to appoint anyone at all. Both sides avoided the obvious answer – that the new governor could appoint a single elector to take the old governor's place – because the result would be no winner in the presidential race and more confusion and uncertainty. Every court involved passed it on like a hot potato, and by noon the next day the case was lodged in the Supreme Court of the United States.

Needless to say, my interview with Lucinda was not at the top of her agenda. I was shuffled around for an hour or two before landing in my original spot in the Palm Room. It was a light, airy space that served as an entryway to the West Wing and provided access to the Rose Garden. Her chief of staff appeared in the doorway.

"Tommy, I know –"

Unsure of her status with the still unconfirmed virus, I held up my hand. "Don't – don't come too close. I'm feeling a little queasy. I don't want you to catch anything." I watched her carefully – she *did* seem a bit flushed.

She looked relieved. "Well – you can't interview the president if you're sick. Go home."

"I will, but – I need five minutes with her about something else. She can just lean in the room."

She hesitated. "Okay. Five minutes."

Lucinda arrived a moment later. "Tommy, I'm sorry. But –"

She *was* flushed, and sweat beaded on her forehead. "It's okay. Don't worry about it. How do you feel?"

She coughed. "Not very well, actually. This Electoral College thing –"

"That's not – listen to me. Don't interrupt."

I decided not to mention Vada. Her name would immediately generate a partisan reaction that would make the story harder to credit. My source would instead be a disillusioned, unnamed co-conspirator. My explanation for infections in the White House, including hers, would be "persons unknown."

When I finished the story, I said, "I don't expect you to buy it without something more than my word for it. But – you look sick to me. Get someone to check your temperature. Look for other things – loss of taste or smell, shortness of breath. How's your throat feel?"

"It's sore. I thought I was catching a cold."

"Maybe you are. But I don't think so." I paused. "I'm not sure when something worse might happen." I handed her the pills. "Take one of these as soon as you can. If you're sick, it'll take care of it. I hope."

"My doctor's –"

"See as many doctors as you want. But – everything else she – he said seems to be coming true, so take the pill. Soon." I held up the "demands." "This is the price for a vaccine," I said. "Even if you agreed to it, which I doubt, I'm afraid the damage is already done. And maybe that's the point."

I drew her to me.

"Tommy, don't. If I'm sick –"

"You're sick, but you're not contagious."

"I hope you're right."

"Me, too." I stepped back. "Good luck."

"What about the other pill?"

"Your medical people may be able to do something with it." I moved toward the door. "I'll do whatever I can to help. Call me."

Later that day the Supreme Court ruled that the governor of Washington could appoint one new voter to her state's slate of presidential electors. When the final tally was made, Jeremiah Jefferson – the dead president's electoral beneficiary – had matched President Vere's 269 votes. The next President of the United States was still undecided.

On the other hand, the contest for the office of Vice-President of the United States was over. Characterized by one of its former occupants as "not worth a bucket of warm piss," the Electoral College vote to fill it was an afterthought. Due to Jefferson's upgrade to presidential candidate, there was only one option – Vada Potts-Jones. While some of those who opposed her voted for Donald Duck or Elvis Presley, most left their ballots blank. As a consequence, she easily won a majority of the votes cast.

THE NEXT few days witnessed an exercise in brutal political power never before seen in the

United States of America. After determining that she was, indeed, afflicted with an unknown virus, the president's first step was to *really* lock down the White House and trace the movements of anyone who had been outside its walls since Election Day. Next, troops were mobilized quietly and sent to the nation's twenty largest cities to search for aerosol trucks that might contain the virus. All this was done within hours in the strictest secrecy.

Against her doctors' advice, Lucinda had swallowed one of the pills and her symptoms cleared up in a few short hours, leading to an all-out effort to replicate the vaccine contained in the other pill. The usual niceties regarding safety and side effects were overruled – the president was their guinea pig and, following a thorough examination, she was found to be perfectly healthy.

It took two days to copy the vaccine, after which various drug companies were secretly ordered to mass-produce it and stand by for instructions regarding its distribution. The object was to slow or stop the spread of the disease, believed to be largely confined to the Northeast. As a precaution, senior officials, armed with the power to shut down virtually every aspect of ordinary life to avoid infections, were dispatched throughout the rest of the country.

Finally, President Vere turned to those already infected. Who could be saved from the worst effects of the virus? Experts from Georgetown University, utilizing the timeframe Vada had given me, calculated their status as of midnight Saturday. At issue was who would get the vaccine and when.

I was seated at Marty's desk when she called.

"Tommy," said the president, "I want you to think again about the conversation with your *anonymous* source." The inflection in her voice told me she wasn't happy with my insistence on a journalist's prerogatives. "I have some hard decisions to make."

"Okay."

"Try to remember *exactly* what he said about symptoms and what comes next."

"He said that symptoms would appear after three days and —"

"Three days after infection?"

"That's the way I understood it. That was the timing for you."

"All right. Then what?"

"He said the — the long-term effects would show up a day or so later."

"A day or so after the symptoms appeared?"

"Yes."

"Did he say anything else?"

"Yes. He said something about the health of the victim." I tried to remember. "That the timing of the 'day or so' depended on the health of the victim." It was quiet on the other phone. "Lucinda?"

"Let's consider where we are," she said. "Take everything he said as true. The aerosol was released at noon last Tuesday. Assume the infections started then. For twenty-four hours some number of people in Manhattan caught the virus from the aerosol. Those same people became contagious for forty-eight hours, and infected more people. That gets us to noon on Friday. Two days ago. Before I even talked to you."

"Right."

"It's now almost noon on Sunday. Two days into the – um, unhealthy people getting sicker. It's possible that *all* the early cases are beginning to suffer whatever comes next. Correct?"

"Yes."

"And the newly-infected will increase by the minute. And on and on and on."

"Yes."

"While all this has been going on, people have been moving on and off the island every day. They're a separate population. Their status, whether from the aerosol or contagion in Manhattan or the spread of the virus beyond New York, is impossible to calculate. That's what the experts say." She stopped. "Tell me again what's going to happen."

Vada's revenge was, as she said, ironic. In some ways it was worse than genocide. It aimed, among other things, to punish the descendants of those who once decreed black "imbeciles" less than human by imposing those same disabilities on them. Manhattan was not chosen at random – for Vada, it was the bastion of progress where the fruits of slavery were most heavily concentrated. Its status as the capital of "white" culture and commerce was an added bonus.

Her virus attacked the brain. Invisible to the immune system, it was designed to quickly reduce the cognitive abilities of the victims who, using the old eugenics terms, would descend from normal to "morons," "imbeciles" and "idiots." Otherwise healthy individuals would ultimately succumb to unrestrained dementia. Along the way, their condition would manifest itself in loss of memory, inability to reason and all the other signs of cognitive impairment, leading to helplessness and complete dependence on others. Death, which might in some respects provide welcome relief, was not hastened by the virus.

After listening to this catalogue of horrors, Lucinda said, "Can it be reversed?"

"I don't know. He said it was irreversible 'within days.'"

"The vaccine is just coming on line. My people tell me it'll be days before we can deliver and administer it. Can you imagine trying to organize something like that in New York? The panic when the symptoms set in? And people will still be going back and forth every day, spreading it further and further like – like the plague." She stopped. "The chances of a successful outcome in Manhattan are practically nil. We have to concentrate on stopping the spread."

"But there are lots of people who probably don't have it yet. And others in the early stages. If you abandon them, they'll all be morons pretty soon. Or worse."

"I'm sorry. I'll try to do something for them, but I have to think about the rest of the country."

Within hours, movement to and from Manhattan Island was shut down without explanation. Federal troops manned all the bridges and tunnels, and turned back anyone trying to enter or leave – no distinction was made between whites and non-whites, sick or non-sick. Navy vessels patrolled the rivers, and fighter jets prowled the skies, ready to commandeer any boat or shoot down any aircraft attempting to escape.

Communications were severed. Cell towers were destroyed from the air, and telephone and Internet services cut off. A news blackout, enforced by threats of treason and execution, was imposed. The media was barred from reporting its own demise.

The reason for all the secrecy was later attributed to the need for calm. The entire country would panic, the story went, if its citizens knew what was happening in New York. As for withholding the vaccine, Manhattan was portrayed as "beyond saving," a circumstance that relieved the public conscience and preserved its sense of virtue. That untold numbers of people had been condemned to suffer the effects of the virus was ignored. Any hint of their fate was quickly denied.

In truth, the president and her party were afraid of the virus's impact on their future electoral ambitions. White people were still by far the nation's largest voting bloc. Trading Manhattan for the rest of the country was deemed good politics and, if the expected toll was taken, many of its citizens would never vote again anyway. The press, incredibly, acceded to this suppression of the facts for the same reasons.

Politics, once defined as negotiations among people trying to live together in some measure of harmony, had become something different, something sinister. It was now a struggle for domination, an effort to subjugate rather than regulate, and every possible means of coercion was fair game for the politician in a position to use them. Someone was always to blame, no matter how farfetched the accusation.

The media had quickly coalesced around President Vere to ensure that she wasn't held responsible for the disease. Indeed, it was viewed as an opportunity rather than a calamity. Beyond the borders of Manhattan, the news of a novel virus was spread quickly, always in optimistic tones. The president, speaking from the Oval Office, assured the nation that she had it under control. Her poll numbers skyrocketed.

The narrative was that the Vere Administration had, in some heroic fashion, detected the virus and, with remarkable speed, created a vaccine. It was now available just down the street, at the local pharmacy or grocery store. Everyone arguably Caucasian – man, woman and child – was required to take it whether he showed symptoms or not, and a "credential" was hung around every neck to demonstrate compliance. A lack of credentials invited the authorities to vaccinate by force. That the victims were all white proved awkward at first, but the press soon solved that problem by ignoring it.

Because of its prominence in the life of the country, most citizens outside Manhattan knew that something was wrong there, but few cared enough to inquire. And no explanation was forthcoming anyway. The administration's response to the virus was a success by everyone's measure.

There *were* moments of panic when supplies of the vaccine ran short, and "hot spots" – sparked by people who had recently visited New York – gave rise to massive quarantines. Many such measures were seen as mostly unnecessary, but "better safe than sorry" was the universal watch-word despite the enormous social and economic disruption. People who somehow avoided the pill gradually lost their minds, but the numbers were few.

In the end, the virus was contained and, despite isolated cases, eventually eliminated. Victims outside Manhattan numbered less than a million. Aerosol trucks were found in several cities and destroyed without explanation. The public was never told that the virus was man-made and, of course, the Vice-President of the United States, a prominent member of the president's party, was never mentioned. It was portrayed as just another implacable disease emerging from the ether. Why it attacked white people only went unexplained.

That Vada wasn't part of the story was my doing but, given the politics that emerged from the virus, it seemed possible that her name might've gone unmentioned anyway. The president was able to "solve" the crisis in a very public way without disclosing that her vice-president was responsible for the disease. For it to become known now would be devastating.

What Vada had done was an enormous crime, but there was no guarantee that others would see it that way. The media, politicians, "thought leaders" – some by outright declaration, others with barely veiled innuendo – asserted that white people "had it coming." Others, as a rule militantly agnostic, claimed that a "higher power" had stepped in to "right historical wrongs." Some argued that whites should "pay through the nose" for the vaccine, if they received it at all. If she were ever called to account, Vada would have her usual cheering section.

The president had complicated things by vowing to "get to the bottom of this epidemic." Unlike the rest of the country, she knew it was not an act of nature. Our time together was uncomfortable now as I refused to tell her what she wanted to know. She nevertheless hewed to her administration's story.

Lucinda's partisans hoped that her handling of the virus would alter the nation's politics. The *Post* opined that "President Vere's swift, decisive intervention in the spread of the disease saved millions of lives," ignoring the fact that no deaths had been reported. The editorial board went on to predict that "this divided country will now unite behind Lucinda Vere and her progressive policies."

In addition to the long-term impact, another, more immediate outcome was anticipated. The tie in the Electoral College had moved the presidential election to the House of Representatives. The president's party had maintained its majority in the House, and formed a new one in the Senate. Winning the White House would mean total control of the government by her partisans. The progressive Utopia was within their reach.

Only the Constitution stood in the way. They had a huge majority in the House, but the Twelfth Amendment required that the vote be by state delegations. Each state had one vote as determined by a majority in each caucus. On that basis, the vote for president appeared to be twenty-four for the president and twenty-six for Jeremiah Jefferson. But the actual vote was still a few days away, and pressure to side with the nation's "savior" was immense. Informal polls among the legislators indicated that two of Jefferson's delegations – Arizona and Ohio – were wavering.

Jefferson himself had become increasingly militant. A vote against him was a vote for racism, he said, and he hinted darkly at the eternal damnation that awaited those who turned against him. The media pulled out all the stops to ensure that he wasn't elected.

Perhaps as an exercise in nostalgia, rumors circulated to the effect that the exhumation of the late president was the true cause of the virus. Microbes escaping from his body had infected the pathologists who performed the autopsies and spread from there. A few of the country's more deranged publications, not to mention a rabid herd on the Internet, subscribed to this notion. Letters to the "newspaper of record" floated the idea that Erwin Muckenfuss had been assassinated.

THIRTEEN

Accounts of outrages committed by mobs, form the everyday news of the times – Abraham Lincoln, 1838

FOUR DAYS after it was isolated from the rest of the world – another cycle of infection through contagion, plus one more arbitrary day – a convoy of inoculated troops, wearing hazmat suits as a precaution, crossed the George Washington Bridge into Manhattan. President Vere had set up a hotline with the mayor but, at some point, the mayor had stopped answering the phone. The unprecedented lack of communication, now being restored, meant that whatever the troops encountered would be a surprise.

It had been ten days since the aerosol was released. The fact of their isolation, of course, had alerted the island's citizens that something was terribly wrong, but exactly what it was was unclear. However, as symptoms appeared and hospitals began to fill up, Manhattan's medical community quickly concluded that a new virus had emerged, resulting in "quarantine" from the rest of the country. The population at risk was, at first, unknown. Death was presumed to be the end result.

Work on a vaccine began immediately. Puzzled by what appeared to be "designer" components of the disease, the scientists found the usual epidemiological protocols useless. Without giving up on a cure, they were reduced to prescribing nostrums for the symptoms rather than the virus. Medical professionals were among the hardest hit.

In the meantime, C-suites and boardrooms in the most powerful corporations in the world began to empty out. Their usual occupants complained of fevers and sore throats and worked from home, but after a few days they stopped working altogether. Many were in the hospitals, others were being treated in their homes, some simply fell off the radar. All showed signs of mental impairment after a few days. As soon as those signs appeared, the other symptoms went away, leaving otherwise healthy people in a cognitive disarray that grew worse by the day.

White rank-and-file employees, many of whom ordinarily lived off the island, could no longer go to work and added to the strain on area hospitals. The people who weren't ill speculated among themselves. Blacks, Asians, Hispanics, even those who worked in close proximity to their white colleagues every day, were unaffected. Unaccountably, they began to suspect themselves of complicity with the virus, carriers of the disease instead of its victims. They voluntarily separated from others and, within days, the island's workplaces, great and small, were empty. The halls of government were no exception. Only a single deputy mayor, a black man of Jamaican origin, manned City Hall.

The national and global economies, heavily dependent on the services provided by New York, seized up at a cost of many trillions of dollars. After a few days, people world-wide began to search for ways to do without them, most often by looking closer to home for lesser, but still serviceable, methods of achieving the same objectives. If and when Manhattan came on-line again, it would find competition where none existed before.

I was part of the press corps that went in with the troops. Vice-President Vada Potts-Jones had volunteered to lead the delegation. The media swooned when the announcement was made.

It wasn't a ghost town in the usual sense. The infrastructure was as it was before. Ethnic and racial enclaves within the borough – Harlem, Chinatown, the East Village – seemed much as usual, though their inhabitants appeared shell-shocked, as if rendered mute and unseeing by the virus, but they could speak and see when prompted. Their lives had been hamstrung by businesses shutting down, but none of them had any idea what was happening beyond what was there for all to see, the near total absence – from sidewalks, streets and stores, from restaurants, parks and museums – of white people. When asked what they thought was wrong, they just shook their heads.

Lower Manhattan and Midtown, on the other hand, were almost totally deserted. The few people in evidence could be divided into three groups – non-Caucasians trying to go about their lives, looters casually picking over what remained in the shops, and white people with no idea who or where they were. The last group was truly terrifying.

They were dressed in nightgowns, uniforms and three-piece suits, none of which were worn as intended. Some had shoes, others were barefoot. They moved with purpose, but no sense of *going* anywhere – I watched one woman walk up and down Central Park South for an hour, talking to herself, until she wound down and collapsed. Any effort to communicate with them was met with silence, gibberish or physical attack. No one called 911, or otherwise took note of their plight.

There was actually another barely visible cohort in the streets – young white children. Seemingly unaffected by the disease, they wandered about in small bands, playing in parks and playgrounds and eating whatever came to hand. They disappeared at night, perhaps returning to homes where adults no longer held sway. Like the Lost Boys, they were in charge of themselves.

Vada, the deputy mayor and the police chief, a black man named Smalls, held a press conference. Rather than rage at the rest of the country, which I fully expected, the mayor and the chief explained what they'd been dealing with for the past week. In response to the first question, the chief said, "The strike's over, not that it matters. Our people are sick. The docs tell me it's a white folks' disease." He paused. "Almost half the force is white. As of yesterday, none of them is able to work and, from what I've seen, they never will be."

"That applies to the rest of city government, in various percentages," added the deputy mayor. "Firefighters, sanitation workers, teachers. The City Council. You name it." He shook his head.

"We're sixty-five per cent white which, I guess, means that sixty-five per cent of us are – disabled."

"There's been a lot of looting out there, Chief," said the woman from the *Post*. "Were there demonstrations? Protests?"

The chief smiled. "No. Just good old-fashioned theft." He stopped. "We've had to prioritize, and property crimes are low on the list."

I addressed the vice-president. "What's the administration doing about treating the disease here?"

"We brought vaccine today sufficient to treat every person on the island. Medics are setting up dispensaries all over Manhattan as we speak."

"Will it cure those zombies out on the street?" someone called from the back of the room.

"We hope so."

"Those – people are my biggest concern," said the chief. "There are hundreds of thousands of them living in these high-rise apartment buildings. We had lots of calls for emergency services at first. Not so much anymore."

"We're afraid there are a lot of sick people in those buildings," said the deputy mayor.

"Why aren't they in the hospital?" said the woman from the Associated Press.

"Well," said Chief Smalls, "they're probably not able to get themselves there, and the hospitals don't have room for them if they did. All our first responders are short-handed. We're reacting on a case-by-case basis, but it's a drop in the bucket." He looked away for a moment. "I'll give you an example. Two days ago, we had a call from the Dakota. It was somebody's maid, and she was hysterical. She

said her people were going crazy. She was right."
He paused. "We took a – an inventory while we
were there. The people living in that building –
there are ninety-three units – are all compromised
to one degree or another. Several didn't answer
their doors. We don't know if anyone was inside or
not."

"Multiply that by thousands of buildings,"
said the deputy mayor, "and you see where we are.
It's overwhelming. Plus, the medical people say
there's really nothing they can do anyway. Let's
hope this vaccine works."

As it turned out, Vada's dispensaries *didn't*
work because the affected population was unable to
get to them. Ultimately, more troops arrived and
began to distribute the vaccine door to door. The
process took weeks, and experts claimed that nine-
ty-five per cent of the white population, including
the children, was covered. None of the "zombies,"
however, doomed to endure Vada's version of slavery, showed any signs of recovering. Manhattan
was an insane asylum. Ultimately, President Vere
appointed a commission to decide what to do about
it.

VADA OFFERED me a lift on her official
helicopter. "We have a stop to make before we go
back to Washington," she said. "The Citadel."

"What for?"

"The whole place is in quarantine now. We're
going to deliver the vaccine."

It was another irony. Due to the presence of
the Secret Service and the helicopter crew, we were
silent during the short hop to Long Island. It was

mid-afternoon when we landed on the pad next to her unit, set slightly apart from the rest of the community. After giving instructions for unloading the vaccine, she summoned an elevator with a key and the two of us descended to her kitchen. "What about a drink?" she said. "Before we start work."

"Sure."

A moment later, she handed me a glass of scotch and a familiar-looking pill. "I'm pretty sure you didn't take the first one I gave you," she said, smiling. "But all's well that ends well."

"Meaning?"

"The vaccine was distributed without any haggling. No one questioned its use. It's reached practically the whole country."

"I thought you wanted a country full of zombies?"

She shook her head. "Not necessarily. We're going to need white people. For a while anyway." She paused. "But don't worry. There's more to come."

"What now?"

"You'll see."

It was too much. She wasn't just an arrogant ideologue – she was a monster. "God damn it, Vada. What's wrong with you? You're worth a billion dollars, you have everything you could possibly need. Why don't you leave the rest of us alone?"

"Because a culture that allows – promotes that sort of inequality is *evil*. Because you and your friends and – and Lucinda Vere aren't sufficiently convinced. You mouth all these slogans about equality and fairness, and it's all BS. You're on top and you plan to stay there, whatever it takes."

Her father had once complained to me about the lack of self-awareness among the media, but it was as nothing compared to that of his daughter. *She* and her fellow billionaires were the problem she was trying to stamp out by poisoning everyone else. "What about your dad? And everything he stood for?"

She shook her head again. "He was a black man."

"So?"

"He beat the system. He's entitled."

"He *was* the system." She didn't answer. "Why not just spread your own money around?"

"Because it would be useless. It wouldn't move the needle at all." She stopped. "It's time to give somebody else a chance."

"Isn't that what elections are for?"

"Elections are for politicians. It's how they get their small share of the pie. The rest goes somewhere else."

"To white people?"

"Of course. Look around." She turned up her glass. "We're taking over."

"We? You and the rest of the one per cent? Revolution from the top?" She didn't answer. "You need soldiers. The *sans culottes.* Who are they?" Again, there was no response. "Whether you like it or not, white people still run this country. It might look like we're ready to surrender, but I wouldn't count on it."

"You'll give up without firing a shot."

Anton had said the same thing. "Why?"

"You'll see."

We sat without speaking. "Why not just wait?" I said. "Things seem to be going your way."

"Maybe so. But not fast enough."

It was the curse of the demagogue. Rather than allow the tides, now running firmly in her favor, to wash over the enemy's fortifications and forever erase his presence, she wanted absolute power now, guaranteeing that there would always be resistance. Even her partisans would be appalled by her methods someday. Like Lucinda, they professed disbelief in the supernatural, but they viewed the alternative, Man, as rational and even good. If that were not so, they would soon find their own heads in the guillotine. The counter-revolution needed to begin, the sooner the better.

I slipped the pill into my pocket. She smiled. "I can't guarantee the level of contagion here," she said.

"If I get sick, I'll take it." She nodded. "We're going to fight you," I said. "I'm not sure how, but we are."

She shrugged. "Have at it. It won't make the slightest bit of difference. It's already done." She rose. "Let's get to work."

It was 9 PM when the six of us finished passing out pills to the Citadel's inhabitants. It was a mixed bag. Long Island had never been cut off, and they knew what was going on. There were few white adults in the compound, and the many children – who had lost their parents to the effects of the virus – were being tended by nannies and other servants. Most of the kids seemed fine, but Vada insisted that everyone take a pill. "Why aren't these kids sick?" I said.

"The virus requires certain hormones to become active in the body," Vada said. "Most of them are too young."

"Why give them the vaccine, then?"

"It doesn't go away. When they're old enough, the symptoms will begin."

"And the pills will stop that?"

"Yes."

I puzzled over her zeal. The woman who had created this crsis now happily promoted the means to resolve it. Why? And what was coming? *What* was already done?

AS THE virus subsided, the media began its inevitable quest for blame and, unsurprisingly, declared the country's white majority responsible. Whites had created an environment in which the virus could evolve and flourish, and only quick action by the government they despised had saved them from mass insanity. It wasn't intentional, of course – it was, rather, a "malignancy" in the air, a "miasma" emanating from their strongholds. Its origins in Manhattan were conveniently overlooked. Evidence for this proposition was not required. It was only necessary that the press report it – uniformly, repeatedly, endlessly – for it to be "true."

Nevertheless, many of the nation's white citizens took it to heart. Why else, they reasoned, were they the only target? They had been punished and, according to their betters, deservedly so. Though pockets of resistance remained, most of them acquiesced in their guilt, and many joined in the emotional flagellation of their brothers.

After all the *sturm und drang,* the election in the House of Representatives was anti-climactic. President Vere carried thirty of the fifty delegations in the first round of voting and, at the suggestion of the Speaker, the final tally was made unanimous by acclamation. "Unity" was proclaimed the new mantra, though evidence for it was thin. With majorities assured everywhere, there was no need to wait for Inauguration Day – the machinery of government was cranked up with a vengeance.

Jeremiah Jefferson, having come so close to the White House, cried foul. Bribery, not cowardice, was the reason his delegations turned on him. He raged at the politicians and the media and was met with a collective yawn. Lawsuits were filed, duly noted by the press, and forgotten.

One of the president's campaign promises had been to restore "normalcy" in America. In her view, normalcy was measured not in terms of adherence to the country's traditional values, but by how much her policies differed from those of her predecessor. Everything he was for, she was against. Some in her own faction balked at this mindless approach to governing, but they were ignored.

Still, an exhausted country tried to rally around her. Everyone went back to work, and trains and airliners carried passengers once more. The violence diminished – the Red Brigade and the White Army called a truce, and the everyday rioters stood down – but remained just below the surface. Earnest Pogue came out of hiding and no one paid any attention.

The culture wars, however, and the rhetoric that sustained them, continued apace. Emboldened by the president's election, touted by the media as "historic" and "unprecedented," her partisans set about establishing the society they had dreamed of for generations, while the even more extreme among them, led by Vada Potts-Jones, clamored for policies never before imagined. With the expropriation of wealth and power in full swing, they turned their attention to the appropriation of hearts and minds.

Proposals were in the works to abolish private elementary and secondary education, to limit Internet services to government-approved platforms, and to tax churches. Radio and television licenses would be allocated at the whim of the White House. The Department of Equity installed a "facilitator" within each of the country's 3,141 county governments to ensure that its mandates were carried out.

Along with the systematic seizure of wealth and property, always by "legal" means, these and other *diktats* were promoted by the press as a form of "reparations" owed by the white majority to the rest of the country, not because of the old slavery they had imposed and permitted, but because of the new slavery – Vada's virus – from which they had been delivered. Despite her skin pigment, President Vere *was* the rest of the country and whatever she demanded was not only good, but right. A brave new hierarchy was in charge, and anyone who objected did so at his peril. For a sizable portion of the population, everyday life became an existential occupation, a concentrated effort to survive the new orthodoxy.

Beyond the United States, the world faced a much different crisis. In contrast to America's self-absorption, people around the globe were riveted to the increasing violence of the weather. Great winds blew across every ocean and every continent save North America, accompanied by unparalleled rain and tides. Millions of people were displaced every day, and desperate cries for help addressed to the Leviathan – America, hitherto always the first, and last, resort – fell on deaf ears. Hurricane Joan, upgraded by a now-enthused weather media to Category 2, meandered west.

The plague of locusts in Africa had come and gone, leaving behind millions of acres of dry, desolate earth saturated with trillions of grasshopper eggs. A single swarm digested 4,000 pounds of vegetation in an hour, and left the desert ecosystem in ruins. Starvation among the population was imminent, their farms were now barren for generations, and another refugee crisis was at hand. God and Allah had punished them again.

Typically, locust swarms died down with the approach of winter but, though the attacks had stopped, the usual signs – mounds of grasshopper chitin strewn across the landscape, dead females with eggs still intact – were missing. Turkey and India reported small-scale invasions, and another swarm had reached the west coast of Africa via the prevailing winds, but what little attention had been paid to the plague was gone.

FOURTEEN

They have pervaded the country, from New England to Louisiana; they are neither peculiar to the eternal snows of the former, nor the burning suns of the latter; they are not the creature of climate – neither are they confined to the slave-holding, or the non-slaving-holding States – Abraham Lincoln, 1838

I SWITCHED off the machine and unloaded the last CD from the recorder. The recordings of the California Suite conversation and my discussions with Vada on the Grapevine were a damning confirmation of the virus conspiracy, one that even her partisans would have a hard time spinning. On the other hand, the confessions regarding Doctor Cohen and the airplane bombs were worthless – she had deleted the actual Interface encounters, leaving no visual evidence of her acknowledged guilt and only silence on the tapes. I found an envelope and slipped them inside.

After turning Marty's computer on, I began to type. Two hours later, it was done: The whole sorry story from our first meeting aboard the Prairie Star to the empty streets of Manhattan to the abandoned children of the Citadel. I considered eliminating names, Vada's included, but it seemed cowardly and less than the truth.

Ultimately, I decided that *I* would remain anonymous, and continue as an "unnamed source" who had confided the events to me, the author of the piece. Scanning the manuscript, I realized that I was no longer editing and revising, I was agonizing over what to do with it. That it would have an impact on the two most prominent women in the country was certain, but what would that impact be?

For Vada Potts-Jones, opprobrium, lawsuits and jail time might once have been assured. The intentional imposition of a cruel disease on more than half the population would've met with universal condemnation, and any partisans she retained would have the good grace to whisper their support. How would it be under the New Régime?

As for Lucinda Trent Vere, the news that her vice-president was a domestic terrorist who had tried to poison millions of her voters would certainly rub off on her. The resulting political firestorm might, at the very least, place her administration on defense for the next four years, leaving no room for the progressive policies she was promoting. The other party would soon be making plans to redecorate the Oval Office. Or would it?

The truth was that the verities I had grown up with were no longer operative. What was once straightforward and all-embracing was now fluid and fragmented, and when the country finally came together — assuming it did — there were no assurances that the new canons would resemble the old —

quite the opposite, in fact. As a consequence, I was operating in the dark.

For all the change, however, it seemed certain that my revelations would damage the Vere Administration, not least because its political grandstanding over the virus would become amusing. Lucinda had nothing to do with weaponizing the disease it carried, but her explanation for it was laughably false. She had taken credit for the vaccine that Vada actually produced, an act that, arguably, won her the presidency. Of all the sins a politician might commit, becoming an object of ridicule was the most deadly. I strained to find an answer to the conflict I couldn't avoid.

I scrolled through Marty's email addresses and found Vada's:

Madame Vice-President:
Attached is a story that will appear in the Star tomorrow afternoon. I have no idea how it will be received, but I wanted to give you a head's up. The president will have a copy shortly.
Corrections or comments are welcome.
Tommy Sawyer

Would she try to stop me? In the old America, it would never have occurred to me to warn her. Exposed as the source of a toxin that poisoned millions, she might've fled the country or committed suicide to avoid public condemnation and prison. Now, I was sure she expected me to tell her story, and planned to cash in on it politically, however bizarre that might seem to me. Or maybe, having orchestrated the worst ethnic assault since the Holocaust, she was merely awaiting exposure and the infamy that accompanied it.

In the old days, the press would've portrayed it as just another "hit piece" from the *Georgetown Star,* while doing what they could to lessen its impact. The reaction might be different now in the country's triumphal newsrooms – turning white people into zombies could seem like the right thing to do. Whatever law or decency mandated, her sycophants in the press would protect her. Providing her an opportunity to embrace or refute the story seemed like the best way to blunt the response from her partisans.

Despite the increasing disconnect between us, I wanted to give Lucinda time to prepare. The virus had paved the way for her election, and she had taken full advantage of it, but that was just the politics of the moment. Although she was losing patience with me and *my* politics, she deserved to know what was coming. It was still impossible to call or email her, so I turned to the computer once more:

> *Madame President:*
> *Enclosed is a report on the recent virus attack. It will appear in the Georgetown Star tomorrow afternoon.*
> *Tommy Sawyer*

After printing the story and the note, I slipped both into an envelope, sealed it, and scrawled an address: "The President of the United States of America, The White House, 1600 Pennsylvania Avenue, Washington, D.C. 20500." The envelope containing the tapes, addressed to my Post Office box in New Hope, went in the mail.

I walked to the White House and turned in at the northwest gate off Pennsylvania Avenue. The guards knew me but, since my name wasn't on the list, it was as far as I could go. "Would you call Wolf?" I said. "I have an important package for the president."

ALTHOUGH MANHATTAN'S human capital had been decimated by the virus, its commercial and cultural infrastructure remained, and those left behind – mostly in European and Asian outposts and on the West Coast – set about repopulating it. Whereas the previous cadre had been shaped over time, the new arrivals came fully formed, indistinguishable from their predecessors now languishing in government madhouses. They took as their immediate task the re-stocking of the island with likeminded people.

Meanwhile, the other coast picked up the slack. California, in particular, assumed leadership in finance, technology and the arts. Newsrooms began to add personnel, and newspapers in Los Angeles and San Francisco vied to become the new "paper of record." The population of the nation's most populous state increased by thousands every day – it was proclaimed a "new Gold Rush for the Golden State." Governor Victoria St. John cheerfully promised new taxes and new "investments in the people of California" while speaking at "Victoria for President" rallies across the country.

Already the world-wide colossus in food production, the California Great Central Valley expanded its output to feed the globe. Increasing productivity combined with the ruthless takeover of private sources of water raised the crop yield exponentially. The Valley cemented its relationship with the Yankee Coalition, and donated many tons of fruit, vegetables and milk to the plague victims in West Africa. Its share of America's food supply was projected to increase by a factor of three.

Those parts of the country that had fallen behind fell further. Instead of being scorned, its citizens were now ignored. Many of their elected representatives, finding themselves powerless, stopped speaking for their constituents and went over to the other side. The partition envisioned by the virus conspirators was achieved in all but name only, but some in Congress and the Administration wanted to convert the *de facto* reality into a *de jure* separation. Vada Potts-Jones, perhaps as redress for her virus co-conspirators, was leading the effort.

President Vere opposed the idea. Her goal was to ensure that the gospel she preached was heard and embraced by every sinner in the country, and that was much easier to do when you could lock them up if they refused. Moreover, Vada had served her purpose and was becoming increasingly troublesome. Lucinda had made her peace with the party's enduring oligarchs, ensuring their wealth and place despite the revolution, and Vada and her band of fanatics threatened to get in the way. My report on the virus turned out to be the perfect vehicle to get rid of her.

The president's campaign to shed herself of Vada Potts-Jones began minutes after she read my story. By the time I returned to the office, there were three messages on my cellphone, all from her. Before I could call her, it rang again. "I wish you'd carry your phone with you," she said. "I've been trying to reach you for two hours."

"Sorry."

"I'm having a meeting here tomorrow. I want you to attend."

"A meeting of?"

"Your so-called profession. You'll know everybody." She paused. "I suppose you have evidence to back up this story?"

"Yes."

"Good. Keep it in a safe place." She paused. "I want you to take out the part about the vaccine."

I knew why, but asked anyway. "Why?"

"I have my reasons. It won't really change your story."

It *would* change the story, but at least she wasn't trying to kill the whole thing. "Okay."

"The meeting's at ten o'clock. It's top secret, so come in by the H Street entrance."

"The what?"

"The H Street – I'll have Wolf call you."

CROSSING LAFAYETTE Square, I stopped to look at the overturned statue of Andrew Jackson, a casualty of the last night of riots before the armistice. His head remained on his shoulders, though his hat – once held high in his right hand – was gone and his horse decapitated. The verdigris cannon that protected him had likewise been toppled and splashed with red paint. A reviled figure among the new breed of "protestors," he was more like them than they knew, though their causes were very different.

It was a dark gloomy day, and the square itself had settled in for the winter. All its color was gone. The bare limbs of ginkgos, elms and willow oaks stood stark against the sky, and the nominally green magnolias were black next to the almost white turf. It was the same story across the street. On the North Lawn of the White House the deciduous trees had lost their leaves and the evergreens – pines, spruce and yews – did little to relieve the colorless monotony. A few shrubs displayed different shades of green, but the masses of hollies and boxwoods only added to the aspect of black-and-white. The rest of the city was equally monochromatic.

Emerging onto H Street, I turned east and crossed 15th Street. Halfway down the nondescript block, I turned right into a blind alley protected by a steel barrier and a barely disguised Secret Service kiosk. The alley led to the rear of what I now knew to be the Annex to the Treasury Department fronting on Pennsylvania Avenue. Wolf Robinson waited beside the heavily barred door. "What's with all the cloak and dagger?" I said.

Without answering, he drew a large key from his coat pocket, unlocked the door and swung it open. "This door opens into the Treasury Annex basement," he said. "There's a tunnel on the other side that takes you under the street to the basement of the main building. Another agent will direct you from there."

Once in the Main Treasury basement, I was escorted down the west side of the building to another tunnel. "This will take you to the basement under the East Wing of the White House," the agent said. "You'll come to a pair of steel doors where you'll need to identify yourself." He smiled. "You're almost there."

I walked down the dingy tile floor, ducking under and around piping and ductwork. At the steel doors, I was interrogated briefly and left to wait while my identity was confirmed, after which the doors opened and I passed through. They closed behind me with a loud hiss.

Except for the surfeit of electronics, it looked like any other conference room, and it was crowded. I *did* know most of them, though not well. The chiefs of all the broadcast and cable news networks, radio conglomerates and Internet platforms, along with the publishers of national newspapers and magazines, were all there. Some of them were new on the job or serving in an acting capacity due to the afflictions suffered by their predecessors in New York. Others had been in place since the Clinton Administration. I was there, presumably, as the publisher of the *Georgetown Star*, but they were surprised to see me since the *Star* and her sister publications had never been on their bandwagon. I was pretty sure my presence had been demanded for reasons different from theirs.

We rose when Lucinda entered the room, and I was struck by the uniformity of the group. She was the only woman in the room and everyone, even the recent replacements, was white. This, despite their never-ending rhetoric about equality and the racism of their enemies. There was no self-awareness, as Marty had said – the media was Exhibit One for Vada's crusade.

The president stood behind a chair at the far end of the table. "Please, sit down," she said. "Thanks to all of you for coming." She paused. "I have something shocking to tell you, and I need your help. It's classified, and everything I say is off the record."

She proceeded to tell the virus story with a few omissions and additions that made it seem a part of the narrative she had already sold to the country. The vaccine wasn't mentioned. "We knew from the beginning that someone in government had purposely spread the virus in New York. We weren't sure who it was, but we didn't want him or her to know that we knew it was man-made, so we pretended it was a natural disaster that we were fortunate to detect early on." She stopped. "We know now who the perpetrator is."

"What about the vaccine?" said the man from CBS. "How was it developed so quickly?"

"We were lucky. Everything fell into place."

"You haven't told us who the government official is," said the publisher of the *Post.*

"I'm coming to that," said the president. "But first I want you to consider what this person has wrought. She is a higher-up in this government. When the story gets out, and I have it on good authority that it will very soon, my administration will face disaster if it's not handled properly. All the things I've worked for, and you've worked for, might be destroyed. Our hopes for this country, so recently born, could be dashed." A tear actually rolled down her cheek. "You must speak against this person with one voice. Anything less will be catastrophic."

A few heads turned toward me. I kept my gaze straight ahead. The president continued: "In the past, your organizations have seen fit to praise this woman – Vada Potts-Jones. The Vice-President of the United States. That has to stop. She's an enemy of the state, and must be treated as such."

Everyone began to speak at once. Lucinda raised a hand. "Please," she said, "one at a time."

"What are you going to do with her?" said the Internet mogul from the West Coast.

"Arrest her. Impeach her. We have to find her first."

"Is she missing?" said the *Post's* publisher.

"Yes. We think she got word we were on to her."

If she stared constantly at her screens like everyone else in the country, Vada knew about the imminence of the virus story at least an hour before the president did. Had she fled, or was she just shopping or playing golf? Lucinda obviously believed it was the former, and she had decided to manipulate the corrupt Greek chorus who protected Vada so as to remove her from the field. Judging from the reactions around me, she would be toast after my story appeared in approximately three hours.

Lucinda sealed the deal: "One more thing. I've decided to create a council of elders to advise the president. A 'kitchen cabinet,' if you will. Some of you will be on it." Her gaze took in every face. "Don't let me down." She looked at me. "Tommy, I need a word with you."

They shuffled from the room in silence, no doubt contemplating the spoils of presidential access. I followed her through more tunnels into the West Wing and, finally, into the Oval Office. "What *are* you going to do with her?" I said.

"Nothing. I'm going to let you publish that story and let them attack her. I want it over as quickly as possible. As long as she stays out of the way, I'll leave her alone." She paused. "I want you to take that message to her."

The notion that she was *allowing* me to publish the story was jarring. Certainly, she had the raw power to shut down the *Star* – we were short on guns in the newsroom and would be unable to withstand an attack – but exposing Vada was apparently more important. "So – no punishment?" I said. "No payback for all those deranged people?"

"I can't afford for this to go on forever. It's bad politics. And there's no telling what she'd say to the press. Or on the witness stand." She stopped. "I can't take that chance. Our cause is bigger than this." She leaned forward. "And tell her something else. If she *does* shoot her mouth off, it'll be the last time."

I raised my brows. "Why don't you tell her? Or get one of your flunkies to do it?"

"I don't know where she is, and I don't want to know. She's toxic, Tommy. To me, to everybody. There's no downside if you do it." She looked at her watch. "I've got a few minutes. Let's go upstairs."

The sex was, unexpectedly, even better than usual, but it felt like I was saying goodbye. Lucinda had become what I had imagined Vada to be, a captive of her dogma without the capacity to uncouple from it. Whereas once we argued about the state of the nation, now there was no room for argument. Her certainty had come between us.

Over the next few days, Vada-Potts Jones went from fashionable *provocateur* to heinous miscreant. Abandoning their campaign against white Americans for the moment, the press shed crocodile tears over her treachery and piled on to a degree seldom seen, perhaps driven by a potential perch on Lucinda's kitchen cabinet. Politicians, some from her own party, joined in. Lawsuits, of course, were filed, but they were hampered by an inability to serve papers on the defendant. Vada had vanished, and no amount of sleuthing turned up her whereabouts. Other than a single unsuccessful attempt via Interface, I made no effort to join in the search – she was gone, and that was enough.

WITH THE election over and the conventional zeitgeist restored, the media cast about for something new to obsess over, and they didn't have far to look. Hurricane Joan, still a Category 2 storm whose winds stretched 400 miles over the Atlantic Ocean, was forecast to make landfall at Nag's Head in three days. From there she was projected to turn north, her eye between Richmond and Norfolk, and threaten Washington a day later.

A half-hearted effort was made to prepare for the coming storm, but city officials, as well as those in charge of the hundreds of federal installations situated in the District of Columbia, acknowledged once again that chance was their only hope of avoiding disaster. Washington suffered serious flooding once every decade, and measures taken to prevent it, if they were taken at all, were never enough. The budget for upgrading the city's defenses had been set at zero for years.

At the heart of its flood control was a levee that stretched from the Lincoln Memorial along the National Mall to what was left of the Washington Monument. This earthen berm was bisected by 17th Street, creating a 140-foot gap that, when flooding was anticipated, had to be plugged. A few years earlier, a movable flood wall consisting of eight steel posts and twenty-seven aluminum panels had been commissioned by Congress, but no one in a responsible position believed it would work. Its assembly in the middle of a storm was problematic – if Joan brought flooding to the District, she would be the wall's first test.

At the same time, on the far side of the world, the plague of locusts had been resurrected. The insects, carried by high violent winds, ravaged Europe and Russia to the north and India and China to the east, while isolated swarms were reported in Malaysia, Australia and Japan. But, stymied by the wide expanse of the world's largest body of water, the Pacific Ocean, trillions of exhausted grasshoppers fell from the sky, their quest to cover the globe denied.

Amidst all the political upheaval, President Vere was determined to sustain the "unity" narrative in order to ensure that her policies endured. It would be harder for some future politician to argue for change if the country came to believe everyone had actually agreed with her. To that end, she appointed members of the opposing party to minor sinecures, made a great show of embracing "women's issues" important to mothers and daughters in the other faction, and promised a farm bill she knew had no chance in the Congress.

The greatest impediment to her unity régime was Jeremiah Jefferson. Once an upright church‑man, he had become a political "character," an un‑hinged partisan who nevertheless had a loyal band of followers. He provided comic relief for the media – cable news delighted in interviews and panel dis‑cussions wherein his election conspiracies grew ev‑er more fantastic. Still, he represented a collective memory the president wanted to expunge, and she had floated several conciliatory trial balloons, all of which he had ignored.

Finally, she hit upon a scheme guaranteed to gain his cooperation as well as score a few points with a large bloc inside her own party. At a recent gaggle on the South Lawn, she had announced a new program, "Giving God a Hand," whereby the federal government would dole out grants to "de‑serving" black churches for "education" and other unspecified "community purposes."

"We'll work with church leaders in deciding how best to spend this money," she said. "It'll be a joint venture between government and God." The first grant, in the sum of $500,000, was going to the Metropolitan African Methodist Episcopal Church, located on M Street a few blocks north of the White House. President Vere would personally hand over the check to its pastor, Jeremiah Jefferson, during services the following Sunday.

FIFTEEN

Alike, they spring up among the pleasure hunting masters of Southern slaves, and the order loving citizens of the land of steady habits – Whatever, then, their cause may be, it is common to the whole country – Abraham Lincoln, 1838

THE MEMORY hole was bottomless. Whether by conscious policy or happenstance, the media had coalesced to suppress the recall of recent events and promote the here-and-now of the Vere Administration. The former president's death, "assassination," and disinterment were forgotten. The violence and disruption, even the virus, were consigned to history. The presidential election, the most unusual and controversial in the nation's history, was notable only for its result. Utopia's labor could not be allowed to befoul its birth.

Hurricane Joan was bearing down on the East Coast. At the same time, though little noted, a major storm system had formed over the North Branch of the Potomac River, and heavy rains caused the river to overflow its banks on the way to the sea. The potential for trouble in the nation's capital was acknowledged in a few quarters, then set aside because it was too late to do anything about it anyway.

I sat at Marty's desk mulling Lucinda's visit to the Metropolitan AME the next morning. Even in these corrupt times, it was a breathtaking demonstration of hubris. I'd been reluctant to criticize her administration, but this was impossible to ignore, however it might affect her and me:

HYPOCRISY? OR GOOD POLITICS?
Tommy Sawyer

It's a given that everything in this town is stunted by hypocrisy. The reasons for that are many, but the primary cause is power. Power is the currency here, and its effect on the brain as well as the pocketbook is profound. What may be vigorously opposed one day is heartily endorsed the next, depending on who has the power and who wants it. The merits of whatever is at issue are secondary if they're considered at all.

The pols will tell you that's how the sausage is made, but it's not necessarily so. There was a time in the not-so-distant past when people had principles and lived by them, and things, important things, still got done. Contrast that with recent decades when nothing of consequence was accomplished, and who had the power was all that mattered.

That calculus has now changed, though the power and hypocrisy remain. The current government and, most particularly, the president, have all the power in Washington but for the (almost cer-

tainly temporary) "negative" influence of the Supreme Court. But there are still a few people who refuse to bend a knee, and a few institutions not yet under the government yoke. Regrettably, Lord Acton's aphorism regarding power sums up the administration's response to these last vestiges of independence.

The pastor of the Metropolitan African Methodist Episcopal Church, Jeremiah Jefferson, has been targeted by the Vere Administration for insufficient obeisance arising from well-known circumstances I won't go into here. Suffice it to say, Reverend Jefferson continues to insist that President Vere's election was illegitimate and, despite every official certification to the contrary, the president chafes at his obstinacy. She plans to bring him to heel with the power of the purse.

Lucinda Vere's government is inarguably more hostile to religion than any administration in the history of the republic. The president herself goes out of her way to denigrate the very idea of religious belief. And yet, she has created a program called "Giving God a Hand," whose sole purpose is to co-opt Reverend Jefferson. Set aside its constitutionality – it's a clear violation of the separation of church and state so revered by the president's partisans, among other defects – it reeks of hypocrisy, personal and institutional, and abuse of power.

I'm writing this on Saturday evening. By the time you read these words tomorrow afternoon, President Vere will have presented Jeremiah Jefferson and his church with a check from the taxpayers for $500,000. One might say he could refuse it, but that's not realistic. Or maybe he and his pa-

rishioners could resist the "strings" on the money, but that's also unlikely. Media and politicians will applaud the whole affair as good politics, but the citizens – those still trying to think for themselves – will see it for the cynical hypocrisy that characterizes every level of our society. It is both a bribe and a bridle, and it will silence one of the president's last remaining critics.

After reading it over, I considered deleting it, but decided not to let Lucinda's ascent to higher office dictate my conscience. Still – we were different now, and this would probably be the end.

About to switch the computer off, I noticed that the Interface icon had begun to blink. I clicked:

"Tommy – I'll call you tomorrow at 7 PM."

I STOOD amongst her hand-picked gaggle beneath the North Portico. It was very cold, and there was a rare dusting of snow on the North Lawn. The pewter sky promised more. We were all underdressed because Washington, despite its current pretensions, was an old Southern town that survived on air-conditioning, and no one was ever prepared for real cold. President Vere joined us, and we started off on our journey to the Metropolitan AME six blocks away.

She clearly relished the moment. She had survived the virus and the election, and she was about to bulldoze the last, minor obstruction in the way of her own personal nirvana. Raised to believe it was her duty to instruct and lead the heathen, she was as one with her Pilgrim ancestors, stripped of the supernatural. It was perhaps disconcerting that her final obstacle should be a member of the tribe for whom she had labored so long, but then the instruction was never truly over.

We passed through Lafayette Square and walked up Black Lives Matter Plaza, formerly known as 16th Street. At M Street we turned east, and slowed to pick our way through the television crews lining the sidewalk. Reporters not invited to be part of her cortège shouted questions. She answered some and turned others aside, almost girlish in her pleasure at the attention. I thought again how beautiful she was despite the creed she embraced.

The church, cheek by jowl with two undistinguished office buildings, was clean red brick with lancet windows and gables over the doors. Its small yard was enclosed by an iron fence, and a newly-planted maple tree, bare of its leaves, stood beside the gate. With President Vere in the lead, we climbed the steps to the middle doors and passed inside.

The pews, including the galleries, were packed. Still photographers lined the back of the nave. Light poured through the festive stained-glass windows behind them, whereas the windows on either side were dark – installed in 1886, their sunlight had been rudely confiscated by ugly buildings constructed more than 100 years later. A large cross hung in the apse, and organ pipes rose on both sides of the chancel.

A murmur of anticipation arose as the president detached herself from us and proceeded down the aisle. A single television camera peered down from the gallery. The Reverend Jeremiah Jefferson, standing beside the pulpit, awaited her. His parishioners, most of whom had probably voted for her ticket rather than his, could barely contain themselves. They rose as she passed beyond the chancel rail and climbed to where Jefferson stood. The choir behind him arranged themselves for a better view. The photographers pressed closer.

She extended an envelope. "Reverend Jefferson," she said, "please accept this offering on behalf of the American people."

Without speaking, he took the envelope from her and turned to lay it in the collection plate behind him. There was a moment's hesitation and then, turning back to her, he produced a gun from his robe and pulled the trigger. As the president fell, the answering fusillade from her failed guardians was immediate and intense, and flashbulbs popped from every direction. The photograph of Wolf Robinson, tears running down his face as he fired round after round into Jefferson's dead body, appeared on front pages around the globe.

The pastor's bullet had lodged in her brain. After six hours on the operating table, her doctors advised the nation that while President Vere's condition was stable, it was still touch and go, and that – oblivious to the irony – the country should pray for her recovery. She was in an induced coma that would not be ended until she died or showed viable signs of improvement. Even if she lived, the qual-ity of her life might be diminished. As the rest of the country grappled with the news, the politicians and the media addressed the unavoidable question: Who was running things now?

Assuming she could be found, the vice-president was Lucinda's constitutional successor and, if she didn't recover, Vada Potts-Jones would be sworn in for a full term as president in little more than a month. Vada was damaged goods, of course – only yesterday the press was calling for prison and impeachment – but now her future was the stuff of partisan dreams and nightmares. Political calculations were ongoing in pow-wows all over town. The future of the republic was once again in the cross-hairs of its most venal cohort.

I SPENT Sunday afternoon musing over our past. Mercifully, recent events were blurred. I recalled our first meeting in her chambers at the Supreme Court, as well as the fatal confrontation with her father, but mostly I remembered the indulgent, indolent hours we spent outside the inferno of her ambition. She was a delight when she forgot about the future.

A blueblood from Back Bay Boston, the last surviving member of her family, Lucinda had followed a modern-day version of the path taken by her very white female forbears – a Latin grammar school, private girls' academy and Radcliffe, then on to Harvard Law and a fancy New York firm. Never married, she pursued her career with a single-minded determination but, despite the reserve, always found time for men – ours was the last of many affairs. I resisted the idea that she might survive as a lesser being.

Just before seven o'clock, I sat down behind Marty's desk and turned on the computer. Vada and her whereabouts were important again, but I was indifferent to her prospects. The endless machinations, and the reckoning necessary to keep up with them, were more than tiresome now, they were repellent. Unfortunately, the country was in a full-fledged crisis again and she was right in the middle of it.

Her face appeared on the screen. "Hi, Tommy."

"Hi."

"Miss me?"

I smiled in spite of myself. "Not really. Where are you?"

"I'm – let's see – somewhere between Minneapolis and Fargo. On the *Prairie Star.*"

"When are you coming back?"

She laughed. "I'm not. Why would I?"

I hesitated. "Haven't you heard the news? Lucinda's been shot. She's in the hospital."

We sat quietly, staring at each other. "Who shot her?" she said at last.

"Jeremiah Jefferson." I paused. "She's in a coma. The docs say she might not make it. The politicos and the press are going berserk."

We were quiet again. "What are they saying about me?" she said.

"They're all over the lot. A few want to impeach you and throw you in jail, but that would take time. And they'd probably end up with the Speaker as president, which they don't like. Most of the others have decided they want you to take over, but you have to come back to do that."

"Why?"

"You need to certify to the House and Senate that she can't do her job. In writing."

"Do they have to vote on it or something?"

"No. As soon as your declaration is received by the Speaker and the President of the Senate, you're Acting President of the United States."

"Acting?"

"If the president recovers, she's president again."

"What are the chances of that?"

"Not very good, I'm afraid."

"And if she doesn't recover?"

"You'll serve out her term. And be inaugurated in your own right on January 20. If you haven't been impeached by then."

She laughed again. "Is being acting president the same as being president?"

"Yes."

She sat very still, blinking. "Can't we do all this remotely?"

"Well – a majority of her cabinet has to agree with you."

"Can't you handle that? She's in a coma, for God's sake. If I fax you a letter, you can take it to the right people, and they can carry it up to the Hill. Problem solved."

The idea of helping her replace Lucinda was repugnant, but without her cooperation the country would wallow in a constitutional morass that might result in true anarchy. "All right," I said. "Send it. I'll see what I can do." I stopped. "Why'd you set up this call?"

"You're still my chronicler. I want to give you the rest of the story."

"Okay. Shoot."

"I think I'll wait until this other business is settled. I'll let you know."

As her image faded from the screen, I reached for the phone. Twenty-four hours later, Vada Potts-Jones was Acting President of the United States of America. Washington, exhausted, awaited her return. Her first official act was to grant herself a full and unconditional pardon for all "felonies and misdemeanors arising out of or pertaining to the recent virus attack on the United States, as well as the distribution of vaccines for the treatment thereof." In the furor surrounding her assumption of the presidency, it garnered little attention.

Thus was the revolution complete. "Politics" had produced a government that almost no one believed in. The counter-revolution was about to get underway.

HURRICANE JOAN and the rising waters of the Potomac River met at Theodore Roosevelt Island, a mile west of the White House. The wind generated a flood that rushed across the Mall as Washington's main levee was quickly breached. Water poured into the city.

Those charged with erecting the 17th Street floodwall were unable to move the posts and panels to the designated location, let alone assemble the wall. Water erupted from century-old storm drains. Official Washington – streets, buildings, open spaces – was inundated. Floodwaters covered the runways at Reagan National Airport.

The water rose so quickly that many federal employees, unable to escape, had to remain in their buildings until it receded. At the People's Plaza, thousands of bureaucrats were forced to abandon the lower floors and move higher in the building. As a result of the flooding, the soil beneath it loosened, the jury-rigged foundation was compromised and, unknown to its occupants, the overload of people on its higher floors sealed their doom.

Though Joan had been reduced to a Category 1 storm, sporadic wind gusts reached 100 miles per hour. One of those gusts caused the People's Plaza to tremble, another pushed it from its foundations, a third drove it to the ground. The loss of life, in the building and on the ground, was catastrophic.

The recriminations began before the water disappeared. Blame for the flooding shifted moment by moment until it finally settled on former officials who went unnamed. As for the People's Plaza, Marty Jones was damned for his "fix," while everyone else who championed the project, including Lucinda Trent Vere, was given a pass. In no case was a current official at any level of government deemed responsible. "Accountability," one of the many meaningless buzzwords used by the political class, was ignored.

It was, in fact, another crisis too good to waste. The Potts-Jones Administration used the disaster to reinforce an old trope – Fortress America. "One-worldism" was abandoned for the moment. The wholesale destruction in Washington, and the resulting disruption of the government's many foreign adventures, inspired yet another appeal for "unity" – "Keep America Great" – to a disgruntled, confused American public. Evil people worldwide were said to be on the march. "National security" was at stake.

In addition to the rhetoric, the chaos provided cover for the ever-increasing gathering of power in the capital. It also allowed the new government, and its allies in the media, to "move on" from Vada's virus scandal. The press, having concluded that her administration would be even more amenable than the one it replaced, had turned on a dime. Anyone with the temerity to mention her role in the virus was told that it was "old news," that the country couldn't be bothered with past indiscretions in the face of current challenges. They succeeded in shutting down debate for the most part, though the anger and resentment festered.

The atmospherics surrounding Vada's investiture as president resembled those that greeted her predecessor, only more so. The ideology was more radical, and her human attributes more satisfactory. No longer would the racial *cognoscenti* be forced to acknowledge a rich, *white* woman of privilege as their leader – they could celebrate a rich, *black* woman of privilege instead. Moreover, she was on record attacking those elements in her party who continued to indulge in wealth accumulation while fulminating against it. Their movement was approaching purity.

But – as self-congratulations swept over the capital, and newsrooms across the country proclaimed the end of history, Vada's government struggled to find its footing. The disconnect between the politicians and the body politic was wider than ever. The governors could no longer even communicate with the governed, much less persuade them. Their overseers in the press stopped sugarcoating the "news," and resorted to commands. The revolution's demise seemed already in the cards even as its partisans admired their victory.

THE DOCTORS had announced that President Vere was recovering from her wound, while remaining silent regarding the impact of the bullet. Eventually the truth leaked out: The bullet had burrowed its way through the frontal lobes of her brain, directly behind her forehead, and permanently affected not only her personality but the ability to regulate her emotions. Problem-solving was hard, and setting and achieving goals almost impossible. A committee appointed by Congress met with her individually and all reached the same conclusion – Lucinda Trent Vere could no longer serve as President of the United States.

With respect to living arrangements, there were no protocols for the current circumstances. The country had a disabled president, an acting president and no vice-president at all so, after a brief negotiation, Vada took up residence at the Naval Observatory and Lucinda was moved to her bedroom at the White House. The unspoken agreement was that she would vacate the premises prior to Vada's inauguration. It required the new president's direct intervention in order for me to see her.

I watched her from the doorway. Head thrown back, she was seated in a leather easy chair next to the window. Her hair was cut close and there was a wide bandage around her forehead.

Dressed in jeans and one of my old shirts with the sleeves rolled up, she looked like a beautiful boy. When her hair grew back and the bandage was removed, she would be the same as always except for the bullet. Her eyes opened. "Tommy."

Relieved that she recognized me, I bent to kiss her. "You doing okay?" I said. She nodded. I perched on the bed. After a short back-and-forth about her new everyday life, I said, "Let's talk about us."

She smiled. "All right."

I had to know who she was now. The doctors had told me I would probably detect little obvious difference – her problems were at the "executive level," a decrease in the cognitive skills necessary to maneuver in the complex world she had inhabited for most of her life. Still, as we talked, I noticed little things.

Always the aggressor in conversation before, she waited for me to speak. Once started on a particular topic, she was reluctant to let it go, repeating herself rather than moving on to something else. She was easily distracted – the overhead fan, a bird outside her window, made her lose track of what we were talking about. The dynamic woman I had fallen in love with, the woman who had operated at the highest levels on the globe, was no longer there.

Her memory was fine. It was as if she had traded the future for the past. She recalled details of our time together that I had long forgotten or never knew. I listened, eyes wet, as she recounted her "conjugal" visit to my hospital bed after my own brush with assassination. We were like an old married couple remembering the highlights of our past.

After knocking on the door, one of her doctors entered the room. I rose. "I'll see you tomorrow," I said. She smiled and lifted a hand, already focused on the new man in the room.

I waited in the hallway. When he emerged from her room, I explained who I was and said, "Can she look after herself? On a day-to-day basis?"

He shook his head. "President Vere can function normally up to a point. What she cannot do is judge among the options we all face at a certain cognitive level – health care, planning a meal, that sort of thing is beyond her. She can choose a dress to wear, apply her makeup, evaluate items on a menu. She can't drive from the White House to the Capitol or conduct a Cabinet meeting or write a book." He paused. "She's okay in the here and now. What comes next is the problem. She needs help with that."

"Does she know she used to be President of the United States?"

"Of course. Just like she knows she used to be captain of her high school basketball team. It's a part of her life that's over."

"Won't she miss it? Doesn't she resent what's happened to her?"

"That's hard to say, but I doubt it. I've seen no evidence of it."

"What about money? Can she manage her own finances?"

"No."

"Is she – is she able to make, um, personal decisions? Who to trust? Who to – love?"

He smiled. "Those are instinctual attributes. They're probably enhanced now."

Vada had chosen to operate out of the vice-president's office until her inauguration. She was waiting for me in the lobby of the West Wing. "Well?" she said.

"She's – different."

"What're you going to do?"

"Apply to be her legal guardian. Her people are all gone, and she meets all the criteria of an 'incapacitated adult.' I stopped. "And I'm going to ask her to marry me." She raised a brow. "I think she can make that decision. I hope so."

We crossed the hall to her office. "Are you leaving Washington?" she said.

I nodded. "I'm fed up with it. And it's certainly no place for Lucinda now." I paused. "I'm taking her home to New Hope."

We sat without speaking. "Did you ever swallow that pill?" she said.

"No. Why?"

"It wasn't the virus. It was the vaccine."

THE DEATH of the locusts on the edge of the Pacific proved to be greatly exaggerated. Rather than simply die in the water, the insects that perished formed a floating mat of hundreds of square miles. Their living brethren, cannibals, landed on the mat, ate the dead and, nourished and refreshed, lifted into the skies once more. Advancing in this fashion, and with the aid of unprecedented winds, they reached Hawaii where they stripped the islands clean of vegetation and, in plague numbers once more, set off for the West Coast. Estimated time of arrival was three days.

The Potts-Jones Administration, so intent on consolidating its power, had paid little attention to the grasshoppers as they circled the globe, but when Hawaii was attacked the government was forced to take notice. Naval vessels were dispatched and airplanes launched to survey the swarms. Their reports were hard to credit.

Taken together, they estimated that the insects comprised a mass that was a half-mile deep and 200,000 square miles in area. Based on numbers from historic swarms in Africa, more than 3 trillion locusts were headed our way. Disbelief was the immediate reaction, followed by "expert" advice that broke down along political lines.

Vada's administration, along with its media stalwarts, had the biggest microphones, but they didn't speak with one voice. The largest group insisted that nothing be done. Locusts were part of our world and, based just on the numbers, far more entitled to their place on the planet than we were. Pesticides of any kind were impossible – not only would they poison innocent insects, they would do untold damage to the rest of the environment. The use of biological agents – bacteria or viruses, or maybe other insects – was likewise dismissed out of hand because of the potential for disrupting "nature." The climate changers were content to note that the locust problem was "certainly" the result of global warming, and say again, "I told you so."

Pundits of all stripes debated the gravity of the coming plague. Some insisted that the swarms would ultimately fall short of the California coast, while others opined that California's crops, so different from the locusts' native vegetation, would prove unappetizing. Scientists assembled teams to study the insects in the air and on the ground. Entrepreneurs proposed fine mesh nets to cover the crops, but time was short and disagreements over patents and licensing stopped the effort in its tracks. A small faction wanted to deploy the nation's military might, a suggestion that brought almost universal condemnation.

In the country at large, polls showed that the people were divided. The "do nothing" camp, citing "media hype," denied the existence of the swarm altogether. When advised of the devastation in Hawaii, they refused to believe it. Others claimed it was "God's will," that the country was being punished by a plague straight out of Exodus. The farmers among them, whose many crops were in various stages of growth, pleaded for help to no avail.

It was left to the entertainment industry, finally, to put the coming assault in the proper perspective. Where the swarms would actually come ashore was uncertain, but the vector they followed from Hawaii, and the winds they rode, indicated they would reach the West Coast somewhere in the neighborhood of San Francisco. Television and movie crews were stationed up and down the coast. Hotels organized "packages," including airfare, lodging and meals, around the expected arrival of the insects. Open-air stadiums sold tickets to the event.

Thousands of "watch parties" were marshalled with prices ranging from $100 to $10,000, depending on the venue and the refreshments being served. The Top of the Mark offered "the most spectacular vantage" from which to observe "this force of nature." Champagne and caviar would be served and formal wear was *de rigeur*. As the locusts approached, media from all over the country descended upon San Francisco.

Mike Beach dusted off his tuxedo and joined the crowd at the Top of the Mark. He described the spectacle for readers of the *San Francesco Press* the next morning:

APOCALYPSE NOW?
Mike Beach

They threw a party at the Mark Hopkins yesterday, and everybody who was anybody was there. They came from all over the country to witness an event of biblical proportions, one visited periodically on other parts of the world, but not seen in the United States for more than 100 years. Like passengers on the Titanic, *the beautiful people ate and drank like there was no tomorrow, but as time dragged on the mirth waned. The guests of honor were late.*

The man who runs the Top of the Mark grew increasingly nervous, despite the fact that his invitations clearly said there was no guarantee they would arrive. "You don't want to disappoint folks like this," he told me. "It's bad for business." The grumbling grew louder, and two or three people headed for the door.

Then someone pointed, and the crowd pushed out onto the terrace. Still miles away on the horizon, the insects looked like a dusty tornado or a whirlwind of dead leaves in winter. As they drew nearer, trillions of iridescent wings turned the sky yellow, and a shadow crossed the sun. The rasping whir of the wings was like a colossal machine. The air crackled like fire.

Huge brown grasshoppers struck the windows and poured through open doors from the terrace. They seemed to attack the patrons, bashing them in the head and face, tangling their hair and crawling beneath their clothes but, in reality, it was all random, mindless. Panic combined with the touch of the swarm made it hard to breath. A seething mass formed on walls and floors and the stench, like that of a putrid corpse, was overpowering.

It seemed to go on forever, but finally the cloud passed as the plague continued east where it would do unimaginable damage to the fields of the Central Valley. The beautiful people at the Top of the Mark, most of whom had fallen into a protective crouch in a vain effort to avoid the insects, ran for the doors, the crunch of grasshoppers beneath their feet echoing in the silence left behind.

The plague may have been a few minutes late, but no one can say they didn't get their money's worth.

The scene in the Central Valley was indeed biblical. The locusts arrived around 4 PM, first an advance cadre then, coming faster and thicker, a massive, writhing blanket of insects rolling and twisting in the wind. Like a close-order phalanx, they fell upon cornfields and tomato patches and grape arbors and, within a matter of hours, rendered them bare and desolate. The noise they made when feeding was like that of flames devouring the countryside.

Like their counterparts in Africa, farmers tried to burn and beat the insects, then resorted to drowning them with firehoses, all to little effect. As the pillage drew to a close the swarms, sated for the moment, rose once more into the sky and turned toward Nebraska and Iowa and points east. They left behind 150 eggs per square inch of soil, almost a billion eggs per acre. At 21,000 square miles, or 13,440,000 acres, the once-fertile ground of the Central Valley was riddled with an almost incalculable number of grasshopper eggs.

The government, faced with the loss of the rest of the country's food supply, finally defied Gaia's cult and defended the nation. Ignoring lawsuits and court decrees, the Air Force outfitted tanker aircraft with special nozzles and, flying above the airborne hoard, sprayed them like mosquitos. Within hours the crisis was over – the accumulation of grasshopper shells in northeastern Colorado was dubbed "the Dead Corner." The eggs in the Central Valley were also sprayed, requiring a cleansing of the soil that left it fallow for years. A few isolated spots were overlooked, leading to a "boil" of hoppers from the ground a few weeks later.

The litigation instituted by hysterical "greens" was over-the-top. A large percentage of the world's food supply had been destroyed and the swarms – absent human intervention – appeared to be perpetual. If high winds became a permanent feature of the weather, they might be a threat to every corner of the earth. Still, the United Nations condemned the "unilateral" extermination of the insects. Given the grasshopper eggs now planted all over the world, it was only a matter of time before it happened again.

I SAT behind Marty's desk for the last time, scanning the front page of the *Georgetown Star.* Despite the death and destruction of the past few weeks, Washington was atwitter in anticipation of the upcoming inauguration. The countless balls were under way, appearances by the rich and famous were reported all over town, and the Inaugural Parade was expected to be bigger than ever.

Ostensibly celebrated as an affirmation of the country's original ideals, the citizens barely noticed. The politicos found common ground for the moment, but the class war – the country's most thoroughgoing antagonism – raged on. The people who really ran the country called it "racism" so as to disguise the real source of the rancor, their smug dismissal of the lives everyone else wanted to live.

Politicians had been their interlocutors from the beginning but, to an unparalleled degree, the people no longer listened. In the past, adversity – wars, plagues, political crises in which everyone *seemed* to be invested – had served to bring them closer together. Recent events had pushed them further apart because no one listened to anyone outside his clan, and everyone, even its partisans, knew the media was counterfeit. Dispensations from on high were ignored or, worse, mocked. More and more, "government" was unable to deliver the acquiescence of the American public to its overlords.

In a moment of more than usual arrogance, they had turned to one of their own, albeit an exotic variety – Vada Potts-Jones – to protect their hereditary prerogatives. She had mouthed their bromides for years, and embraced the vassalage they imposed, but she had proved to be more than they bargained for.

The virus, for which she was no longer answerable, had turned many of their number into idiots. Her policies since assuming the presidency were increasingly hostile to the perquisites of their class. They longed for the days when one of their *very* own, Lucinda Trent Vere, had manned the watchtower. A few even whispered good things about Lucinda's predecessor. Nevertheless, comforted by their historical inevitability, they withdrew to their enclaves and waited for Vada to go.

She had carried her obsession with the eugenics movement to the White House. After appointing a "truth" commission to establish its impact on the black community she had, more ominously, directed the Department of Justice to track down the descendants of every eugenics proponent for the past 100 years. The states were compelled to send their sterilization files to Washington in order to identify families associated with the victims.

According to the *Star,* the president was weighing another round of reparations, this one aimed at the casualties of the eugenics régime. Part of the process was going to be a public apology, memorialized by a monument on the Mall, from those whose ancestors perpetrated the crimes to those who, as a result, were without any ancestors at all. "What good will that do?" said the *Star's* reporter. "That's just a slap on the wrist."

"Well – you'd be surprised," said President Potts-Jones. "It's really just a final acknowledgement. They've been punished more severely than you think."

Nodding, I looked at my watch. It was time to pick up Lucinda. About to log off, I noticed a new headline posted a few minutes earlier: "OB-GYNs Puzzled by Drop in Patients." I nodded again. It was the vaccine, not the virus.

EPILOGUE

*So the Lord scattered them abroad
from thence upon the face of all the
earth: and they left off to build the
city. Therefore is the name of it
called Babel; because the Lord did
there confound the language of all
the earth . . .* Genesis 11: 8-9

TWO MONTHS after what became known as
the "White Virus" struck the United States, physi-
cians around the country began to report an alarming statistic: Among white women of child-bearing
age, the rate of new pregnancies had dropped to zero. White women in mixed marriages were likewise
uniformly barren as were the wives of their male
counterparts. The women themselves were unable
to explain it, and the usual tests for fertility – for
both sexes – revealed nothing. The impact was nationwide and, as time passed, showed no signs of
reversing itself.

Expert speculation centered on the virus itself. Perhaps it was another effect of the disease,
but that failed to explain why the great majority of
the white population, who had used the vaccine to
avoid the virus, couldn't have children. Other ex-
planations – a new virus, sunspots, the wrath of
God – were proffered, none of which seemed satisfactory. The likely answer was obvious to all, but

experts and media alike were loath to disturb the enlightened gulag they had created and the woman responsible for it.

At first, the news was greeted with the same impulsive sentiment as the virus – it was only white people and they deserved it. Those who had cheered the recent savaging of whites in America, a cohort that included many white people, cheered some more. Not only would Governor St. John's "underdogs" have a seat at the table, pretty soon they would have the table all to themselves.

After the initial delight, a different reaction began to set in. The loudest critics of the country and its creators – the legislatures, the courts, the media, the universities, the arts and entertainment complex – were overwhelmingly white, and their members had all swallowed the pill. For those of an age who could still have children, the new reality was staggering. The right to procreate, their most fundamental liberty, had been stolen from them. Those who already had children would have no grandchildren. Frantic people demanded a solution.

As the months passed, and no answer was forthcoming, anger took the form of diatribes against former President Vere, the woman who had rushed through the vaccine and, thus, was presumably responsible for their lack of fertility. The media in particular, unable to come to grips with the fact that they were the last of their kind, was especially shrill. Editorials suggesting some kind of public revenge appeared daily. President Potts-Jones was silent at first but, after communications between the White House and New Hope, she called off her dogs.

And so it was that the defiled "idiots" of the past and the woke victims of the present gained their revenge on the unborn oppressors of the future. It was not without cost, of course. The people who now lacked a posterity stopped planning for one and retreated into whatever dystopia – drink, drugs, ennui – was available to them. Many committed suicide.

Those who, by virtue of their ancestry, still had a future, found life a lot harder to live. Of the working population of 160 million, almost eighty per cent – from farmers to engineers to clergy, from school teachers to childcare workers to pilots – were white. Their withdrawal from the country's social and economic life meant many fewer options available to the rest of the populace. The lives they had grown accustomed to, however circumscribed, became impossible. Government revenues plummeted, as did college enrollment and the tuition it produced. Infrastructure decayed, poverty soared and people really starved.

The wokest of the woke, who reveled in human suffering, applauded. Many others prepared to leave. The vast expanse of America began to slowly empty out. The experiment begun 250 years earlier was over.

Still, government carried on. The Department of Equity was re-populated and moved to a deserted Pentagon. The estate tax was raised to 100 per cent for those who died without issue. The progressive agenda was passed in Congress by acclamation. And, in what was widely seen as an effort by the president to remove her as a viable opponent, Victoria St. John was named Vice-

President of what was left of the United States of America.

A new monument on the Mall, the Vada Potts-Jones Climate Clock Tower, was erected in record time. Just above the clock itself, the medallion from the Peace Plaza – inscribed with her initials – blazed like a malevolent, golden eye watching over the remains of the city. "Auld Lang Syne" was the national anthem.

THE END

Meet our author

ALAN THOMPSON

Born in Danville, Kentucky, on January 31, 1949, Alan Thompson grew up in his beloved Chapel Hill, North Carolina. A 1966 graduate of Chapel Hill High School, he received his B.A. from the University of Kentucky in 1970, and his J.D. from the same institution in 1973. He practiced law for forty years, primarily in Atlanta, Georgia, and now resides near the South Carolina coast.

Alan's civil trial work extended to dozens of jurisdictions throughout the United States, Australia and England, and he contributed to several professional journals and treatises dealing with his particular area of expertise, construction law.

He began writing fiction seriously in 2008, and his first novel, *A Hollow Cup*, was published in 2011. *The Black Owls* was released in 2013, followed by *The Kingfishers, Gods and Lesser Men, Lucifer's Promise, The Nun's Dowry, Juvenal's Lament, The Onyx Unicorn, The Order, Wolf Isle* and *The Peninsula.* He and his wife Barbie have two sons, one a lawyer in Salt Lake City, the other a retired Navy Commander who lives in Minneapolis.

You can learn more about Alan and his work at his website, mindsonshelves.com.